Hard Blue Midnight

Gavin brought the folded leather belt down over Rayne's ass. She shrieked when the belt fell across her cheeks but her cry was muffled by a gag. The leather strap gleamed with her juices.

'You like that, don't you?' Gavin said. 'You need a good strapping, you disrespectful bitch. Who do you think you are?'

Rayne whispered a protest, incoherent through her gag.

'It's too late to apologise. You need to be put in your place.'

She nodded furiously. Gavin dropped the belt and smacked her right buttock as she wiggled her hips in a desperate invitation. He unzipped his trousers and was so lost in the sensation of reaming her that he didn't even hear the door creak as Lori pushed it open another half an inch to get a better view of this extraordinary scene.

Hard Blue Midnight

Alaine Hood

BLACK LACE

Black Lace books contain sexual fantasies.
In real life, always practise safe sex.

First published in 2003 by
Black Lace
Thames Wharf Studios
Rainville Road
London W6 9HA

Design by Smith & Gilmour, London
Printed and bound by Mackays of Chatham PLC

ISBN 0 352 33851 2

1

If she weren't so in love with the past, Lori would be having more sex in the present. She had always been obsessed with history, especially the kind that unfolded behind bedroom doors. But ever since she had opened her vintage clothing shop, the only history being made in Lori's bedroom was a chronicle of modern celibacy.

Inspecting a lingerie set from the 1920s, Lori wondered if the owner had suffered from the same frustrations. The style of the garments suggested that they had been part of a trousseau, but the satin slips, crêpe-de-chine brassieres and lacy knickers were in pristine condition. Apparently the bride had never worn the items, much less had them ripped from her body by a horny groom. Some careful hand had folded them in muslin and kept them sealed away from time.

Lori held one of the slips against her body and walked over to the mirror. The baby-blue satin matched her eyes, and the dropped waistline floated against the crest of her hips. Most of the lingerie she sold had been made for women smaller than Lori, but this long slip looked like it might fit her tall frame.

The shop was empty. Lori stripped off her shorts, pulled her T-shirt over her head, and let the slip fall over her shoulders. Her nipples tightened as the cool satin glided across her skin. Lori loved lingerie from the 20s. The knickers and teddies were so sexy and free, made for women who craved adventure and fun. Lori ran her hands across her belly, smoothing the garment along her stomach and thighs. Her narrow hips and small breasts filled the slip perfectly. The blue brought out the apricot tones of her summer tan.

Lori studied herself with a more critical eye. If she were to wear this slip for a man, what would he see? A sexy woman, or a mouse hiding in second-hand glamour? She wriggled out of the slip and put her clothes back on. Now she looked like herself again. Comfortable. Familiar.

Lori Marwick's wardrobe consisted of jeans (cut off at the thigh in summer), a T-shirt, and an Irish fisherman's sweater. Her long blonde curls were tamed into a simple French twist. She wore no jewellery except for a pair of earrings that she had inherited from her great-aunt Lorelei, the seductive ghost for whom Lori had been named.

The filigree gold earrings were tantalisingly sensuous, like the hints of scandal that flavoured the old stories about Lorelei Price. An adventuress in sex and art, Lorelei had fled her home-town for Paris in 1928. In her absence rumours flourished: she had become famous for her erotic photographs in Europe; she had squandered her savings and turned to prostitution; she had worked as an artist's model and become the mistress of a famous photographer. Growing up in the shadow of those tales, Lori had wondered if she could ever live up to her exotic namesake. Compared to Lorelei Price, Lori Marwick was as scandalous as unbuttered toast.

Lori's customers didn't seem to mind. In the summers her shop was crowded with collectors from Boston and New York. During the school year the shop teemed with local teenage girls, who bought velvet empress gowns and silk negligées to wear with their combat boots and nose rings. Several years ago Lori had invited one of those rebels to work in the boutique after school. Hiring Melanie Paxton was the best professional move that Lori ever made.

Harem bells jangled as the rebel herself burst through the door. Melanie's cheeks were flushed under their patina of makeup, and her eyes glittered behind smoky kohl circles. Lori knew that glitter well. Melanie, who had just returned from the San Francisco Vintage Clothing Expo, had made a glorious coup. Her shoulders sagged under the weight of half a dozen shopping bags.

'Got any champagne?' Melanie asked.

'Maybe a magnum or two. Why do you ask?' Lori hugged her friend.

'When you hear about my latest brainstorm, you're going to want to celebrate. The toys in these bags are going to make us obscenely rich.'

While she was away, Melanie had reinvented herself again. Her waist-length chestnut locks had been dyed a glossy shade of eggplant and cut in a geometric pageboy with bangs. Instead of her usual long, filmy dress and bare legs, she was clad in skintight black suede.

'What have you done to your hair?' Lori moaned.

'That pre-Raphaelite look was too frou-frou. This is much more sophisticated. Besides, it's perfect for the new direction we're going to take.'

'What new direction?'

'The secret to our future success is in these bags.' Melanie let the bags fall to the floor. 'First, let me tell you about my idea. The name of the shop is Chimera, right?'

Lori nodded warily.

'A chimera is a foolish idea, a fancy. Well, let's take our fancy to a new dimension.' Melanie walked through the boutique, her hands moving through the air as she shaped her vision. 'You come into the shop, and you see our selection of clothes. Evening wear, day wear, accessories, and so on. Then you move on to night apparel and lingerie, entering a more intimate world. Finally, at the very back, you find yourself in a realm of pure fantasy, a place of risk and exotic pleasures.'

'What are you talking about?'

'About this!'

Melanie reached into one of the sacks and pulled out a leather riding crop. She fumbled through another bag and produced a plastic dildo of alarming proportions. The gigantic pink tusk looked like it could serve as a tool of pleasure or an implement of war.

'Oh, Mel,' Lori laughed. 'We could never get away with selling anything like that. We'd be rolled out of town in a barrel lined with nails.'

Melanie pouted. 'You said you wanted to start offering a selection of non-vintage items. Some new accessories to boost our revenue.'

'I was talking about contemporary jewellery, maybe a few designer scarves. Not sex toys from the Marquis de Sade's boudoir.'

'In San Francisco these items are chic. On Market Street I saw a businesswoman wearing a black leather corset and pearls under a silk jacket. Who says women wouldn't want to do that here in Morne Bay?'

'San Francisco is a sexual mecca; Morne Bay is a Methodist mecca. No one's going to wear corsets in public here, unless it's under their long woolen underwear.'

'You're exaggerating. This place isn't that uptight.'

'Oh no? Remember that uproar five years ago when we started selling vintage lingerie? Take that controversy and multiply it by a thousand, and you'll get an idea what their reaction would be if we turned this place into a bondage basement.'

Melanie's pout darkened into a scowl.

'I wasn't talking about a bondage basement – and the proper term is 'dungeon', by the way. I just thought we could add a few toys. Gradually, not all at once. We can start by converting one of the dressing-rooms into a sex nook. We'll line the room with shelves, and fill them with spicy books, dildos, and scented oils. On one wall we'd display the serious stuff: whips, handcuffs, masks, studded collars and corsets. Then we'd cover the nook with a lace curtain. We'd only let customers back there if we knew they were open-minded.'

'And those customers would tell their open-minded friends, who would tell their not so open-minded friends, who would tell the hardcore conservatives like Maggie Hanover, who would bring the town council into the store carrying torches. And what about all those nice old ladies who let us prowl around in their attics? Do you think they'd sell us their clothes if they knew we were operating a sex shop on the side?'

'Fine!' Melanie cried. 'Let Maggie and her crowd bleed all the sexuality out of this town.' Her eyes glittered. 'Sometimes I think you're just as bad.'

Lori sighed. She shouldn't have been so quick to brush off Melanie's idea. As a part-time clerk starting out in high school, Melanie had boosted the regular clientele by twenty-five per cent. After she graduated, Melanie had started going out on purchasing expeditions, hunting for clothing at estate sales and thrift shops all up and down the coast. Her magic had transformed Chimera into a sought-after cavern of treasures.

'I'm sorry, Melanie. Look, I may be a prude, but the last thing I want to do is put out your creative light.'

'You need to open up, Lori. I hate to see you spend the rest of your life in a shell.'

Lori reached out to touch Melanie's cheek. Enjoying the satiny texture of her friend's skin, she let her fingertips skate along Melanie's jaw line and down her throat. Melanie's cinnamon eyes softened. The citrus tang of her perfume overwhelmed the scent of the lavender bouquets that filled the shop. Lori blushed.

'I don't understand the appeal of bondage or sadomasochism.' Lori turned away from Melanie and began fussing with the box of clothes again. 'It all seems so forced to me, so overdramatic.'

Melanie leaned against the counter. 'A little sexual drama can change your life. Trust me, I know.'

'Since when did you become such an expert?'

'Since I took a crash course in sexual submission. While I was in California I met a French professor who's a dedicated scholar of the Marquis de Sade.'

'You're crazy,' Lori said. 'I suppose you let him break in that riding crop on your bottom?'

'My bottom was just the beginning.' Melanie licked her lower lip. 'One night he ordered me to meet him at a coffee shop on the second floor of a bookstore. He told me to take a seat at a table beside the window. The window is about twenty feet high, and you can see whoever's sitting at the table from the feet up.'

'Let me guess. He made you wear a miniskirt.'

'With no panties. While he watched from below, I had to spread my legs, let my skirt ride up my hips, and play with my pussy under the table. I had to bring myself to orgasm in front of him and about a hundred strangers strolling by on the sidewalk.'

'It's a miracle you weren't arrested.'

Lori's lips tightened, but her thighs were tingling. She imagined herself sitting at the table, spreading her legs, teasing and tweaking her clit while a sexy man, a near stranger, stood below and watched her through the darkness. And as Lori neared her peak, the stranger's hand disappeared into his pocket and massaged his swollen cock.

I'm getting to be as bad as Melanie, Lori thought. If I had her nerve, what would I be capable of?

'If you could just meet the right lover, all this would make sense to you.' Melanie motioned to the bags of toys lying at her feet. 'You have to find a dominant male who makes you wet just by looking at you.'

'I can't even find a dominant male to buy me lunch.'

'Don't worry, you'll find someone. I know it. You're so ripe with potential, you've got juice seeping out your pores.'

'What an enticing image.'

'You're definitely enticing. And I know someone else who thinks so.'

'Who? I thought all the hot men were lined up beside your bed, Mel.'

'Mmm. Now there's an idea. But I'm saving this one for you. He's divine.'

'Where did you meet him?'

'He was flying back from an architects' conference in San Francisco. When I spotted him at the airport I did some heavy manoeuvering to get the seat next to his on the plane. Once we started talking and he found out who I worked for, he couldn't stop asking questions about you. He's driving up to Morne Bay tomorrow.'

'You're joking.'

'No, I'm not. He wants to meet you. I told him it's been a nuclear winter in your bedroom lately, so he knows the situation is urgent.'

Lori slapped her friend's arm. 'Who is he? What does he want?'

'You'll have to wait and see.'

'Tell me!'

Melanie gathered her shopping bags. 'I'd love to, but I've still got a few hours left in my vacation, and I intend to squeeze the last drops of pleasure out of every minute.'

'You're a merciless tease.'

'Not a tease, just merciless. Meet me at the Dockside at seven. We'll have a few drinks, some girl talk, and I'll tell you who he is. I promise.'

Melanie danced out of the shop. The harem bells gave a taunting jingle as the door closed behind her.

* * *

Melanie's apartment was a suite of rooms on the second floor of a rambling Victorian house. As she stepped through the door, she inhaled the familiar scents of faded incense and patchouli oil. Pushing aside swathes of lace and velvet, she entered her parlour, which she had decorated to look like a gothic bordello. She sank onto her favourite piece of furniture, a leather beanbag the colour of merlot.

This corner of the room was Melanie's temple of self-love. Beside her beanbag sat an antique bookshelf where she kept her collection of erotic fiction and memoirs. Against the opposite wall stood a lacquered chest of drawers that held a treasure trove of vibrators, dildos, and ticklers. Add a box of handmade chocolate truffles and a bottle of icy champagne, and this corner became Melanie's version of paradise. Occasionally she even let a man join her here.

Melanie stretched her arms behind her head and sighed. Her body, deprived of sex for the past twenty-four hours, hummed with desire. She reached over to the bookshelf, closed her eyes and chose a book at random.

Her hand lighted on one of Anaïs Nin's journals from the early 1930s. The book's pages were crinkled from so many loving readings. Melanie turned to one of the intimate encounters between Anaïs Nin and June Miller, the description of the two women conjuring up images of herself and Lori. Melanie, with her heart-shaped face, rosebud lips and exotically painted eyes, might be Anaïs. Tall, graceful Lori had June Miller's fine, abundant golden hair and classical features.

Melanie snuggled into her beanbag and pulled up her black suede miniskirt. She strummed her bare pussy in a leisurely rhythm while she read. Ever since her Sadean professor had introduced her to the delights of exhibitionism, Melanie had been going without panties. Lori had been intrigued by Melanie's story about the coffee house. If only Lori could find the right man to drive her to those limits, she would discover a dimension of pleasure that she had never known existed.

Melanie's fingers ventured deeper, opening her inner shell to find her swollen clit. Lori would look so angelic lying here on the beanbag, her Botticelli hair loose around her flushed face, her eyes closing with pleasure as Melanie covered her breasts with butterfly kisses. Melanie rubbed her clit in swift circles. With her other hand, she reached under her silk sweater and pinched one of her nipples in a matching rhythm. Lovely. She'd bring herself to a quick peak, then bring out a few toys and start again.

Just as her cunt was revving up for a climax, someone knocked on Melanie's door. For a second she considered ignoring the knock and coming anyway. Then she smiled. Maybe whoever was at the door could help her finish what she'd started. Melanie stood up, her knees wobbly, and wriggled around until her tight skirt and sweater fell into a socially acceptable position.

Her landlady's nineteen-year-old son leaned against the doorframe. He had arranged his body in a nonchalant, slightly hostile posture that he had probably practised for hours in front of his mirror. Melanie laughed.

'Who are you trying to look like?' Melanie asked. 'James Dean? Or is it Elvis?'

'I just came up to welcome you home.' Neil scowled. 'What's so funny about that?'

Neil had an adorable scowl. All of his frustrated lust and teenage insecurity were written in that frown. It was a good thing he didn't know that the look shot Melanie straight between the thighs.

'There's nothing funny about it at all. Thank you for the welcome.'

She leaned closer to Neil and kissed him on the cheek, lingering next to him so that he could smell the musk that wafted from under her short skirt. His nostrils flared.

Neil was gorgeous. He had knocked Melanie out the first time she saw him, some five years ago. Tousled black curls, crystal-blue eyes and those skittish-pony nostrils added up to one hot fantasy. But when Melanie had first moved into the house, Neil had only been fifteen. Melanie wasn't interested in being the first woman in Morne Bay to be pilloried for statutory rape.

By the time Neil had reached legal age, he had a steady girlfriend. Melanie, too, had moved on to other projects. She was dating several men in town and had taken on more responsibilities at Chimera, including the purchasing trips that took her away from home for days at a time. She stopped hanging around the mailbox to see if she could catch a glimpse of Neil's bare back as he mowed the lawn, or his denim-clad ass as he stood on a ladder to clear out the rain gutters. Now, suddenly, he was here, not an awkward boy but a young man with a distinct shadow along his jaw and a man-sized bulge in his jeans. And Melanie was standing six inches away from him, her inner thighs as slick as peeled peaches.

'I like what you did to your hair,' Neil said. 'You look like Cleopatra.'

Melanie smiled. The boy might be complimenting her hairstyle, but his eyes were devouring her body. Melanie took one step closer to Neil. Her erect nipples skimmed his chest and his breath stirred the hair around her neck. Slowly, as if approaching a wild mustang, Melanie placed her hands around his neck. Neil stayed where he was, trembling as he tried to control himself.

'You know what, Neil?' Melanie purred. 'You are exactly what I needed.' Melanie pulled him into the apartment, then closed the door and pulled her sweater over her head. Her pink-crested breasts bounced and

Melanie shimmied a little to prolong the motion. 'Do you like my tits?'

Neil nodded. His mouth opened as if he wanted to speak, but only a moan came out.

'Would you like to taste my nipples?'

With a tenderness that surprised her, Neil took Melanie's breasts in his hands and cradled them together, so that he could reach both nubs with a single swish of his tongue. Back and forth, back and forth, until Melanie was the one who couldn't speak. When he started nibbling, she moaned. The orgasm that she had delayed was roaring back to life.

'Wait,' she gasped.

'You don't like it?' Neil's worried eyes probed hers. 'If I'm doing something you don't like, just tell me. I'll try something else.'

'You've had a lot of practice?'

'I've only had a little practice. But I've read a lot of books.'

'Let's get some more practice in bed.'

Melanie took Neil by the hand and led him across the room. She lay down on her back, with her buttocks propped on the edge of the bed, and let her skirt ride up her hips, exposing her naked bottom and swollen sex. When she spread her thighs, her lips made a liquid sigh.

'Lick me,' she said.

Neil knelt between her thighs. He lapped at her in a slow rhythm, his tongue swirling around her folds, deliberately avoiding her aching clit. Melanie groaned. Now she knew how men felt when their balls ached from delayed climax. Her clit was an outraged burr of frustration. She reached down to rub it herself, but Neil grabbed her hand.

'Not so fast! I'm going to do that.'

'Then do it,' Melanie begged through gritted teeth.

The boy focused all of his attention on Melanie's pearl, first tickling it with his tongue then taking the tiny globe between his lips and sucking. Pleasure shimmered through her body. Through her haze, she heard Neil unzipping his jeans, and had an overpowering urge to sit up and grab his hard-on. But when Neil took her clit between his teeth and began oh-so-tenderly to grind, Melanie knew that his cock would have to wait. Her back arched as her hips bucked through wave after wave as she came.

When she floated back to consciousness, Melanie opened her eyes to find Neil leaning over her. His blue eyes looked stunned.

'God, you're hot,' he whispered. 'Are you OK?'

'Darling, I am so far beyond OK that I can't even describe it.'

Neil grinned. 'Do you think you could do that again?'

'I think I could manage it. But let's take care of you first.'

Melanie slid a finger into her hole and glazed his lips with the clear honey, letting him suck her juices off her finger. She rolled over on top of the boy and made a trek of kisses down his chest. He tasted so fresh, all salt and soap and sweat: the taste of a brand-new man, still moist from the cocoon. Melanie longed to see his cock, which was pressing insistently against her belly, but she wanted to save it.

Neil's muscles quivered with the effort of holding back his orgasm. When she began to lap up the dew that had gathered in the pool of his stomach, a sob escaped from his lips. His cock pulsed underneath her, begging for mercy. Melanie sank lower, until the shaft was lodged in her damp cleavage. Eyes closed, she glided up and down, luxuriating in the sensation of Neil's vibrating prick.

'I can't take it. Please let me come!'

'Lie still. You can wait.'

Melanie glanced at her lover's face. His jaw throbbed. The poor boy wouldn't be able to stand this torture much longer. Melanie sat up, allowing herself to see the quivering prize. She sighed. A solid rod of dark-pink muscle, gleaming with the sweat from her breasts, rose above Neil's open fly.

Neil's penis was not excessively long, but it was delightfully thick, and was crowned with a head like a small, shiny apple. Around the base of the shaft, damp black curls clustered. A bead of white fluid hung trembling at the slit. Melanie touched it with her tongue. Salty, slightly bitter, a sexual ambrosia, the taste of his fluid started her loins pounding again. She straddled his leg so that her vulva was pressed against his knee. Against her overstimulated lips, the coarse denim of his jeans made an unbearable friction.

Melanie swept her tongue all around his cock's head, then took the overripe fruit in her mouth. She threw her whole body into the task of sucking him. Her hips bucked in rhythm with her lips as she dived up and down, taking him deeper down her throat with each motion. With one hand she reached into the opening in his jeans to grab his firm, heavy balls, and with the other she took hold of the root of his penis, so that she could rub his cock and balls in a simultaneous massage.

The rubbing combined with her sucking was pushing Neil over the edge. He lifted his hips off the bed, pushing himself further down her throat, making her lips ache as she struggled to take in his girth. He really was so very, very wide. She had to have him inside her. Just when his body braced for the climax, Melanie broke away.

'Melanie, no! Oh, God.'

With one fluid motion, Melanie planted herself on Neil's cock. She gasped. His thick cock stretched her channel to the limit; one more centimetre, and she would have been crying out in pain. Neil seized her by the waist and began to thrust up and down, his hips slamming against her buttocks. The passionate percussion was more than she could bear. Melanie grabbed her breasts and pinched her hard nipples. That stimulation was exactly what she needed to fly over the edge. Seconds later, he grabbed her ass cheeks and drove himself into her as far as he could go. His teeth clenched, then he shouted as the climax shook him from head to toe.

Melanie collapsed onto her new lover's chest. In the steamy, sap-scented sheets, they stroked each other lazily.

'You held out longer than I did,' Melanie murmured.

'Barely. When you licked the tip of my cock, I thought it was going to blow.'

'How did you keep from coming?'

Neil grinned. 'I tried to remember the stages of photosynthesis from biology class. First a plant is exposed to light. Then it creates chlorophyll. Then –'

'Enough!' Melanie laughed. 'I prefer human biology.'

Every woman should have a younger lover. Older men were exciting, especially when it came to dominance and submission, but they always wanted to extend their control into every corner of her life. Melanie had too much wildness in her blood to be anyone's submissive.

Neil's penis was already stirring against her thigh. Melanie reached for the beast, and it surged up to fill her hand.

Younger men. Oh, yes.

2

Lori spent most of the afternoon sorting clothes in the back of the shop, with only her thoughts for company. Who was this man who wanted to meet her? Melanie had called him divine, but Melanie's definition of divinity was warped. Add to that her tendency to embellish, and this mystery man would probably turn out to be a tax auditor.

Still, Lori itched to know who he was. She hadn't had a date in almost a year. Most of the time she could convince herself that she was happy with her life. She had a thriving business, she owned a house, and she had a wonderful friend in Melanie. But on solitary evenings, when she stood at her bedroom window and watched the bay, she often caught herself leaning against the sill as if she were waiting for something – or someone – to come to her across the water.

At six o'clock Lori closed the shop. With an hour to kill before she met Melanie at the Dockside, their favourite local tavern, Lori decided to take a stroll on the beach. The fog had cleared, making way for a stunning sunset. Watching the sheer pinks and yellows that tinged the sky, Lori misjudged her distance and got caught in the tide. By the time she got back, her shoes were full of seawater, and the salt wind had whipped her hair into a sticky mess. She decided not to stop at home to freshen up, but to head straight for the Dockside to meet Melanie. An evening of drinks and girl talk didn't exactly call for fancy dress.

Naturally, Melanie turned out to be sitting with a man. An extraordinary one.

Even in the gloom of the bar, under the tacky foil-spangled fishnet that hung from the ceiling, the stranger looked elegantly handsome, dark and restrained. His long hair, tied back in a loose ponytail, gleamed like sable against his crisp white shirt. Lori usually found ponytails in men affected, but this man wore the style with the effortless grace of a Celtic king. The carved planes of his cheeks and jaw spoke of a world of ancient stones and shadows, and his eyes had soft animal depths that matched his hair. Melanie's date was her best conquest yet.

'What happened?' Melanie asked when Lori approached their table. 'I heard you sloshing from across the room.'

'I got stuck on some rocks on the beach. My shoes are drenched.' Lori blushed. She wished she could smooth her hair, which was probably springing out in all directions, but she already felt self-conscious enough.

Melanie's date smiled. 'You remind me of a mermaid in sneakers. Only a classical beauty could pull that off.' He tilted his head, as if to see her more clearly. 'The resemblance is amazing.'

Lori's blush deepened. 'You mean I look that much like a drowned sea creature?'

'No. You look that much like Lorelei Price. You have the same profile, that swan-like neck. I can't see the colour of your eyes in this light, but if they're anything like hers, they must be a pale blue bordering on silver. Of course you don't get that much detail from her black-and-white portraits, but I've read descriptions of her in the society pages of old Paris newspapers.'

Melanie pulled out a chair for Lori. Someone had already ordered her a gin and tonic. Lori took a long sip.

The Celtic king turned to Lori. 'I'm Gavin MacLellan. I bought the land where your great-aunt had her first studio. I just finished building a house on the site.'

'You're the one who built the Ice Cube?'

Lori had heard about the New Yorker who had bought her great-aunt's property. He had torn down the old cabin overlooking the sea and replaced it with a house that seemed to be made entirely of glass. Kayaking on the bay on sunny afternoons, Lori could see the flashing white of its reflecting windows. She had never imagined that the architect of that shimmering box would look like this. Locals referred to the house as the Ice Cube.

'Don't be provincial, Lori,' Melanie scolded.

'I'm sorry. I didn't mean that the way it sounded.'

'Of course you didn't. Gavin's one of the leading architects in New York. When he's not building fantastic vacation homes, he designs towering erections.' Melanie propped her chin on her hands and gazed at Gavin. 'Will you tell us about your erections?'

Gavin laughed at Melanie's joke, but his eyes remained on Lori. 'Don't apologise. I know what the local residents say about me and my glass house. What kind of lunatic would build a place that's a greenhouse in summer and an icebox in winter? I have to admit, it was a crazy dream. When I found out that Lorelei Price's property was for sale, I took that as an omen. I had to make my dream a reality.'

'It would be incredibly sexy to live in a house made of windows,' Melanie said. 'Can you imagine the opportunities for exposing yourself? Undressing by candlelight in front of the glass, doing a striptease in the darkness, making mad love in front of dozens of your neighbours . . .'

'Or dozens of seals and gulls. The house looks out to sea, and it's surrounded by woods. It's a lot more private than you'd think. Not that your ideas aren't tempting. For the right woman, the place could be an ideal setting for exhibitionist fantasies.'

Again, Gavin's attention was fixed on Lori. In fact, he

hadn't stopped staring at her since she walked into the bar. The truth finally dawned. Gavin wasn't Melanie's date. He was the mystery man Melanie had met on the airplane – the man who wasn't supposed to arrive in Morne Bay until tomorrow.

Melanie caught Lori's eye and read her thoughts.

'I guess I should have explained what's going on here,' Melanie said, all innocence. 'Gavin is the man I was telling you about this afternoon. I tried to call and warn you that he'd be joining us tonight, but you weren't home. He was supposed to be here tomorrow, but he got here early.'

'I couldn't wait another twenty-four hours to meet Lorelei's grand-niece,' Gavin said.

Gooseflesh sprang up on Lori's bare legs. She shifted in her seat, accidentally brushing against Gavin's knee. Once she had made the contact, he prolonged it, holding his thigh against hers with a light pressure that might have been accidental. Lori prayed that it wasn't. When was the last time she had met a man who made her whole body vibrate with a casual touch?

'But I didn't come here to talk about my house,' Gavin went on. 'I came here to talk about a book.'

'A book?' Lori echoed. She wished she could touch Gavin's hair, to lose her fingers in those rich depths. She wondered whether he had the same sleek pelt on other parts of his body.

'I'm writing a book about your great-aunt. I laid the groundwork of research in France, and a publisher in New York accepted my proposal. When Melanie told me about you, I couldn't believe my luck. I was just about to dig into Lorelei's past here in Morne Bay, when Melanie dropped you in my lap.'

'There isn't much to write about,' Lori said. 'Nothing's left of her but rumours. Her father had all her photographs burned when she left the States. We don't even know what happened to her after she went to Paris.'

'You mean you never tried to investigate?'

'I've been too busy living my own life,' Lori said with a defensive laugh. 'Running a vintage shop, I spend too much time in the past as it is. After a long day of sorting through grimy old clothes, or trying to convince some elderly widow to sell her grandmother's junk jewellery, I don't have much energy left over for my own family history.'

'That's a shame. Your great-aunt's life is a fascinating mystery.'

'How did you find out about her?'

'A collection of her work was exhibited two years ago at a gallery in Montparnasse, as part of a show of women photographers from the 20s and 30s. As soon as I saw those photos, I knew I had to see them collected in a book. I want to give her the reputation she deserves.'

'But you're an architect. Why would you care about those old photographs?'

A metallic taste had filled Lori's mouth, making it impossible to finish her thought. She hadn't felt jealous of her great-aunt since her gawky adolescence, but suddenly that bitterness was flooding back. Lorelei Price had had passion, courage, and a powerful gift. What did Lori have to offer a man like Gavin MacLellan?

'Architecture is my career. Erotic photography is my passion. Especially when it's done by artists who understand the bond between creativity and sexuality. Lorelei was one of those artists. Her eye was like a lens that exposed her subjects' secret fantasies. Her nudes aren't posed; they're acting out dreams, obsessions, as if the camera weren't there. She took erotic photography seriously, and doing that as a woman back then took guts. Guts and talent.'

'Lori's just as talented as her great-aunt was,' Melanie said. She clasped her friend's hand under the table. 'You'd never know it by the way she dresses, but she's got a great eye for fashion and design. Lori's a hidden treasure.'

Lori gave Melanie's hand a grateful squeeze.

Gavin smiled. 'That treasure isn't as hidden as you might think.' He turned back to Lori. 'I've got a proposition for you. I want you to be involved in this project. I'd like to arrange for you to meet my editor in New York.'

'Lori would love to go to New York. I'm always trying to get her to leave town. Not forever, of course. Just for a hot sexual interlude in the city.'

'Melanie!'

'I'd love to be the one to take her,' Gavin said.

Lori's cheeks blazed. She tugged at one of the tendrils of hair that had fallen out of its pins. Gavin watched the gesture. His eyes travelled from the nape of Lori's neck down to her collarbone, leaving imprints like kisses along her skin. Lori shivered.

'Are you cold, Lori?' Gavin said. 'You could wear my jacket.'

With mock concern, Melanie looked at her watch. 'Eight thirty already? It's past my bedtime. I think I'm going to go home, peel off all my clothes, and slide into the sheets. Would either of you – or both of you – like to join me?'

'I'll stay here, if you don't mind,' Gavin replied. 'But thank you.'

Melanie stood up and shimmied into her black mohair sweater. 'Thank me for what? You bought the drinks, sweet prince.'

'Thank you for introducing me to Lori.'

Gavin's hand sank onto Lori's knee. His fingers were

cool and dry, but his palm held a core of heat. Lori lost her breath.

Melanie bent down and kissed Lori on the cheek. '*Ciao, bella*. Don't do anything I wouldn't do.'

Then Melanie was gone.

'Would you like another drink?' Gavin asked.

'No, thanks,' Lori said. 'I'm not much of a drinker. One gin and tonic, and I'm ready for bed.'

Gavin's eyebrow arched. 'Are you?'

'No. I mean yes! I mean, I wasn't saying that we should have sex. Or that we shouldn't.'

Lori's hands flew up to cover her face, and she knocked over her glass. She cried out as a stream of melted ice trickled onto her thigh. She grabbed a handful of napkins from a basket on the table.

'Let me take care of it.'

Gavin caught Lori's wrist with one hand. With the other he eased her chair away from the table, then trailed his forefinger from the crest of her knee to her inner thigh, following the rivulet of cold water. Lori's eyes fluttered shut. She released a long, unsteady breath.

'I took you literally when you mentioned bed. I'm afraid I'm a very literal man.'

'I'm sure you are.'

Lori was trying to collect herself, but Gavin's fingers were resting on the most sensitive spot on her thigh. Then he turned the caress into a friendly pat and sat up in his chair. From the way he twisted his hips as he straightened his body, Lori wondered if he were hard. She wished she were bold enough to touch him. If she were Melanie, her fingers would be dancing up his inseam by now, testing the tension in his thigh muscles, delaying the journey towards his crotch so as to make the final discovery as rewarding as possible.

'If a woman wants to make love with me, she has to

be direct about it. My head is always buzzing with cost analyses, building codes, blueprints. I've lost the art of sexual innuendo.'

'I can't imagine that's true,' Lori said. If it were, her panties wouldn't be slippery, and her heart would be beating at its normal pace. 'I'd better go home now.'

Gavin helped her to her feet. 'Let me drive you.'

'I only live a couple of blocks away.'

'Then I'll walk with you.'

'That's not necessary. I walk at night all the time.'

'Alone? A woman like you?'

Lori reached for Gavin's arm. When she touched his skin, a muscle twitched under her fingers. 'This is Morne Bay, not Manhattan,' she laughed. 'But I'd love to have you walk me home.'

They walked in silence, their arms joined and their hips brushing against each other now and then. Lori could feel a bite in the air, but the night still held its summer softness. Maybe it was the chill that gave her that restless feeling, that longing to seize whatever she could before the winter came.

'Here we are.' Lori stopped in front of Chimera and dug into her shorts pocket for her keys.

'Is this your shop?'

'Yes, the shop is on the lower floor of the house. I live upstairs.'

Gavin took Lori by the shoulders and turned her around to face him. In the moonlight he looked more than ever like a figure from a Celtic legend.

'Why are you here with me?' Lori asked.

She was surprised to hear herself say it, but she couldn't hold the question back any longer; not with Gavin looking at her with such deep wanting. She had to know if she could claim any of that lust for herself.

Gavin's eyebrows rose. 'Because I want to be.'

'But why? Because I look like Lorelei Price?'

'No. Part of you is Lorelei, that's true. I can't pretend I wasn't stunned by the resemblance. But you're the reason I'm standing here. Lorelei Price has never been a sexual fantasy for me.'

'Then what is she?'

'Before I decided to become an architect, I wanted to be a photographer. I wanted to do what Lorelei did – run away from home and create a new identity; take photos with extraordinary power. But my father made it clear that unless I chose a more stable profession, I'd lose his support: financially and emotionally. At the time I didn't have the guts to make it on my own, so I took the safest of all possible roads. I became an architect, like he was.'

'My mother wanted me to be more like my great-aunt,' Lori said. 'Isn't that ironic? When I graduated from art school, she thought I'd go to New York. Instead I came home and took over the family antique shop. She couldn't believe it when I stopped selling furniture. To her, vintage clothes are just overpriced dust rags.'

'What are they to you?'

'Shreds of sensual memory. Almost like skins. Touching another person's clothing can be so powerful. Wearing it can be almost like a kind of erotic possession.'

'Erotic possession,' Gavin repeated. 'Have you felt that before?'

'Not yet. Maybe that's why I hardly ever wear the clothes I sell. Sometimes the sensations are overwhelming.'

'Don't you ever want to be overwhelmed?'

Gavin cradled her face in both hands, thumbs resting behind her jaw. Lori had never known that those twin spots held such secrets, that a delicate pressure there could send waves of pleasure rippling down her spine. The hairs along her neck rose in the draft of his breath, like tiny grasses blown upright by a warm wind. Lori sighed, and Gavin lifted her face and kissed her: not a suggestive kiss, but a very literal one, an insistent press of smooth lips against hers, a demand expressed in a firm flicker of tongue. He held her by the waist and pulled her close, letting her ease against the warm length of his erection. She opened her mouth, and their tongues met, playing against each others' lips.

Lori raised one thigh so that the ridge of Gavin's cock fitted into the groove between her legs. She was so wet she could hear the liquid sounds of her own arousal as she moved against him.

'I've always wanted to be overwhelmed,' Lori whispered.

'Take your hair down,' Gavin said hoarsely.

Lori's fingers trembled as she searched for the pins buried in her curls. It seemed to take hours to loosen the coil, hours of standing under Gavin's coal-black gaze. Her nipples rose in the cool night breeze. Finally her twisted hair fell down her back in a silky tumble. She shook it loose, and its damp, springy weight rolled down her back.

'You're lovely. Too damn lovely to be hiding in this town.'

He lifted the cloak of her hair and let the strands fall through his fingers. Then he seized the mass of it by the roots and pulled firmly. She gasped. Other men had caressed Lori's hair, but no one had ever held it that way, with that combination of roughness and gentle authority. His grip was electrifying.

'Fuck me,' she begged.

Gavin's hand slid under the ragged edge of her cutoffs and hooked the waistband of her panties. He tugged at the slip of fabric, running his fingers along the gusset in a slow, rhythmic motion, as if weighing Lori's question.

'I want to.' He took her hand and placed it on the swell of his cock. She could feel its impressive length throbbing through the cloth. His fingers cradled one of her breasts, chafing the erect nipple with his thumb. 'But I'd rather not take you on a public street.'

'I was thinking of my bed.'

'So was I. All evening.'

'Then come upstairs with me.'

Without releasing her, Gavin edged back a step. 'I know what I want, Lori. I want to make sure you want the same thing.'

'But I do –'

Gavin stopped Lori's protest with another kiss.

'Come up to my house tomorrow night. We'll talk about it then. Eight o'clock?'

Lori nodded. Her mouth was too dry for speech, and her nerves buzzed with frustration. When Gavin backed away, she wanted to throw herself on him and drag him upstairs. Instead, she watched his lean, muscular form walking down the street. Under the soft illumination of a street lamp, he turned and looked back.

When she made her way, wobbly-kneed, up the stairs to her bedroom, Lori had to remind herself to breathe.

3

At sunrise Gavin gave up the struggle to sleep. He had hoped to catch a few hours of rest, then go over his conference notes and finish his presentation for Monday. But his thoughts refused to settle, his eyes registering nothing but visions of Lori's lips, and his cock stood at attention, refusing to subside. He could have soothed the thick organ with a few quick strokes, but Gavin was going to make his body wait. If Lori wanted him tonight, she would have the full force of his lust.

His married friends assumed that Gavin MacLellan led the extravagant sex life of a wealthy Manhattan bachelor, but in truth Gavin could count his recent lovers on one hand. From the way Lori had kissed him last night – hungry and awkward and terrified all at once – he would guess that her track record was the same. When he broke the kiss and looked down at her softened lips, every muscle in his body had burned to fuck her. Her beauty was so familiar to him that he felt he could see through her clothes to the silken nudity underneath.

That familiarity was exactly why he'd stopped. When he made love to this woman for the first time, he wanted to see Lori Marwick, not Lorelei Price, responding to his touch. Lori deserved nothing less than her lover's full attention.

Throughout the evening Gavin had looked for similarities between Lori and her great-aunt. So far, he had seen mostly differences. Where Lorelei Price had been brazen and socially defiant, Lori Marwick was soft-spoken and protective of her public image. Where Lorelei had been overtly sexual, Lori was subtly sensuous. Yet under Lori's demure exterior, Gavin had seen plenty of passion. He could still hear her moaning 'Fuck me' when he took hold of her hair. A passionate urgency had shaken her body when she responded to the dominant gesture. Did he dare hope that on top of her beauty and intelligence, Lori shared one of her great-aunt's darker hungers?

The telephone on his bedside table rang. Gavin grabbed the receiver.

'Hello?'

'Well, good morning, Sunshine. I didn't expect you to be so eager for my call.'

Gavin's spirits sank. Sandpaper glazed with honey – that was the image that came to mind whenever he heard Rayne Hughes's voice. The sound used to make his prick leap. This morning it made him wither.

'You did remember that I was going to call this morning, didn't you?'

Gavin winced. 'Of course.'

'Bullshit. Ten to one you're not even alone.'

'As a matter of fact, I *am* alone, Rayne. I'm just worn out from the San Francisco trip. The conference was a waste – nothing but politics. I could have used the time to work on the book.'

'Funny. When we were living together, you had a lot more stamina. If you're really that tired, I should call back later. You'll want to be in a good frame of mind when you hear what I've got to say. Seems we've got a bit of a problem.'

Gavin steeled himself. He could almost hear the hiss of Rayne's silk stockings as she crossed one leg over the other – her power gesture. Legs of a gazelle, brain of a cobra. He knew how to turn those fine legs into jelly, how to soften that keen mind into mush. Dozens of men wanted to give Rayne pleasure, but only Gavin knew that she took her pleasure with a double shot of pain.

Only Gavin knew that when the pain had been delivered, and the spanking or flogging or whipping was over, Rayne liked to be cuddled like a little girl.

'What's the problem, Rayne?'

'I've been talking with the publisher about the Lorelei Price book.'

'And?'

'How can I put this? He's having second thoughts about the project and, frankly, so am I. What you've written so far is tantalising, but tantalising isn't good enough. We need more meat, more conclusive facts about Lorelei Price's life, at least some evidence of her influence. So far all you've got is a woman who ran away from home, went to Paris, and took dirty photos.'

'Damn it, Rayne, there's a lot more to Lorelei than that. Even without the biographical component, you've got her whole body of work!'

'Sure, she took some stunning shots. And I'll grant you that from what you've shown me, she was a promising artist. But frankly, I smell a cover-up. Either you haven't worked hard enough to get to the core of this woman's past, or you're deliberately withholding something.'

'Haven't *worked* hard enough? I've been to Paris three times, let my career slide, spent thousands of dollars on travel and overseas phone calls –'

'Which is why I can't believe that you don't have a clue about what happened to her.'

Gavin took a deep breath. He pressed the receiver against his forehead. He should have known this would happen. Rayne had a nose for deception. Not that he had been deceiving her – he had only been drawing out his research, double- and triple-checking all his facts. If Rayne knew what he had found, she would nix the project altogether. *Sorry, darling,* she would say, *but it's just not worth the risk. My career is everything to me. Especially since I'm alone now.*

'Listen,' he said. 'I've got something new to bring to the table. *Someone* new, I should say. This person could make a huge difference to the outcome of the project.'

'Oh?'

Gavin inwardly begged for Lori's forgiveness. As soon as Melanie Paxton had told him about Lori, he had planned to seek her help on his book. But he'd never expected that he would be using Lori as a pawn in a power game with his editor.

'She's the grand-niece of Lorelei Price. Named after her, actually. She's the only one of Lorelei's living relatives I've been able to talk to. She never met her great-aunt, of course, but she's familiar with the family legends.'

'Legends aren't what I had in mind. I was thinking of facts.'

'Lori Marwick could be a goldmine of facts.'

'You sound so defensive! Are you protecting the little goldmine from your ball-breaking editor?'

'Stop it, Rayne. Would you give me a chance to get to know this woman?'

Gavin felt the deep-freeze on the other end of the line. Suddenly the conversation had careened into personal territory.

'Get to know whatever pitiful slut takes your fancy,' Rayne said.

Gavin ignored the bile in Rayne's remark. 'I want you to get to know her, too. Let me introduce you to her. I'll bring her to New York. Please, Rayne. Can't you look past our personal history and see how important this book could be?'

Rayne sighed. 'Fine. You can bring her with you when we meet on Friday. But I'd better be beaming with satisfaction by the time the meeting's over.'

'You will be.'

'Just remember, the publisher signed on for a biography,

not romantic fiction. If there's anything in Lorelei Price's past that you're trying to cover up, I'm going to find out about it. And if I don't like what I find, you can forget about your precious book.'

Rayne hung up the phone. Gavin left his fingers wrapped around the receiver. Rayne would be staring out of the window now, her eyes fixed on the skyline. Her angular features would be set in a mask of flawless glamour. A casual observer would never guess that Rayne was in the grip of a ferocious rage. Gavin knew the full depth of her anger. He had lived with it for three years. As he imagined her sitting alone in her office, he almost felt a pang of tenderness for his former lover.

Almost.

A memory came to him unbidden: Rayne standing with her wrists bound above her head, her raven hair cascading to her heart-shaped ass, her face blurred with joy as Gavin stroked her buttocks and thighs with a deerskin flogger. Her porcelain skin reddened as he increased the strength of the blows, so gradually that she couldn't identify the moment when her pleasure crossed over into pain. Her moans turned into cries as she begged him for more. More, always more. Even when the flogging brought her screaming to a climax, and he cradled her shuddering body in his arms, Gavin knew that Rayne's hunger wasn't sated.

'Oh, Lori,' Gavin said out loud. 'What the hell am I getting you into?'

Lori woke to the sounds of Melanie moving around in the shop downstairs. A glance at the clock informed her that she had slept till almost noon.

'Damn!'

Lori threw off her quilts. In eight hours she would be seeing Gavin again. When she showed up at his house, she wanted to give him nothing less than a total metamorphosis. Melanie would help her. It was the least the little witch could do after the surprise she pulled last night.

After settling her nerves with a cup of tea, Lori went downstairs. Each time she walked into the shop, she felt a thrill of pride at the way she'd transformed her parents' antique business. As soon as she had decided to sell vintage clothing, Lori had remodelled the old house, adding a display window that filled the shop with light. The showroom had been repainted, with creamy crown mouldings and pale-coral walls. Bouquets of dried French lavender sat on antique piecrust tables, and every article of clothing, down to the scraps of lace and ribbon in the wicker odds-and-ends basket, had been lovingly cleaned. The stronger garments hung on gleaming chrome display racks, while the more fragile articles lay folded on shelves.

A bedroom next to the showroom held Lori's sewing machine and three dressmaker's dummies. Here Lori repaired the tattered rags that Melanie scavenged from flea markets and auctions, and altered old gowns to fit women who were taller than their Victorian and Edwardian ancestors. A second downstairs bedroom had been turned into a fitting area, with three dressing stalls, gentle track lights and cheval glasses.

At the counter Lori found Melanie taunting a customer with glimpses of her cleavage. The poor man's eyes were misty with lust. Draped over his arm was a pea-green woolen wrapover coat with padded shoulders, circa 1940. Even Lori had to admit that the thing was ghastly. Leave it to Melanie to foist it off on a vulnerable male.

'Lori! I've been telling this gentleman about my ideas for the boutique. He thinks selling erotic merchandise is a terrific idea. In fact, I was just about to show him some of the items I brought back from San Francisco.'

'But Melanie,' Lori said with lethal sweetness, 'we haven't decided whether to sell those items.'

Undaunted, Melanie turned back to her victim. 'If you come back in a few weeks, I'm sure we'll be offering anything you've dreamed of. Maybe more.' She led the man over to the cash register and rang up his purchase. 'Your wife is going to *love* that coat. The fabric is so durable, she'll get another fifty years' wear out of it.'

As soon as her customer had left, looking bewildered with his purchase, Melanie pounced on Lori. 'So tell me! What happened with Gavin last night?'

'Not as much as I wanted.'

'How far did you go?'

'He kissed me at the door, but he wouldn't come upstairs.'

'What? Is he crazy, gay, or both?'

'Neither. He cares about my feelings. He wanted to wait.'

'You've got to be kidding. What's he waiting for, your wedding night?'

Lori smiled. 'Hardly. I'm going up to his house at eight. I intend to finish what we started.'

Melanie checked her watch. 'You have less than eight hours to get ready. Let's close early.'

'Don't be silly. We haven't stopped running a business just because I –'

'Because you're about to get laid? What's more important than that?' Melanie took a step back and scrutinised her boss. 'I love you, Lori, but you're a mess.'

Melanie took Lori by the shoulders and pushed her over to the mirror. Lori's French twist had drooped into a lopsided bundle. She had forgotten to put on shoes before she came downstairs, and her old T-shirt was splattered with tea.

'I see your point,' Lori said. 'We'll close at five instead of six.'

'Four,' Melanie insisted. 'We close at four, or you'll have to get ready alone.'

'Fine,' Lori sighed. But in spite of her disarray, she had never seen herself look so happy.

While Lori watched the shop, Melanie prowled through the racks, searching for the perfect gown, shoes and accessories. After an hour of exploration she let out a whoop of triumph, then rushed upstairs to lay out her selections in Lori's bedroom. She reappeared half an hour later, only to dash out of the shop to run errands.

'Back in a few minutes!' she cried.

Melanie didn't reappear until four o'clock.

'How could you leave me alone all afternoon?' Lori moaned. 'I'm a wreck!'

'Hush,' Melanie said. 'When you see what I've got in store for you, you'll be overjoyed. After tonight you'll be in debt to me forever.'

Lori let Melanie blindfold her with a scarf and lead her up to her apartment. An unfamiliar fragrance filled the rooms: not quite musk or ginger, more like a spice than a fruit. Melanie guided her into the bathroom, then untied the scarf. Lori laughed with delight at the sight that greeted her. The rim of her tub had been lined with candles, which formed a ring of soft flame in the dimmed bathroom. Rose petals floated on the bath water, in which scented oils formed swirling rainbows. Irish dulcimer music drifted from the bedroom. Yards of gauze draped from the shower rod formed a hazy background to this vision of sensual indulgence.

'We must be in the wrong apartment,' Lori said. 'This is not my bathroom.'

'Yes it is. Take off your clothes,' Melanie ordered. 'I'll be right back.'

Lori eased herself into the tub inch by inch until she was submerged in the steamy depths. She leaned her head against the edge of the tub and closed her eyes, then spread her legs, letting the water flow through the creases of her sex, and imagined that the undulating water was Gavin's tongue. His lips had been warm and firm, his tongue insistent. He would know how to pleasure a woman with his mouth. Lori moaned. Her fingers wandered down between her legs and parted her lips. One by one she touched the places that were most sensitive. Her clit sent shock waves through her body as she massaged the little button with her fingertip. Here he would lick her, and here, and here . . .

Suddenly Lori realised that her fingers were no longer moving on their own. A second hand, cool and soft, lay on top of hers, guiding her motions. Lori opened her eyes to find Melanie sitting on the edge of the tub. Her full, moist lips were parted, and her lush brown eyes gleamed. Her skirt was gathered up around her thighs, and as she helped Lori play with herself, she was rubbing her own pussy with her free hand.

'Caught you, didn't I?'

'Melanie! I was only washing.'

'Of course you were. And I'm helping you.'

'But I can't do this . . '

'Shhh. You can do anything you want. Just lie back and let me show you something lovely.'

Lori closed her eyes again and gave in to Melanie's nimble touch. The younger woman's fingers seemed to be everywhere at once: caressing, tickling, plunging into Lori's openings. Lori opened her thighs as wide as the tub would allow. She let her worries float away into the warm water and surrended herself to Melanie's expert attentions.

'Let me see you play with your breasts,' Melanie said. 'You have such delicious nipples – like pink gumdrops. Squeeze them for me.'

Lori obeyed, kneading her nipples into tight peaks. The bath water churned. Melanie's fingers moved faster as her hands did double duty on Lori and herself. Lori opened her eyes to see her friend biting her lower lip, clearly holding back her own orgasm. Her naked thighs squeaked on the porcelain as she slid back and forth, wildly fingering herself. Her cheeks were hot pink, her nipples dark and hard under the sheer fabric of her blouse. Melanie's arousal was all it took to send Lori into a keen climax. Both women cried out as waves of shared pleasure washed through them.

'Oh my,' Melanie gasped, as they both caught their breath. 'I almost fell in with you.'

'You definitely got soaked,' Lori said, touching the wet hem of her friend's skirt.

'We both did.' Melanie smiled.

'That was wonderful, Melanie. Exactly what I needed.'

'Well, that was just a little warm-up for tonight. Here's something else to help you relax.' Melanie leaned over and poured champagne into two glass flutes that sat on a tray on the floor. She handed one of the flutes to Lori.

'Champagne? Isn't it a bit early?'

'Lori, life is supposed to be an adventure. Stop fretting and enjoy the ride.' Melanie raised her glass. 'Here's to the hottest sex you've ever had.'

The dry champagne tickled Lori's throat and sent a buzz of anticipation through her body. If sex with Gavin turned out to be as hot as the kiss he'd given her last night, she probably wouldn't live to tell her friend about it.

After they had polished off their drinks, Melanie handed Lori a fluffy white towel.

'Now get out and dry yourself,' Melanie said, 'and I'll lay out your gown. We'll pretend I'm your French maid. Keep your back turned until I'm ready.'

While Lori dried off and rubbed jasmine cream into her skin, Melanie busied herself with laying out a dress, stockings, and shoes.

'OK, you can look now,' Melanie said. Lori turned.

'Oh, Mel, not that one!'

Melanie had selected the most stunning evening gown in the shop. The simple barrel silhouette sparkled with thousands of black beads, which formed a geometric pattern reminiscent of Ancient Egypt. The deep V-shaped back neckline would fall only centimetres above the wearer's buttocks. Lori could already feel Gavin's lips roving across her shoulder-blades and down her spine, hovering in the dip of her lower back before brushing along the swell of her buttocks.

'Why not?'

'The backing is chiffon. It's too weak. Think about all those beads stressing the fabric over the past seventy years.'

'But it's in good condition. You said so yourself.'

'Good condition to sit in a collector's closet, not to wear on a date. One little rip, and the whole thing will fall apart. Besides, how am I supposed to wear panties and a bra?'

'You're not. That's the whole point. You'll wear thigh-high silk stockings, and nothing else. Oh, shoes, of course. And maybe a necklace.'

'I can't.' Lori sank onto her bed. 'That dress is worth too much.'

'Lori, this is a piece of cloth. Whoever made it meant for it to be worn by a beautiful woman, not stuck in a closet.'

'Do you know what keeps bothering me? The idea that I'm trying to be like Lorelei. That Gavin only wants me because he's so fascinated by her. Even that dress . . . it might as well be something from her wardrobe. All my life I had to hear about Lorelei Price – how glamorous she was, how sexy and creative. Now I've finally met someone I really want, and he only sees the parts of me that remind him of her.'

'Did it ever occur to you that you've been trying too hard *not* to be like her? That you don't let yourself seem sexy because you're afraid of competing with Lorelei and losing?'

'Maybe.'

'I saw the way Gavin looked at you last night. He damn well wasn't staring at Lorelei Price. Will you try the dress on?'

Lori stood up. She threw off her bathrobe and lifted the dress off the bed. Its heavy folds glittered like the sea under moonlight. Melanie helped her into the garment. A sprinkling of beads drifted off the bodice. Before Lori could notice, Melanie kicked the beads under the bed. She fluffed out Lori's hair, then turned her around to face the mirror.

'You're looking at a woman who's about to get a life,' Melanie announced.

'I do have a life!' Lori protested. But when she saw her reflection in the mirror – golden hair billowing across her tanned shoulders, black beads shimmering across her curves, face glowing in the discovery of her own beauty – Lori realised that her life was about to change.

4

Driving along Shore Road, Lori already felt like a changed woman: proud, cool, an object of mystery. Salt air blew off the sea through her open jeep, caressing her face and throat as if the night wind were her lover.

The land where Lorelei's cabin once stood lay on an isolated outcrop of Shore Road, at the end of a dirt road that wove through pine and birch trees. As she negotiated the rutted trail, Lori felt grateful for her jeep. Those three acres had been her great-aunt's first adult purchase, the site of her infamous photographic studio and the setting of more erotic encounters than anyone would ever know. As much as he had railed against his daughter's sins, Lorelei Price's father had refused to sell the property, as if he hoped in some unacknowledged part of his heart that she would come back to the cabin. After he died, Lorelei's sisters had sold the place. The next owner had left the land untended for decades, letting wild raspberry bushes choke the ramshackle building.

Now the cabin was gone. As Lori pulled into the clearing, she gasped at the sight that met her eyes. A structure made of windows, fully illuminated, rose against the sky. Through the glass panes she could see the stars, the moon and the bay below, as if the house were suspended in the darkness. If the residents of Morne Bay had mocked this dream, it was only because they had never been invited here at night. At the heart of that golden box stood Gavin MacLellan, standing at a counter in what must be the kitchen and uncorking a bottle of wine.

It wasn't the breeze that made Lori's skin tingle. In black trousers and a black turtleneck sweater, Gavin was a vision of masculine beauty. The tight wool of his sweater revealed the elegant topography of his arms and chest – every ripple and swell stood out in relief. With his black hair swept away from his face, the planes of his cheekbones and brow gleamed in sculpted perfection. As he efficiently pulled the cork from the bottle, Gavin bit his lower lip. Lori's mouth went dry.

The shriek of alarm bells shattered the stillness, and harsh light flooded the clearing. Lori froze.

The door of the house flew open. Moments later Gavin appeared, shielding his eyes with his hand. 'Lori?' he called. 'Are you out there?'

'I'm here. I think.' She pressed her hands to her ears. 'Am I under arrest?'

'I forgot to turn the damn security system off. I think I'd rather be robbed than have to hear that racket every time anything moves out here.'

Lori followed Gavin into the house, shrugging off her black woollen shawl.

'The system is faulty,' Gavin went on. 'And I've had a hell of a time trying to get anyone to look at it in the off-season –'

Then he really saw her. The irritation left his eyes, and his face slackened in awe.

'Good Lord,' he said. 'You're exquisite.'

His fingers grazed Lori's cheek and trailed down her neck and came to rest in the hollow of her throat. He lifted the airy masses of hair away from her shoulders and draped them behind her back.

Lori opened her mouth, intending to deflect his compliment with a joke, but she changed her mind. If there was anything she needed to learn from Lorelei Price, it was self-assurance. She raised her chin, met Gavin's dark gaze, and held it, until the tension of confronting his desire was more than she could bear. Then Gavin kissed her: just a light kiss, slightly flavoured with the smokiness of his mouth, a kiss to sustain her until later. Her nipples stiffened against the lining of her dress, and the hollow between her inner thighs turned into a dish of melted butter.

'Melanie was right,' he said.

'About what?' she asked, when she had caught her breath.

'You *are* more beautiful than Lorelei Price. How does a diamond like you stay buried in this rocky coastline? You could be in New York, in Paris or Milan. Designing, studying, even modelling, if you wanted.'

'At my age, modelling's probably not an option,' Lori said with a laugh. 'But I've always wanted to travel.'

Gavin walked back to the kitchen to pour the wine. Lori followed him through the house, admiring the burnished-honey sheen of the hardwood floors against the velvet backdrop of the night. The only furnishings in the main living area were a black futon on a wooden frame and a low glass table, which was stacked with books. Thick, glossy art books sat in pyramids across the floor.

'You've never done any travelling? Why not?'

'I've lived in Morne Bay all my life, and my family has been here for generations. I hate to be away from the ocean for more than a couple of weeks. Besides, I enjoy the isolation.'

'According to Melanie, you're too talented to be living in isolation. She thinks you should design clothes that sell on Fifth Avenue.'

'Melanie means well, but she's wrong. The only clothes I love are old ones, ones that have already been worn. It's not the designs that attract me as much as the idea of the people who wore them.'

Gavin handed her a glass of Merlot. 'So you're

attracted to history the same way I am. Physically, sensually. Even sexually.'

'That's it exactly. I always feel sad whenever I send clothes out to be cleaned. Especially when they still have a scent of their owner: perfume or a sachet or even perspiration. When I smell the fabric, or even touch it, I sometimes have flashes of another woman's experiences. I can feel her desires.'

'That's an unusual gift, erotic empathy. As long as you don't lose touch with your own desires.'

'The past can be very seductive.' Lori sipped her wine.

'It's easy to lose yourself in other people's lives. When I look at what I've been through in the past couple of years – buying this property, collecting everything I could by Lorelei Price – I wonder if I've gone crazy.'

Lori stiffened at the sound of her great-aunt's name. She walked over to the window and looked out at the bay, broad and still and seamed with moonlight. The lights of incoming boats twinkled on the water, and the glow of the town's windows along the curve of the bay reminded Lori how far she was from her safe, familiar house.

'I don't think you're crazy,' she said. 'Everyone says Lorelei was fascinating. It's too bad you'll never meet her.'

Gavin set his glass down on the floor, walked up to Lori and slipped his arms around her waist. Although his reference to Lorelei Price had stung her self-esteem, Lori's body was more than receptive. Her hips moved back of their own free will to meet the hard cradle of his pelvis.

'How do I get it through your head,' Gavin murmured, his lips moving against her cheek, 'that you're the one I want to be with?'

'I guess you'll have to prove it,' Lori said.

'How's this for proof?'

Gavin drew Lori close, letting the bulk of his erection sink into the groove between her buttocks. She swallowed.

'That's . . . convincing,' she said weakly.

'Look at yourself in the window. You're breathtaking.'

Gavin pushed her hair over her shoulder, baring her neck, then swept his fingers across the valley between her shoulder-blades. His fingertips massaged their crests, as if he were shaping her shoulders into wings.

Lori sighed and arched her back. Gavin's hands slipped under the opening of the dress and glided upwards to cup her breasts. Starting at the nape of her neck he began to kiss her spine, moving downwards bead by bead. At the same time he tugged at her nipples, coaxing them into peaks. Each time his lips left her skin, the imprint of his warm mouth turned cool in the open air. Lori closed her eyes. She was hovering over the water in a glass box, floating on a sea of sensation. The stem of the glass between her fingers was her only reminder of the everyday world.

Gavin's hands left her breasts and roved hungrily down the long, curved course of her thighs. He sank to his knees and, as he breathed in the jasmine-scented warmth that rose from her body, took the hem of her dress and pulled it slowly upwards, baring her silk-clad legs inch by inch: first her slim ankles, then her taut calves, and finally her thighs.

When he saw that she was nude above the lace tops of her stockings, Gavin groaned and buried his face in the warm hollow where her thighs curved into her buttocks. The dress was gathered around her waist, revealing her long legs and the golden froth of her pubic hair. In one abrupt motion, Gavin stood up again, took Lori firmly in his arms, and ground his hardness against her.

'I want you so much,' he said against her throat. 'I'm going to take you right here.'

It occurred to Lori that the passengers on the boats outside could see the two of them on the verge of making love in front of the window. To the old Lori, that thought would have been mortifying. But this new creature wanted to be seen, completely naked, being fucked like the desirable woman she was.

Lori melted under the pressure of Gavin's cock. The dark, dangerous scent of his arousal was making her dizzy. Her knees wobbled, and her heart pounded so hard that its beat threatened to knock her off balance. Wrapping her arms around his broad back, she dropped her drink. Glass shattered; red wine splashed across the golden floorboards.

'Oh, God, I'm so clumsy! I can't believe it. Let me clean it up.'

She started to fall to her knees, but Gavin grabbed her wrists.

'Stop. It doesn't matter.'

'But the floor is going to be stained!'

'The floor can wait. I can't.'

He turned Lori to face the window; just as well, because the intensity of his eyes was more than she could bear. She leaned against the glass, her palms splayed over the darkness. Gavin pushed her skirt up again, more roughly this time. The dress was an elegant trap. Lori tried to shake the garment off, and in her haste the inevitable happened. The old chiffon tore, releasing a thousand beads that leaped in chaotic, sparkling patterns across the floor.

Startled back into reality, Gavin and Lori watched as the beads' frenzied dance went on and on, the bits of glass seemingly propelled by an energy of their own. After a few moments the last of the beads settled into stillness.

'Fuck me,' Lori said. 'I want you to fuck me now. I don't give a damn about this old rag.'

Lori let the dress fall around her feet. She kicked herself free of it.

Gavin stared. On the surface he seemed overwhelmed by the scene: the sea of beads, the sight of Lori's nude body, the force of her demand. But his body knew precisely how to react – his erection was straining so hard against his trousers that it pulled his belt away from his waist.

Lori braced herself against the window, spread her legs and tilted her ass upwards. Her breasts dangled like pink-tipped ornaments. She didn't recognise her face in the glass: fiery, glittering, demonic. Her hair billowed over her shoulders in an electric cloud.

'What's the matter? Are you afraid we'll break your glass house?'

'Hell, no. You want to be fucked, you've got it.'

In the dark glass she watched him reach around the front of her body to touch her sex. He played with it roughly, his fingers yanking at her pubic curls then digging through her slick folds. The sound of him unbuckling his belt, struggling to release himself with one hand while he fondled her with the other, drove Lori crazy. Soon she felt the length of his cock against her ass cheeks. She longed to see the details that made his organ different from any other: the relief map of veins, the hue of the aroused skin, the ridges and creases that held his unique musk. A droplet of her juice spattered on the floor.

'Touch your pussy,' he ordered. 'Show me how you rub yourself.'

She reached down and clutched her lower lips. They were so slippery that there was no friction; she might as well have been reaching into a bowl of warm pudding. Using all five fingers she spread herself open. She could see her sex glistening in the glass, held wide for all to see. Her clit twitched and Lori rubbed the tiny knob, bringing herself to a near peak.

'That's enough.' Gavin yanked her body back. 'I'm going to give you exactly what you asked for.'

'Please. Please! I can take whatever you can give.'

Gavin laughed, a harsh, choking sound. 'I'll remember that.'

Then the smooth head of his cock was pushing its way through her lips, and with one long stroke he penetrated her halfway to the hilt. Lori cried out. Her cunt wasn't used to being filled.

'You want more?'

'I want all of it!'

Gavin had her by the hips. She watched his reflection in the window as he thrust into her. Knowing that the whole town below, and the passengers on the boats, could be watching the same scene sent her to the brink. Her orgasm mounted like a thunderhead. Her legs, trembling on the frail support of her high-heeled shoes, burned with the effort of staying upright.

While he rocked inside her, Gavin began to explore the puckered bud of her anus. When he eased his finger into her tight opening, her muscles tried to push him out, but as she gave in to the intrusion, she felt herself relax. The sensation was odd, nothing like the demanding greed of her cunt. Gavin's finger circled inside her, opening her further. The unexpected invasion of his hard finger, combined with the smooth strokes of his cock, was too much to take.

Lori gave a shattering cry as her body tensed from head to toe. She fell against the window, breasts pressed against the glass, and let the orgasm shudder through her. Gavin followed her through every spasm.

Whimpering, Lori drifted down. Her body was still raw; her nerves leaped at the slightest nudge. When

Gavin began to thrust towards his own peak, she climaxed again. She could feel his arousal building to a crisis. His fingers dug into her waist as he girded himself for his climax.

'I'm going to come,' he said through gritted teeth, 'all over your sweet ass.'

In one smooth glide he pulled out. The sensation of his shaft leaving her body was almost as powerful as his entry, and Lori summoned up the last of her strength to keep herself from collapsing. Gavin let out a sharp cry. Molten fluid bathed her buttocks, trickling in a hot runnel down the cleft.

Lori dropped to her knees. She had never felt so open, so exposed. Her breath had clouded the window with mist. She wiped a clear space in the glass, and caught a glimpse of her face, shining like a new star, before her gasps steamed the window again.

'The house didn't break,' she said in wonder.

Gavin knelt down beside her and took her in his arms. He was shaking too, his body radiating a damp heat.

'I'm as surprised as you are,' he said.

'I've never felt anything like that before.'

'How did you feel? Tell me.'

Lori let her hair fall over her eyes. She didn't want to re-enter the world yet. Tonight, in this house, on the land where Lorelei Price had lived, Lori had been possessed.

'I felt like Lorelei,' she whispered. 'Will you show me her photos tonight?'

Gavin buried his face in the moist jungle of Lori's hair and laughed.

'For once, I have no interest in those photos. The only thing I want to do tonight is carry you to bed, strip off my clothes, and make love to you again.' He took Lori's hand and placed it on his penis, which was already half erect again. 'Could you handle me one more time?'

Lori gripped his cock. She twisted around to face him and pulled him into a long kiss, her tongue penetrating his mouth as eagerly as his cock had probed her earlier. His penis swelled in her hand.

'I can handle you a thousand more times,' she said, when she allowed the kiss to end.

5

The night passed like a lush erotic dream, alternating between passages of slow-motion ecstasy and surges of blinding heat. Lori refused to stop making love to Gavin until her fingers had memorised his body, until the shadows had turned silver and he was begging her for rest.

After a few hours of sleep Lori opened her eyes to find herself inside a box of sunlight, afloat on acres of glittering blue. The beauty of the morning sea was so dazzling that she had to recover for a moment before she could take in the other details of Gavin's bedroom: the drafting board and high stool in one corner, an upright roll file filled with neatly rolled blueprints, a wooden table that held a blue ceramic bowl. Lori recognised the bowl as the work of a potter who lived down the road. The light playing on its glaze turned the simple object incandescent.

The thought that Gavin appreciated the beauty of a local artisan's work was comforting to Lori, who felt a bit like a scullery maid waking in the master's bed. The master himself was nowhere to be seen.

Lying beside her on the sheets, spread across the valley that his body had left, were six black-and-white photographic prints stored in archival envelopes. Lori sat up and lifted one of the photographs. Through its clear protective jacket, the old paper felt warm against her fingertips. She propped it against her knees and studied the swirls of black and white, the creamy shadows and areas of stark relief. What kind of dreamscape was this?

Lori turned the picture around, and the light and darkness fell into place.

Three bodies lay together, their limbs intertwined. The outlines of the composition were milky, blurred, but the longer Lori gazed at it, the more details emerged. The delicate lighting couldn't hide the tension in the subjects' bodies. A series of rippling shadows that might have been a range of sand dunes were actually two columns of muscle, and the slope of sand beneath them was the skin of a bare thigh. Two pricks met, head to head, across a pelt of cloudy hair. The streaks of light that crosshatched the organs made them appear to be in motion.

Two cocks were duelling over a woman's sex.

The woman's mound was tilted, as if she were wriggling with pleasure, turning first towards one man then the other, teasing them with her furred warmth. What a dilemma, to have the choice between those two fine organs! Both cocks were beautifully formed and dark, engorged with blood.

The contrasts of shapes and tones in the composition set off a waterfall of images in Lori's mind, sending her into a fantasy. She imagined that her own body lay interwoven with two men, whose pricks butted against each other in a battle for Lori's cunt. She rearranged the scene so that her lovers lay side by side on their backs, while she swept her lips back and forth between the continents of their skin.

After this mild teasing, she took one erection in each hand and tugged them closer together until the pearls of juice seeping from their cock-heads intermingled. One after the other she lapped at the heads.

'Those photos give you ideas, don't they?'

Gavin walked in, looking tanned and muscular in a plain white T-shirt and tight, faded jeans. On the tray he carried, coffee steamed in two heavy white mugs, and quarters of fresh cantaloupe twinkled in a white bowl next to a plate of croissants. He set the offering down on the mattress.

Lori pounced on the tray, snatching a piece of fruit. 'You must have sold your soul to get this! Melon's not even in season.'

'I have my sources.'

'I bet they're female.'

'Possibly.'

Gavin sat down next to Lori. He pulled the chunk of golden fruit from her lips and replaced it with his mouth. He smelled of soap, laundered cotton and fresh sea air. She tasted a ghost of her own musk in his kiss.

'I wanted to give you some time to look at these by yourself,' Gavin said. 'What do you think?'

'I've only looked at one of the prints so far. I picked it up and got lost in it.'

'The three lovers?'

Lori nodded.

Gavin picked up the print. 'That's one of my favourites. It shows her natural instinct for framing an erotic shot.' With his forefinger he drew a square around the shadowed hollows of the lovers' bodies. 'She's drawn to the parts of the body that are most engaged in the sex act, whether that be the genitals, eyes, lips, hands or feet. She knows how to capture the essence of the lovers' experience in a single scene.'

'The picture looks so spontaneous. I always imagined her working with a big, boxy camera on a tripod and posing her models.'

Gavin took one of the croissants and tore it apart with his hands, golden flakes drifting onto his hard, muscled thighs. Lori watched his full mouth move as he ate. His lips were swollen and bruised from Lori's love bites.

'She did use traditional studio equipment, but she was also experimenting with smaller, more portable cameras. She borrowed a 35-millimetre Leica from one of her wealthy clients and started taking pictures all over Paris – in cafés, in the Bois de Boulogne, and in some of the city's most famous bordellos. Her work was getting more fluid, less structured. You can see the influence of that here. Lorelei had the best of both worlds: an unconstrained creative gift combined with classical studio training.'

'It's strange to think that she had her first studio here. Right where you built this house.' Lori looked around at Gavin's bedroom, then out at the water. 'You know, something has been happening to me since I came here last night.'

'What do you mean?'

'I feel like I'm changing.'

'Does that bother you?'

'No. The strangest part is that it doesn't. I've never talked to any man the way I talked to you last night. Telling you to fuck me, letting you take me in front of the window. I would have been too scared of looking like a fool, or turning you off. I probably would have turned *myself* off. Instead, I loved it.'

Gavin smiled. 'So did I.' He glanced down at his crotch, inviting Lori to see how aroused he was. She stroked the bulge as she continued to talk.

'When I was looking at the print, I drifted into this fantasy about being the woman in the photograph. Is the woman Lorelei?'

She picked up the photo and handed it to Gavin. He turned it over and studied the back. '"Three friends, 1930",' he read aloud. 'She wrote that here in pencil. The woman in the photo wasn't your great-aunt.'

'How do you know?'

'I'll show you.'

Gavin brushed the crumbs off his jeans and stood up. He left the room and came back holding a manila folder, which he gave to Lori. She opened it. Inside was a sheaf of word-processed typescript.

'What is this?'

'Read a page or two. You'll see.'

Lori scanned the papers. Every few pages were marked with a date, beginning with June 1928 and ending with August 1934. She caught references to a sea voyage, Paris, a hotel in Montparnasse; an exotic supper at a Hindu restaurant, a fully-clothed frottage session in a smoky jazz club. Then Lori saw the signature at the bottom of the page: 'Still your lover, Lorelei.'

'How did you get these? This is her correspondence from Paris!'

Gavin nodded, grinning like a schoolboy. As Lori examined the letters, her eyes fell on scenes of heated intimacy, descriptions of lavish Parisian homes and decadent parties with artists, aristocrats, and anonymous lovers.

'Where are the original letters?'

'In Paris, with a woman named Geneviève Pommier who insists that she owns them. She allowed me to have the letters transcribed – for an astronomical fee, of course. Obviously she thinks she's found the goose that laid the golden egg. She wasn't about to let me keep Lorelei's original documents. The only reason she sold me those photos was that they were printed on proof paper, and they aren't in the best condition. She probably tried to sell them somewhere else and found out that they had no commercial value.'

'What does this woman have to do with Lorelei? Why does she have her things?'

'She's the daughter of a woman named Nanette Pommier. Nanette was Lorelei's assistant and protégé. When Lorelei vanished, Nanette ended up with the entire body of her work.'

'Who were all these letters addressed to?'

'Justin Maxwell, her lover back in the States. He was one of Lorelei's professors at Beardsley College. Married, of course. He paid for her trip to Paris. The only condition was that she couldn't contact him again. But she loved Maxwell, and she didn't want him to forget her. More than anything, she wanted to make him jealous.'

'So why didn't Maxwell end up with the letters?'

'Lorelei didn't send them. She kept all of her correspondence to this man sealed and postmarked, but the letters were never mailed. When she left the hotel where she was living, she stuffed the letters under a mattress. By the time Nanette found them, Lori had disappeared.'

'I've heard about Justin Maxwell,' Lori said. 'But I never knew about these letters.'

'They were quite a discovery,' Gavin said. 'Without that correspondence, I couldn't be writing this book.'

Lori took the photo back and studied it again.

'If the woman in this photo isn't Lorelei, then who is she?'

Gavin took the letters out of Lori's hand. He leafed through the pages until he found the letter he was looking for, then handed the typescript back to Lori.

'Read for yourself,' he said.

Dear Justin,

The contents of this letter could make you ill with jealousy, so if you're feeling the least bit unwell, put it aside for another time – maybe when you're in bed with your wife.

I've been thoroughly enjoying the freedom you bought me. I don't know how much pleasure a human body can stand, but I think mine has reached its limit. I'm too worn out this morning to do anything but lie in bed and write.

Yesterday the photographer I work for left me alone in his studio while he went downstairs to spend the afternoon with one of his mistresses (in France, you see, married men like to keep their lovers close by, not send them overseas). About an hour later, three visitors came to the door, a young woman and two male companions. All three were stunning – and more than a little tipsy. The woman explained that she had 'posed' for my boss in the past, and I immediately understood that she'd been more than just his model. After a few drinks, she'd come to look for him. When I told her I was his personal assistant, she burst into tears.

'You're too pretty to cry,' I told her. 'Why don't I take your picture?'

While I rummaged through my employer's props, looking for a piece of brocade or an exotic cape for her to wear, the model began to undress. The little angel wanted me to photograph her nude.

I was happy to oblige – the girl was exquisite. Her tiny breasts curved up like tulip petals, the nipples wide and silky pink. Her flat belly and slim thighs were dimpled with pretty gooseflesh, and her pelt of brown fur must have offered little protection from the chill in the studio. She was a perfect example of a *garçonne*, one of these sexless flowers that are all the rage these days. Probably some farmer's daughter – the cafés of Montparnasse are full of luscious country girls. They all want to be models, dancers, or the mistresses of famous artists. Many turn into prostitutes.

The sight of the naked girl excited her friends. Both men sported tents in their trousers, and I was feeling a bit randy myself. While I was arranging the lights, praying that the damn fuse wouldn't blow, the men stripped and joined her on the rug. The little angel was sweet and willing, not like most of her kind. I've gotten so bored of those Parisian *mannequins*, with their nasty tempers and their sour breath and their sexless bodies.

I got few good shots of the three of them before the angel gave in to the effects of Pernod and passed out on the chaise longue. By this time, her friends were more interested in each other. I knew that the photographs wouldn't be a success. I was working with a slow exposure, and my subjects were too passionate by this time to hold any poses for me. Then the more dominant of the pair, a burly blond American, suggested that I put down my camera and join them on the rug. His Italian friend apparently spoke no English, but he beckoned me with a wicked smile.

I peeled off my skirt and shirtwaist as I stepped across the room, enjoying the rapt attention of my audience. Their pricks were as alert as their eyes. I sank to my knees so that I could enjoy the contrast of their erections. The Italian boy's member was almost purple, its smooth head as dark and shiny as a grape. His shaft was draped with the folds of a velvety foreskin. An opal droplet was already forming at the slit.

The American thrust himself in between us, butting his penis against my cheek. The shaft was as smooth and taut as a German sausage, except for a magnificent forked vein that rose along the base. His hair was a marvel, silky and golden. I wove the crinkled strands through my fingers and gave a sharp tug, which made him whimper.

Without releasing the American's fur, I sank the fingers of my free hand into the woolly depths of the Italian boy's black curls. I then pulled my lovers closer together, so that the heads of their cocks were touching.

Though I've admired many a cock in my life, I had never had the luxury of comparing two such fine roosters as these! Each organ stood at a distinct angle, each bush released a distinct odour. I closed my eyes and breathed them in. The Italian's skin had a gingery scent, and his musk was riper than the American's. His fleece had a slightly gritty texture, while the American's pelt was so smooth that it seemed to melt between my fingers. By now I was as good as drunk. Clutching one penis in each hand, I licked the two heads, then tried to take both of them into my mouth at the same time. This set off a battle, with my two lovers fighting for a place between my lips.

I decided to lavish my affections on the Italian. I clutched his shaft and slid his foreskin back and forth under my palm; through the thick folds I could feel the map of his veins. He murmured something sweet and imploring in his native tongue. I took him all the way down my throat. His hips swayed, and he crooned in ecstasy.

The boy wouldn't need much coaxing to reach his peak. I cradled his balls in one hand, while inserting my forefinger into his back passage. His muscles bit my finger. I gripped his balls more tightly. He froze, shook violently from head to toe, and came in my mouth in a series of hot pulses, shouting like Lucifer tumbling from heaven.

I then turned to my American. I have to admit that I was daunted by the size of his prick. I licked my palms, took hold, and set to the task with an industry that would have made my Calvinist ancestors proud.

In rhythmic waves I pulled at the American's sex, using not just my hands, but my arms, shoulders, and back. He was already so swollen that I thought he might burst. I gripped the root, opened my mouth wide, and inch by inch I swallowed him. My lips hurt, my jaw ached, but a stream of moisture gushed from my sex.

The Italian heard the pitter-pat of my juices on the floor and came to my rescue. He knelt down behind me and reached around to slide his fingers between my lower lips. He found my pearl right away, strumming the nub with such skill that I knew he was as experienced at loving women as he was with men.

I wiggled back to give him even more access, and he took this as an invitation to penetrate me, with one finger in my slippery cunt and another in the tighter hole behind. I sank down onto my lover's hand. He cradled me against his body, rocking me in a motion that was at once sensuous and comforting. Through my fog of ecstasy, I realised that I had never been filled so completely.

By this time I was wild. I began to work my fingers up and down the American's shaft in a swift glissando. I sucked the crown of his cock, applying the most pressure to the ring of the head. The contrast of sucking with the lightning motion of my fingers pushed him over the brink. His body stiffened, and he bellowed like a bull. I yanked him out of my mouth. With every contraction his giant shaft quaked, sending an arc of spume through the air. He was an impressive shooter, this American. I was dazzled!

But not for long. The Italian tightened his hold on my body. As the American sank to the floor, the boy brought me to a masterful peak. I clenched my teeth and rode his hand like a horsewoman rushing to the end of a race. My cry was more like an Apache yell than a shriek of pleasure – loud enough to wake the dead.

It was loud enough to wake the little angel, who opened her eyes to see me bucking to a glorious finish. As I settled down to earth, I saw her pretty face droop with disappointment at the fun she'd missed. A drop of liquor may be good for the digestion, but a woman who souses herself is likely to miss much greater delights.

I hope you enjoyed my little story, Justin. Maybe

there's a lesson in it for you, too – a lesson about what you've lost.

Still your lover,
Lorelei

After she had finished reading her great-aunt's letter, Lori was grateful that she was lying down.

'Well? What did you think?' Gavin asked.

'Are you sure Lorelei wrote that?'

'You sound like you wish she hadn't. Does it embarrass you?'

'I'm not embarrassed, I'm overwhelmed.'

'Lorelei was a strong woman. She wasn't ashamed of her own pleasure.'

'I wish I could be like her.'

'You are.' Gavin sat up. 'Let me show you something.'

He leafed through the folder that held Lorelei's letters and pulled out a sheet of paper. It was a photocopy of an old photograph, a portrait of a woman in profile. Her short blonde curls framed her temples and cascaded over the top of a sequined headband, from which rose a single feather. Until now, Lori had only seen two photos of her great-aunt, both taken before she left the country. In one of them she was a grinning, snaggle-toothed seven-year-old, squinting in the bright light of a summer afternoon. In the other she was a teenager, her arms wrapped around the waists of her two sisters, her face in shadow under the brim of a floppy hat.

Lori stared at the portrait. 'She does look like me. I mean, I look like her. I never knew how much.'

Gavin smiled. 'I told you there was a strong resemblance.'

'Do you have the original of this?'

'Yes. It's in a safe in New York, with my other research materials.'

'Can I see it someday?'

'Of course. You'll see everything, once you start working with me on the book.'

'Were you serious about that? About wanting my help?'

'Absolutely. I want you to design the book for me. I want this book to have a personal feel, a sensuality that's almost palpable. I don't want it to look like a typical biography. You have a natural empathy with the past. I want you to translate that into something that strikes the reader whenever she turns a page.'

'The way the scent of an old dress rises from the cloth.'

'That's right. That's what I'm looking for.' Gavin's dark eyes gleamed. 'Among other things.'

He pushed the sheet away from Lori's body. The scent of her sex mingled with the fruity perfume of the melon. Lori moaned and slid down among the sun-warmed bedclothes. Gavin took a wide slice of melon from the bowl and brushed it across his lips.

'This would taste much sweeter with your juice on it,' he said.

Lori parted her legs, and Gavin eased the tip of the half-moon slice between her pussy lips, which opened eagerly to the unfamiliar shape. He hadn't peeled the rind off this piece of fruit, and the rough texture stimulated Lori in a way she'd never felt before. At her gasp of surprise, Gavin began to pull the melon back and forth, creating a delicious friction. Even the hard edges of the fruit wedge felt strange and exciting.

Gavin pressed Lori's clit with his thumb as he penetrated her more deeply. She raised her hips, urging him to rub her. His thumb moved in slow circles. Lori's lips tightened around the melon slice, until she felt the soft, cool flesh give way, the pulp of the fruit mingling with her own hot fluids. Lori squeezed as hard as she could, until the rind dug into her flesh. The bite of its corners, combined with the abrasion of Gavin's thumb, brought her to a stinging crescendo of pain. She cried out at the sharp discomfort, which melted into pleasure as her climax rippled through her.

Gavin smiled as he watched Lori come. Obviously he did not intend to let the cantaloupe go to waste. He pulled the softened melon out of Lori's cunt, brought it to his mouth and bit into the glistening flesh.

'I was right. It's much sweeter now.'

He held the melon out to Lori and she took a bite, curious to taste the flavour. At first she thought Gavin must be crazy; the slick fruit wasn't sweet at all. It tasted briny, slightly bitter. Then, under the saltiness of her own juices, the cantaloupe's succulent honey exploded in her mouth.

'Sometimes the true taste of a fruit is hidden.'

Gavin laughed at Lori's startled expression. He leaned over to kiss her, his erection pressing into her thigh. She helped him pull his T-shirt over his head. His coppery nipples stood to attention against the golden expanse of his smooth chest. When she placed her lips to one of the dusky points then nipped at it with her teeth, he yelped.

Lori smiled. Somehow, in the madness of last night, she had left Gavin's nipples unexplored.

'I want you to lie down on your back,' she ordered.

Gavin stood to strip off the rest of his clothes, then let Lori guide him down on the bed. She straddled him, clasped his wrists above his head and set to work on his nipples, licking and kissing them, transforming them into cut gems.

'Suck my cock,' he whispered.

Lori shook her head, tickling his chest with her long curls. He clenched his jaw as she ground the pebbles between her teeth. Under her belly she could feel the wetness of his pre-come. His cock shifted as if it might find its way into her cunt by sheer will, but she kept the rigid organ pinned. His fingers clutched her curls, trying to urge her downwards, but she was enjoying her torture far too much to stop.

'I have to fuck you.'

'Not yet.'

'Now!'

If penetration was what Gavin needed, she would give it to him at her own sweet pace. Still holding his wrists, she hovered over the tip of his cock, her soaked pubic curls tickling the silky head. The erect muscle twitched. Lori glided back and forth, letting herself be slowly split. Then she began to ride it. Gavin closed his eyes. His pulse beat so hard that its tremors shook Lori's body. She had never felt the sheer high of sexual control before. Now she knew how Lorelei Price must have felt every day of her adult life – strong, passionate and richly sexual. When Gavin began to drive his hips upwards, the speed of his pounding matched the beating of her heart.

'I'm going to come,' he groaned. 'God, am I going to come!'

In one quick movement Lori slid off her mount. She knelt between Gavin's thighs, gripping his cock with both hands. The first spurt of jism christened Lori's cheek, and she stroked his prick until the rest of the come rose in a white fleur-de-lis, splashing her lips and throat.

As they lay together in the dazed aftermath, Lori wondered what was in store for her. When she went back to her normal life, she wouldn't be the same woman who had met Gavin at the bar last night. The past twenty-four hours had cleared her vision. The gossip about Lorelei Price had formed a veil between Lori and her great-aunt, preventing her from seeing her ancestor's full power – and seizing that power for herself. Watching the flush recede from Gavin's sculpted cheeks, watching his eyes close in satisfied tranquility, Lori knew that the veil had been torn for good.

6

Separating herself from Gavin was torture, but Lori finally untangled herself from his warm, musky sheets.

'Don't tell me you're leaving.' He reached for her hand to pull her back into bed. She toppled into his arms, and he began to nuzzle her neck.

'I've got an appointment with my lawyer this afternoon,' Lori protested. 'And tonight I'm taking Melanie out to dinner. It's her birthday.'

Gavin smiled. 'Buy her a drink and charge it to my tab. Hell, buy her a bottle of Dom Perignon. She gave me the best gift I've had in years.'

'If I'm really that great, how about lending me some clothes? Otherwise I'll have to drive home naked.'

'Are you kidding? I'd give a year's salary to see a naked blonde driving a jeep.'

Lori bit Gavin's shoulder. He shouted in mock agony.

'Well, you're going to have to find another blonde to live out that fantasy,' she said. 'I've got a respectable reputation in this town.'

After a quick shower, Lori dug through his closet until she found a pair of shorts and a T-shirt. Gavin's clothes drooped comically from her slender frame, but she had nothing else to wear. The beaded dress was now a pile of glittering glass.

In the bedroom Gavin dozed among Lorelei's scattered photos and papers. Lori leaned over to kiss him goodbye. As their lips met, his cock stirred again. Lori wished she could grab it, to feel it grow even firmer in her hand, to watch the head emerge from the soft foreskin. Another hour of sex with Gavin would be so much better than a meeting with her hatchet-faced attorney.

'Don't forget about Friday,' Gavin murmured as Lori was leaving his bedroom.

'What's on Friday?'

Gavin raised his head from the pillow. 'We're going to New York. Don't you remember? We planned everything last night.'

'Did we?'

'Yes, darling. You have erotic amnesia. Somewhere in between orgasms last night, I told you that I'd arranged a meeting with my editor on Friday afternoon. I want you to meet her.'

'Shouldn't you talk to her first? Make sure she approves of you working with someone?'

Gavin sat up. 'I already told her about you. Rayne Hughes is a cautious woman, but she'll come around. Take Lorelei's photos and letters home. Get to know your subject. If you know what you're talking about, she'll warm to you. The meeting should be short and sweet, and then we'll have the rest of the weekend to cause trouble in New York.'

'The whole weekend? But I can't leave Chimera for that long. I have to . . .'

Lori stopped, wondering exactly what it was that she had to do. She couldn't remember the last time she'd done anything spontaneous. A small business owner had to be responsible, dedicated, or she wouldn't survive. But shouldn't life consist of more than survival?

'If you've got another commitment, I'll reschedule the meeting with Rayne. I won't hold you to any promises you made in post-orgasmic bliss.'

'No. I don't have anything urgent to do. I'll meet you here Friday morning. Maybe I'll even have a few mock-ups to show your editor.'

Gavin grinned. 'Perfect. You're perfect.'

'Almost,' said Lori. Then she dashed away, cradling the folder with Lorelei's photos in her arms.

Back at home, Lori hurried up the back stairs to her rooms. A quick glance in the mirror showed her a face shining with joy; her eyes were as clear as fresh water, and her cheeks were a pearly pink. Lori stepped out of Gavin's clothes, then held his T-shirt to her mouth for a moment, breathing in his scent.

In the past, a night of hot sex would have been followed by a storm of questions, fears and self-recriminations. A thousand doubts would have rained on Lori's happiness: had she seemed too awkward in bed? Too eager? Too needy? Would her new lover call her today, or would he wait till tomorrow? Or had he already fled the country in fear of a permanent relationship?

Today Lori's conscience was blissfully clear. No doubts, no guilt. Lori hummed as she glossed her lips with a clear pink gel. Even with only this small trace of makeup, she looked gorgeous. This is how Lorelei Price must have felt after a long lovemaking session – not weakened, but empowered.

Lori threw on some clothes and left her damp hair loose, then sneaked out of the house down the back staircase and walked the five blocks to her attorney's office. The briny ocean breeze aroused all her senses. Last night had sent her libido into overdrive; by the time she knocked on Howard Mather's door, Lori's panties were wet from the memory of Gavin's touch. She thought she saw the lawyer's nostrils flicker as he ushered her into his office.

'Can I get you some coffee?' he asked, eyeing Lori's uncombed curls and rumpled clothes. The offer was polite enough, but the attorney's raised eyebrow said, *You look like you need a cup of strong black coffee.*

'No, thanks,' Lori said. 'I've got another commitment later, so I'm in a hurry.'

'I've prepared your partnership agreement,' Howard Mather said, frowning. 'I was hoping we'd have some time to review it.'

'Wonderful. I'd love to stay, but I've got a hundred things to do. Why don't I take it with me and get back to you if I have any questions?'

'Please. Sit down for a minute.'

Howard sank into his old leather chair. With the knobby tips of his fingers he began to worry the brass studs on its arms. Lori recognised the habit. Howard was concerned about his client. Ever since Lori's father had died Howard had taken a paternal interest in her future, an interest that was more oppressive than reassuring.

With a sigh Lori sat down in one of Howard's guest chairs. The partnership contract lay on his desk, temptingly out of reach. Lori wished she could grab it and run, sparing herself the lecture that was sure to come.

'I know you don't think this is a good idea, Howard. But Chimera is *my* business. The shop doesn't belong to my parents anymore. There's nothing wrong with taking a partner, especially someone who's invaluable to me.'

'If you want to show Miss Paxton that you value her, give her a bonus,' Howard said. 'Making her a partner is premature. She's too young to contribute significantly to the business. A partner should bring something more to the table than youthful enthusiasm.'

Lori bristled. 'Melanie has already brought much more to the business than enthusiasm. Sales have risen consistently in the past three years, mostly due to her efforts. If anything, she's more of a businesswoman than I am. I was running on automatic pilot until Melanie came along. She's aggressive, she's creative, and she's a wizard with numbers. You know I can't keep books to save my life.'

'But can you trust her with your books? She's a newcomer to Morne Bay.'

'Anyone who can't trace their roots back at least two centuries is considered a newcomer around here. Melanie's family has lived in Morne Bay for fifteen years, and I've been her mentor for half that time. I've watched her change from a snotty teenager into an assertive, confident woman.'

'She got into some trouble a while back.'

'She was caught shoplifting once. When she was thirteen. The store's owner didn't press charges.'

'Shoplifting,' Howard repeated, giving the word a sinister weight. He propped his elbows on his desk and made a prim steeple with his fingers. 'Are you sure there hasn't been anything worse?'

'Of course not.'

'Whether you'd care to admit it or not, Miss Paxton has a bad reputation in this town. If you take her on as a partner, that reputation is going to taint you as well.'

'A reputation for what?' Lori's cheeks burned, and she stiffened in the hard-backed chair. 'For having a healthy sexual appetite? For making love to more than one person in her lifetime?'

'You can't see the problems that await you if you let the Paxton girl into your business. But I can. You don't know what's good for you, young lady.'

'Don't talk down to me. I'm not a child.'

'Things could go very wrong for you if you go ahead with this. Your business will suffer. I'm warning you.'

Lori stood up, towering over the attorney. She had never spoken sharply to Howard Mather before. She had never been anything but a good little girl in his presence. But today she didn't care what he thought of her. She didn't care if she never saw his pious face again.

'Morne Bay has never done anything for the women in my family. For the first time in my life, I can truly sympathise with my great-aunt. Nothing has changed in this town since she left. It's no wonder she never came back – she had no use for hypocrites like you.'

Lori snatched the partnership contract off Howard's desk. With her vision blurred by rage, Lori barely saw the old man's flabbergasted face. In the resounding echo of the slamming door, she couldn't hear him dialling the ancient rotary telephone, but she knew that was exactly what he was doing. By tonight, everyone would know that Lori and Melanie were going to be business partners. The gears of the local gossip engine would be oiled with malice.

For the first time in her life, Lori couldn't care less.

The tavern glowed with the undulating light of a pine fire. That deep flagstone fireplace was one of the reasons Melanie loved this restaurant, and for her birthday the proprietor had agreed to light it for her. Few men could resist a birthday request from Melanie, especially when she was dressed in smoky burgundy velvet that clung to her breasts and hips as if it had been poured over her skin.

Melanie had chosen a secluded booth close to the fire. Her cinnamon-brown eyes were translucent in the light of the flames, and her glossy lips were the colour of ripe currants, contrasting dramatically with the creamy pallor of her skin. She had piled her hair on top of her head in an auburn mound, and vintage art deco earrings dangled from her ears.

Lori recognised the earrings as part of Chimera's inventory. Fourteen-carat gold with rubies – they were more than costume jewellery. Had Melanie decided to take them for herself as a birthday gift? As Lori bent down to give her friend a kiss, the spectre of Howard Mather rose in front of her eyes. *Can you trust her?*

Melanie patted Lori's cheek. 'Don't worry, I'm only

borrowing these for tonight,' she said, noting Lori's glance at the earrings. 'They'll be back in the display case tomorrow morning.'

Lori blushed. Guilt plucked at her conscience. 'You look stunning. Keep the earrings. You deserve them.'

'Really?' Melanie beamed and touched her earlobe. 'I hope you don't mind, but I invited someone to join us for dinner.'

'Of course I don't mind. It's your birthday.' Lori paused. 'This isn't another surprise for me, is it? Because after meeting Gavin, I don't think I could take another one.'

'No, this isn't a surprise for you,' Melanie laughed. 'This man is all mine. Wait till you get a look at him. He'll be a bit late, but it'll be worth it.'

'I'm glad he's coming late. I want to give you your present.'

Lori opened her handbag and pulled out a manila envelope. Her hand shook a little as she handed it to Melanie. Melanie was twenty-five years old today, a mature woman with a strong sense of herself, a powerful sexual energy, and a clear idea of where she wanted to go. Until this moment, Lori had never considered the possibility that Melanie might turn down the partnership offer. Now she realised that the younger woman would have many more opportunities in her future, most of them far better than this. Suddenly Lori felt shy, and more than a little scared. What if Melanie said no?

Melanie nibbled her lower lip as she opened the envelope and read the agreement. Lori stared down at her lap, her fingers winding themselves into nervous knots. Melanie was quiet for a long time. When Lori looked up, she saw that her friend's eyes were sparkling with tears.

'Take some time to think about it,' Lori said. 'It's just an offer. More like a gesture, really, to show you how important you are to me. You'll have lots of offers for other jobs. You might want to start your own business, for all I know. But I wanted to make the first bid on you. If you join me, half of everything is yours. Of course, that's not saying much.'

Lori's words were drowned out as her friend jumped from her seat and enfolded her in a hug that literally took Lori's breath away.

'I never dreamed you'd do this, Lori. How can you think I'd go anywhere else? The answer's yes! I'll sign the contract right now, before you change your mind.'

'I won't change my mind. And I don't want you to sign anything yet. Take a few days to think about the proposal. Read the fine print. I want you to be sure this is right for you.'

Melanie sat down again. 'It's right for me. It's exactly what I want.'

Lori wasn't the only one to notice Melanie's excitement. At a nearby table an elderly couple held their soup spoons suspended in mid-air as they strained to hear the women's conversation. Lori thought of the prudish Howard Mather and what he had said about Melanie's reputation.

'You know,' Lori said, 'if the business keeps growing, we might think about leaving Morne Bay. We could set up shop in Boston. Maybe even New York.'

'We could go anywhere! How about San Francisco? Then we could sell sex toys, leather corsets, anything we wanted.'

'We certainly could.'

'Lori, look.' Melanie wriggled in her seat. 'He's here.'

Lori turned. The hostess was leading a young man across the room. The boy would have looked spectacular carved in marble, but he was equally devastating in an Oxford shirt and jeans.

'Who is that? He looks familiar.'

'It's Neil!' Melanie whispered. 'My landlady's son. You

didn't recognise him, did you? He's been working on a fishing boat all summer. Went to sea and grew up.'

'You can say that again.'

Neil walked up to the table like a pilgrim approaching a shrine, his gaze fixed on the holy grail of Melanie's bosom. He held out a clumsily wrapped box, which Melanie accepted with grace.

'Happy birthday, Melanie,' he said, with an endearing trace of a stammer. 'I wanted to give this to you now, but you'd better not open it till later.'

'Thank you, darling. I'll save it just for us.'

'And you're Lori, right?'

'That's right.' Lori rose to shake Neil's hand. His palm felt a bit clammy, but his handshake was firm; strong fingers, with just enough calluses to generate an enticing masculine friction.

The boy stood as if frozen between the two women. He didn't seem to know where to look. His eyes travelled from Melanie's ripe cleavage to Lori's long, loose hair, back to Melanie's jutting nipples, and across again to Lori's bare legs. Lori wore an ivory silk shift that was slit on both sides. She had accessorised the simple dress with chunky gold jewellery – a choker and bracelet that appeared molten in the tavern's low lights – but those accents couldn't draw attention away from her spectacular legs.

Lori suggested that Neil slide into the booth beside Melanie. As if in a trance, he obeyed. Lori sat down next to him. She would have liked to talk to Melanie about the partnership agreement, but she was glad Neil had come. He was wonderful to look at, with his heavy black curls and crystalline blue eyes. He had full, carved lips and a classical cleft chin. Lori found herself wishing she could stroke the curve between that chin and his lower lip.

He's a boy, she scolded herself, *and he's Melanie's date. I had better behave.*

Lori unfolded her napkin and placed it on her lap, then ducked her head to hide her smile. When was the last time she had had to order herself to behave?

The waiter served the trio a bottle of complimentary champagne. Inexpensive stuff, it tasted a bit sour at first, but after the first two glasses it went down like air. They polished off the bottle, then ordered a second one to go with their appetiser course. Melanie ordered raw oysters.

'Here's to natural aphrodisiacs,' Melanie declared. She gave her friends a sultry look as she held up her champagne flute. 'Let's see where they take us.'

Neil laughed, his cheeks turning fire-engine red. The champagne had relaxed him, but he was obviously still nervous. Before she knew what she was doing, Lori found herself giving him a comforting pat on the thigh. Maybe not so comforting – the boy jumped as if she had delivered an electric shock. Lori sneaked a peek at his crotch. No doubt about it – he was hard. And Lori could guess how he got that way: with a little help from Melanie's nimble fingers.

'So, birthday girl,' said Lori sweetly, 'when did you become ambidextrous? I've never seen you hold a glass with your left hand before.'

'My right hand is otherwise occupied,' Melanie replied, pursing her lips. She leaned forwards until her breasts nestled against the table. From Neil's shocked expression, Lori could tell that Melanie's fingers had found their goal. He sputtered into his champagne. Lori couldn't help laughing.

'I'm sorry, Neil. I'm not making fun of you. It's just that I know Melanie so well.'

'Then you know what I'm doing right now, don't you?' Melanie purred. 'Why don't you help me?'

Neil looked at Lori, his gaze a mute plea for her touch. She slid her hand underneath the table – the tavern was equipped with thick, heavy tablecloths that hid any suspicious activity – and stroked his knee. Gradually she moved upwards towards his groin. When she reached the crest of his straining cock, Lori's hand met Melanie's. The women smiled as their fingers intertwined.

'Should we order dinner?' Melanie asked.

Neil moaned. 'I won't make it all the way through dinner, Mel.'

'Eat a couple of oysters,' Melanie coaxed. Twelve oysters on the half shell lay on a bed of ice in a silver bowl. 'We promise not to torment you. You'll need lots of nourishment to get ready for what's coming.'

She winked at Lori, who realised that Melanie had planned this whole scenario. As recently as two days ago, Lori would have been shocked at the tableau that Melanie was suggesting. She might have agreed to it eventually, but only after weeks of discussion and self-analysis. Tonight she was ready: so ready that she had to part her thighs to accommodate her swelling pussy. From what she had felt beneath the denim of Neil's jeans, he was very well-endowed.

Neil ate one of the oysters, tipping his head back to swallow the silken flesh. He licked the brine off his lips, then took another. He held the shell out to Melanie, who gulped the succulent tidbit with relish. Then it was Lori's turn. Neil extended the oyster to her lips and tilted the spiny bowl so that the broth flooded her mouth. She looked into his blue eyes as she sucked the meat straight out of the shell. But before she could swallow the shellfish, Neil's smooth lips were pressed to hers, his tongue dancing inside her mouth.

While Lori was catching her breath, Neil turned to Melanie and kissed her too. Lori was glad that Melanie had reserved a table in the shadowed corner of the tavern. She took advantage of their concealed position, squeezing Neil's erection through his jeans as he prolonged his kiss with Melanie. The young man gave an imploring groan, and Melanie broke away. Her cheeks were rosy with arousal, her eyes dreamy from Neil's kiss.

'Waiter!' Melanie trilled, waving to catch the man's attention. 'We're ready for the check. Please hurry. It's my birthday, and I've got to get home to open my presents.'

The most clear-headed of the three, Lori drove them to Melanie's house. Glancing in the rearview mirror, she could see the lovers pushing themselves against each other, kissing as if they were feeding from each other's lips. Neil scooped Melanie's breasts out of the deep neckline of her gown and teased the nipples with his tongue. Lori just hoped he could restrain himself from pulling up Melanie's skirt and entering her. She didn't want to drive the jeep off the road as she watched.

In the dim light, Melanie's breasts were creamy fruits tipped with dark stems. Lori's pussy clenched. In a very short time, she would have the chance to taste those nipples too. She had always harboured a hidden curiosity about Melanie's breasts. Would they really be as flawless as her cleavage promised?

The drive to Melanie's house was mercifully short. The trio toppled out of Lori's jeep and into each other's arms. The women giggled and whispered as they led Neil up the staircase to Melanie's boudoir.

'My mom's in Boston, visiting her sister,' Neil said. 'We can make as much noise as we want.'

'I don't know about that,' said Melanie. She propped her fists on her hips and frowned. 'Lori is a respected businesswoman in this community. And now that we're going to be partners, I'll have to conduct myself properly too. At least a dozen people saw the three of us groping each other in the tavern. By tomorrow morning the whole town will know that we went home together. This could ruin us.'

Lori and Neil stared at each other. Neil's look of disappointment, as he saw his fantasy being withdrawn, could have melted a heart of granite. Lori was stunned by how much Melanie's words sounded like Howard Mather. Had she somehow found out about the attorney's threats?

'Oh, you two!' Melanie cried, throwing her arms around her friends. 'I was only joking. Do you really think I give a damn about what anyone thinks? I just want to strip you both naked and eat you alive.'

Neil laughed with relief. Lori shivered. Melanie held them both until they relaxed, and the embrace melted into a three-way caress.

Lori was still shy about the situation. Except for her encounter with Melanie in the bathtub, she had never made love to a woman before, much less to a man and a woman at the same time. But as she revelled in the separate sensations of touching a hard male body and a supple female one, her doubts dissolved. A new instinct for pleasure had taken over Lori's cautious imagination.

Melanie broke the circle, taking Lori and Neil by the hand and leading them to her bedroom. While they waited, she lit candles all around the room. From the swell of Melanie's parted lips, the quick rhythm of her breathing and the visible swelling of her nipples, Lori could tell that her friend was aroused, but she lit the candles with ceremonial grace, creating a constellation of tiny lights. Lori had always thought Melanie's bed was over the top, with its baroque mahogany frame and heaps of foamy pillows. Tonight, with the candles shedding a mellow glow across her antique lace coverlet, the bed reminded Lori of an illuminated stage.

'Wait,' Neil said. 'I have to go get your present. We left it in the jeep.'

'Couldn't I save it for later?'

'You have to open it now,' Neil insisted. 'I'll be back in two seconds. Don't go anywhere.'

After he left, Melanie approached Lori and kissed her on the cheek: a friend's kiss, this time, full of warmth and affection. Lori marvelled at Melanie's power to communicate her feelings through her body. Her bold sexuality could change to sisterly affection with one shift of her hand, one tilt of her head.

'How do you feel about this?' Melanie asked. She tugged at one of Lori's curly locks. 'I know it's something new for you. But I had a feeling that you were ready.'

'I'm ready,' Lori whispered. Intoxicated by the soft light and the scent of Melanie's perfume, the thought of the hard young man who would return any second made her weak. 'I'm more than ready.'

Neil bounded into the room, brandishing the long box. He gave it to Melanie with a flourish. Even with sex on her mind, Melanie couldn't resist a present. Her eyes shining, she tore through the wrapping, then broke into peals of laughter when she opened the box and saw its contents.

'Neil, it's gorgeous. And this is the perfect time to break it in.'

She showed the gift to Lori, who gasped. The hand-carved dildo had a satiny wooden shaft and an intricately carved head. Just by looking at it, Lori could tell that its ridges and notches would fit into all the right places, stimulating a woman in the most sensitive crevices of her body.

'May I hold it?'

Melanie handed the instrument to her friend. Lori held its lovingly crafted bulk in her open palms, just feeling its weight. She ran her forefinger along the underseam, which was carved with a serpentine motif. Unlike the comical plastic phallus that Melanie had shown her the other day, this was an object designed for the subtlest sensual pleasures. It was beautiful to look at and magical to touch, and the scent of the wood would mingle with the smells of the juices that seasoned it.

'Where did you find something like that around here?' Lori asked.

Neil grinned with pride. 'I made it.'

'Neil, I can't believe it! Melanie didn't tell me you were so talented.' Lori's gaze shifted from the beautiful phallus to Neil's slender fingers. She recalled the calluses on his palms, and realised that he must have earned some of them from his incredible woodwork.

'I've been working on it for months,' Neil said. He turned to Melanie. 'I was thinking about you the whole time I worked on it. About your body, the way you're made. The way you would feel when I put this in you. So if I ever had the chance to make love to you, you'd be satisfied.'

'I'll never forget this birthday,' Melanie said. 'I've had two of the best gifts of my life in one night.'

'And you're about to get a third.'

Neil bent to kiss the dip of Melanie's bare shoulder. He pulled down the neckline of her dress so that the fabric slid over her shoulder, baring her breast. While Neil suckled at Melanie's nipple, Lori unclasped the barrettes that held her friend's hair in place. As her hair tumbled down, its strands releasing a cloud of fragrant warmth, Melanie shook her head. Lori unzipped Melanie's dress. The burgundy velvet gown slid to the floor, revealing that Melanie wore no panties, only black lace garters and stockings with her high-heeled pumps. Lori took a moment to drink in her perfection, the dips and swells of Melanie's pale, curvy body. Being here with Neil and

Melanie was so decadent, but it also felt profoundly right. Sharing Neil would seal their friendship in a way that few people in this town could ever understand.

Neil guided Melanie to the bed. She lay down and arranged herself into a provocative position, her thighs parted.

'Since I'm the birthday girl, I get to give the orders,' she said. 'I want to start out by watching the two of you together. Neil, let Lori take your clothes off.'

The young man happily complied. He let Lori linger over the buttons on his shirt while his erection grew to fill the crotch of his jeans. Melanie's sex made a light smack as she parted it with her fingers, stimulating herself to the sight of Lori kissing Neil's hard, ridged stomach. She reached for the wooden dildo and eased it into her cunt, and Lori stopped for a moment to watch her friend penetrating herself with the exotic instrument. Melanie pushed the faux cock deeper into her body, until it was settled comfortably inside her. Then she lay back to watch.

Lori turned her back to Neil, in an unspoken invitation for him to unzip her silk shift. The dress shimmied down the length of Lori's nude body and formed a pool on the floor. Neil made a low sound deep in his throat, and Lori turned and let him see her from the front. His mouth fell open as he drank in the sight of her lean brown limbs and her high, round breasts, with their alert nipples. Lori knew that her skin, in the candles' soft light, must look like honeyed satin. Candlelight was so sexy, so kind.

'You're beautiful, Lori,' Melanie said. 'All this time I've known you, I've never known how beautiful you are.'

Neil nodded in mute agreement. The head of his penis was thrusting against his waistband. Lori unbuttoned his bulging fly.

'Doesn't he have a lovely thick tool?' Melanie said.

'Yes, he does.' Lori tried to encircle the rod with her thumb and forefinger, but it was too wide.

'Give him a lick. He tastes wonderful.'

Lori helped Neil step out of his jeans, then knelt to inhale the warm air that came from his groin. Melanie was right; his scent was clean, fresh. She smelled soap, with an underlying trace of his young male essence. The shaft of his penis was slightly wider than the glans, and the whole organ was so engorged that it gleamed. Its tender slit was already seeping. Lori rolled her palm around the crown, moistening her skin, then administered a gentle rub-down from root to head. Neil whimpered.

'Go ahead. Taste him,' Melanie urged. 'But be careful. He looks like he might burst.'

Neil's thigh muscles quivered as Lori grasped the base of his rod and began to lick it in long, slow strokes. She savoured the feeling of every indentation, every vein under her tongue. Deliberately she lavished attention on his shaft, ignoring its sensitive tip, so that he wouldn't be stimulated to the point of orgasm. Neil groaned. She shook her head, so that he could feel the cloud of her full hair brushing his thighs. Although she knew she had to hold back, Lori couldn't resist tasting a few drops of his fluid, and sipped at the tiny hole, letting the droplets spread across her tongue. Suddenly Neil pulled away, breaking her hold on his shaft.

'I'm too close,' he panted.

'Good boy,' Melanie said. 'Save some of that for me.' She seemed close to coming herself, her hips rocking up and down and her eyelids fluttering. With skilful movements she pulled the dildo back and forth, giving it a small twist each time. She caught Lori watching her and smiled.

'Why don't you take over for me?' Melanie asked.

Feeling hesitant, Lori straddled Melanie's thighs. She

had no idea how to use the dildo on her friend, but both Melanie and Neil were waiting for her to try. Neil lay down on the bed next to his lover.

Lori tossed her hair back to get a better view of Melanie's sex. Her outer lips were stretched taut around the dildo. Lori gripped the base of the phallus and pulled, but Melanie's shell-like inner lips tugged at the tool, as if reluctant to let it go. Melanie laughed.

'You're going to have to work a little harder than that.'

'But I don't want to hurt you.'

'Go ahead, shove it back and forth. Give me a good screwing. I'll let you know if it starts to hurt.' Melanie clutched a handful of Neil's curls with her free hand. 'Neil, my clit needs attention too. It's as ripe as a cherry.'

Neil burrowed through the folds of Melanie's sex until he found her swollen love-knot. While rubbing his erection against her thigh, he suckled at her breasts and tweaked her clitoris, and she murmured encouragement to Neil as he paid court to her lush body. His gifted fingers played across her slick pubic pelt while Lori pulled the dildo in and out of Melanie's passage. Lori was reluctant to push as hard as her friend had requested. A slow, measured pace seemed more suitable at first, but as Lori's pulse quickened, so did the speed of her thrusts.

Melanie lifted her bottom off the bed and spread her thighs into a full split. A deep flush spread from her breasts to her cheeks, her eyes had closed, and her mouth was open and gasping in time to Lori's penetration. Lori couldn't believe the rush of power she was feeling, penetrating another woman. Was this what men felt, whenever they made love?

Lori's desire was blended with a dose of envy. She had never before been jealous of her friend, but suddenly Lori wanted to be the one being reamed by the ornate dildo, the one being bitten and sucked by Neil's hungry mouth. Lori began to work the dildo back and forth at a much faster rate – harder, harder, until she was giving Melanie a vengeful pounding. Instead of protesting, Melanie cried out with joy. Poor Neil was in agony, so turned on by Lori's aggression that he had to grip his balls to keep from exploding.

'Please let me fuck her,' Neil begged. 'Let me be inside her when she's coming.'

In one long, cruel stroke, Lori pulled the dildo out.

Melanie shrieked in disappointment, but her irritation was replaced by ecstasy as Neil took Lori's place and entered her. He threw his head back, losing himself inside her well-oiled channel. Both of the lovers were at the brink; Lori could feel the heat rising from their bodies as Neil's muscular buttocks rippled with each thrust.

Melanie's climax started with a silent shout. For one long moment she held perfectly still, her entire body straining upwards, then she let go. The sight of Melanie in full-blown orgasm was too much for Neil. His cries joined hers as they bucked and shuddered. Seconds before he ejaculated, Neil pulled out and sprayed Melanie's mound with thick milk.

Splayed out on the bed, Melanie turned her flushed face to Lori. 'Will you lick me clean?' she gasped. 'I want to come again. Please, make me come again.'

Neil backed away. The boy looked like a stallion who'd been ridden for hours. His nostrils flared, and his curly mane was drenched with sweat. Pulses beat in his temple and throat. Breathing raggedly, he collapsed on the bed.

Lori climbed between Melanie's thighs. Her friend was already writhing, anticipating this new pleasure. Instead of sating her lust, Neil had only unlocked it. Her lovely face was feverish with greed. She raised her hips, exposing her inner lips and auburn thicket, thick with Neil's fluids. Lori didn't know where to start.

'Lick me like a cat,' Melanie instructed. In the midst of her excitement, she seemed to remember that Lori had never eaten another woman's pussy before.

Lori bent her head to Melanie's steaming bush. She began by lapping away Neil's seed, a more salty taste than Melanie's pungent juices. Together they formed a heady potion, and Lori was soon intoxicated. Once she got used to the scent of Melanie's musk, her tongue delved deeper, and she teased the inner whorls of Melanie's cunt, deliberately skirting her enlarged clitoris. Lori quickly felt herself learning how to do it properly. She took the nub lightly between her teeth and sucked.

'That's amazing,' Melanie moaned. 'Don't stop. If you stop, I'll die.'

Melanie began to rock her hips. She took hold of two long locks of Lori's hair and guided her movements: now faster, now more slowly; now round and round, now up and down. Before long the women were working in unison to guide Melanie to her second orgasm.

At this point Lori decided that Melanie's cunt was being neglected. She inserted her finger, then changed her mind and replaced her finger with her thumb. With her thumb buried in Melanie's cunt, she sought Melanie's anus with her forefinger.

'Oh, yes, that's it. Fuck me in both places.'

Melanie widened her straddle so that Lori could dive into the recess between her plump cheeks, and her finger soon reached its goal. Gently she probed Melanie's bottom until the tight hole yielded to her touch. Lori loved the contrast of the loose, wet vagina with the taut, elastic anus. Within seconds both openings tensed. Lori tightened her grip and nibbled Melanie's clit.

Each pulse of Melanie's climax sent a rivulet of fluid

into Lori's mouth. This time her cries were softer but more beseeching. As she descended, Melanie stroked Lori's hair lovingly.

'Thank you,' Melanie whispered. 'Thank you for everything.'

'Let me fuck you, Lori,' Neil pleaded. 'You haven't had a chance to come yet.'

Lori looked up to see Neil lying back on a cloudbank of Melanie's foamy pillows, stroking his hard-on. Melanie helped her roll over on her back, so that her head rested on the cushion of Melanie's pubis. Neil mounted Lori and, as he plunged into her open cleft, Melanie reached down to squeeze and tweak Lori's nipples. Neil was very wide, wider than Gavin. Less than a dozen thrusts with that cock sent her toppling over the edge, and her orgasm was sudden, hard, and brutal in its intensity. When Lori came down, she was startled to find her legs wrapped firmly around Neil's back.

The boy smiled. 'I never thought I'd get the chance to satisfy two women in one year, much less in one night,' he said.

'Oh, we're just beginning,' Melanie laughed, caressing Lori's breasts. 'We haven't even tried all the configurations of this trio yet. I still have to make love to Lori.'

'And I have to make love to Neil's dildo,' Lori added. 'Where did it go?'

The three of them looked around for the artificial phallus, but it had rolled out of sight. More enchanted with each other's flesh than the ornately carved wood, they fell into a damp, giggling heap.

'Now we're partners in every sense,' Melanie murmured into Lori's ear.

7

Like a blossom bending to meet a hummingbird, the model hovered above her lover's tongue. Her knees were bent in a pretty squat, and his hands gripped her thighs as she straddled his mouth. She pinched one of her nipples between two varnished fingernails. Around her neck she wore a dark shawl, which framed her pale breasts. Its fringes dangled on either side of the man's face, twin curtains concealing his identity. But the woman's face, a portrait of joy, was clearly exposed. Her head was tilted back in concentration, and her sleek black bob dipped down to shadow her neck. Her rosebud lips formed an O, and her eyebrows were lifted, as if she were startled by her own pleasure.

On the floor next to the couple sat the remains of a tea party. The Japanese teapot had been overturned, spilling its contents across the floor. One of the cups was intact, but the other had been cracked in half. Half of the cup lay on the floor next to its mate. The other half hung like a shattered helmet from the head of the man's erect cock.

Lori turned the print over. The words 'Tea Ceremony' had been scribbled on the back, in a bold, curvy hand.

Lori smiled. In the dignified silence of Morne Bay's public library, Lorelei Price's images bloomed like obscene flowers. Lori sat at a corner table in the reading-room, where no one was likely to look over her shoulder. Her great-aunt's prints and letters lay spread around her, concealed by a stack of books about Paris. As she studied the pictures, Lori scribbled rudimentary drawings and notes on a sketchpad. Later she would convert these sketches into page mock-ups to show Gavin's editor.

Lori was slowly reading her way through the letters that Gavin had loaned her. She was dwelling on every detail, searching for clues. So far she had traced her great-aunt's life in France from the day she stepped off the ship at Le Havre in 1928 to the day she decided to break off with her employer, the fashion photographer Jules Réverte, and set up a studio of her own. By 1930 she had built up a reputation as a portrait photographer, but her real business lay in providing erotic images to a handful of wealthy clients. Society matrons whose husbands were distracted by the flocks of beautiful girls who filled the city begged Lorelei for more seductive images of themselves, which they could use to lure their straying mates back to the marriage bed. Fashion models with a craving for adventure offered themselves as subjects for her erotic tableaux. While her native country sank into an economic depression, Lorelei prospered in Paris.

Everything about the city bewitched the young photographer. Lorelei went to the cinema whenever she could, danced the Charleston and the tango in music halls, listened to jazz in cellar clubs. She seemed to be in constant motion, lost in a whirl of friends and lovers whose names evaporated like bubbles in champagne. When she went dancing she wore a gold lamé dress, so short that it proved to all of Paris that she was a natural blonde. She bought a pair of knickers printed with crossword puzzles, and invited two of her rival suitors up to her studio to see which one could complete the acrostics first.

Using an old tour guide, Lori located the street where her great-aunt had lived in Montparnasse. She found the places where Lorelei's favourite cafés stood: the Dôme, the Dingo, Le Boeuf sur le Toit. Lori closed her eyes and imagined her great-aunt laughing with friends, sipping champagne, smiling at a new lover from underneath the brim of a cloche hat.

Then there were the bordellos. The more time she spent in Paris, Lorelei wrote to her lover Justin Maxwell, the more fascinated she became with the city's *maisons closes*:

> The *maisons* make me realise how far I've come from my Puritan roots, for these places are perfectly legitimate here. Knowing how curious I am about such things, a male friend of mine has taken me to visit several bordellos, where we have enjoyed watching the girls hold private performances for us.
>
> The more functional *maisons* have comfortable bars downstairs, where the girls meet prospective clients before retiring to one of the chambers upstairs. These tiny rooms have no more aesthetic appeal than the inside of a water closet. I prefer those establishments where function is given over entirely to form, where the décor is more extravagant than my wildest fantasies.
>
> Last week I visited one of these dream creations, a *maison* called the Bouquet d'Étoiles. Each room was decorated according to a different theme. Because my friend Pierre is a frequent client, he was allowed to take me on a tour of this fabulous palace, where one can visit the bedchamber of a Venetian courtesan, the interior of a Turkish harem, the depths of an African jungle and the shrine of an Egyptian goddess within a single hour.
>
> But the rooms are the least of the curiosities at this establishment. The reason for its popularity is not the sumptuous décor, but the amazing variety of women one can choose from. As the madam escorted us through the ornate bar, she whispered a discreet commentary about each of the flowers in her garden.

'Mimi is a contortionist – not a bone in her body. Giselle's tongue is so long and graceful that she can moisten a man's member from top to bottom in one swoop. Denise has not two perfect breasts, but three. And Clotilde has the rarest gift of all: a love knob long enough to satisfy those women who crave the softness of their own sex and the hardness of the other.'

Pierre took the madam aside and, after a brief discussion, led me to the harem room. I made myself comfortable on the floor, sinking into a bank of satin cushions while he removed his clothes and dressed in a robe that the madam had provided. I could hardly wait for the spectacle he had arranged. I longed to have my camera with me, but I would have to make do with having the night's visions imprinted on the lens of my imagination.

After several minutes the curtains of the tent opened, and Clotilde and Giselle appeared. Clotilde was a petite blonde, Giselle a plump redhead with an ample bottom. Both women wore the briefest of garments: short sheer drapes that crossed over their shoulders and barely covered the shadows of their mons. They held hands and smiled, looking for all the world like mischievous schoolgirls. Pierre's manhood stood erect, in tribute to their beauty, growing so large that it parted the panels of his robe. He is a tall, auburn-haired man with a smooth, well-muscled body and a cock like veined pink marble. The women lost no time in settling him down on a pallet on the floor so that they could have their way with him.

With the candles casting amber light over their intertwined bodies, and the billowing Moorish tapestries bathing them in rich shadows, the three were figures from another world. Giselle began to practise her lingual magic on Pierre's manhood, her long pink tongue winding around his organ like a serpentine vine. Her full bottom wriggled as she worked. Giselle sat behind Pierre's head, her hands reaching forwards to dandle his nipples. She allowed her friend to lick Pierre's prick into a gleaming sword, then began her own part of the dance.

I have never seen anything as strange and exotic as Clotilde's body. The madam didn't lie when she said the young woman had a rare gift. If you are repelled, my dear, by my description of her anatomy, rest assured that you would be utterly enchanted by her in reality.

Clotilde rose to her knees and inched forwards until her vulva was hanging above Pierre's mouth. In order to show her jewels to their best advantage, she had trimmed her mound of Venus, leaving only a feather of blonde hair to cover it. Her puffy pink lips were shaved bare, and they pouted like the petals of a shy orchid. But when Pierre took hold of her hips and began to lap at her sex, the orchid blossomed. I gasped as her labia parted to make way for a clitoris of miraculous length, which swelled even further at the stimulus of Pierre's tongue. Noting my surprise, Clotilde leaned backwards, exposing her entire vulva for my view. From the red heart of her sex, her clitoris unfurled like a pink stamen.

No botanist in the depths of the lushest tropical forest could have felt more wonder than I did at that moment, or more longing to capture some evidence that I had seen such a treasure. My eyes literally ached for my camera. I have heard the clitoris disdainfully referred to as a 'cock *manqué*,' a button that falls short of the splendour of the penis. But no one seeing Clotilde's organ could compare it to the male member. For that matter, it is nothing like its female counterpart. Clotilde's clitoris is an instrument from another species, a hermaphroditic gem, more like flora than fauna.

What an extraordinary sight! While Giselle sucked lavishly on Pierre's manhood, he bestowed a similar favour on Clotilde's clitoris, so that the three of them were joined in the most unusual union I have seen. Clotilde was the first to succumb. Her eyelids fluttered, and her pretty face flushed as she approached her summit. Pierre gave her clitoris an extravagant pull, which sent her into a transport of joy. He came himself seconds later, casting his liquid pearls across Giselle's quivering breasts. Seeing that her two lovers were fatigued, Giselle brought herself to a climax by riding Pierre's thigh.

After we had treated Giselle and Clotilde to a bottle of champagne in the bar, Pierre and I walked back to my hotel. I was silent for once, folded up in the mink I had received as payment for a portrait of an aristocrat's mistress. When Pierre asked why I was so quiet, I told him I was marvelling over the things I've seen and done in Paris, and thinking how far I'd come from the life I lived at home. In Morne Bay I felt like a freak of nature, a woman who carried on a sham of a career while keeping her true passions squirrelled away like filthy secrets. In Paris those passions have blossomed into a calling. Seeing wonders like the ones I witnessed tonight, I wonder how I could have been ashamed of my real work. How can there be shame in the frank beauty of the naked body, the infinite variations of desire?

As Pierre and I passed a café, I caught a fragment of a song sung by a bawdy chanteuse, who strolled through the crowd with her skirts lifted almost to her waist. 'There's no shame in being shameless,' she sang, as if she had chosen her lyrics to match my thoughts. 'There's no joy in being alone.'

Pierre laughed and put his arm around me. I did not tell him that I was thinking about you, Justin. Paris has turned my shame into joy. Unfortunately, it has not made me love you any less. You are the one thing I regret.

Lori put the letter down. Her fingers burned, as if she had been caught rifling through someone's personal belongings. In a sense she was doing just that. But wouldn't Lorelei have wanted someone else to know how Paris had transformed her? Wouldn't she have wanted someone in her family to know what had become of her?

The possibility that her great-aunt could be alive, living somewhere in Europe, had crossed Lori's mind, but she knew that was very unlikely. Gavin's sources believed she was dead, and a search on the library's internet terminal produced no sign of a Lorelei Price in any of the major European cities. 'Would I go home if I could?' Lorelei wrote in 1934. 'A lot of my expat friends have cleared out of Paris, but I can't stand the idea of going back to the States.'

Miraculously, my business is better than ever. It seems that every aristocratic beauty who buys a gown from Molyneux or Schiaparelli must have her photograph taken – first in the gown, then out of it. Women who would die of shame in front of a male photographer unfold their wings for my camera. Being in the studio with me is as intimate as being in a sister's bedroom – as intimate as being with a version of oneself. Men love to model for me, too, because the eye of desire rests on *them* for a change. Everyone wants my photos: the more decadent, the better.

Last Saturday I was invited to a picnic in the Bois de Boulogne with the strangest party of women that I've ever seen assembled. The wives of two French politicians had decided to treat their husbands' mistresses to an afternoon of outdoor pleasures. Consider this – the mistresses outnumbered the wives by three! Two wives, five mistresses, one photographer, and a picnic basket that could have fed every resident of the 14e arrondissement. What followed was a sapphic orgy of mythic proportions, a riot of moaning and caterwauling and passionate licking that lasted until twilight. By the time it was over, every woman was sated, and I had a set of deliciously scandalous photographs. Do I want to go home? Not on your life!

The unemployment rate in Paris continued to rise, but Lorelei managed to scratch out a living as a studio photographer, relying on portraits of high-society clients. *Le tout Paris* was determined to enjoy the dazzling displays of creativity that continued to burst forth from artists, musicians and fashion designers even as the economy slid further into decline and French politics fell into disorder. In love with Paris, Lorelei wanted to hold her lips to the city's pulse as long as she could. Had she still been in Europe in 1939, when England and France declared war on Germany? Had she survived the bombing of Paris in 1940 and seen the occupation of Hitler's troops?

Lori couldn't understand her great-aunt's decision to stay. Lorelei Price didn't seem to be a foolhardy woman. Was her father really so hard and unforgiving that the prospect of going home was more frightening than the risks of war?

Memories of old family rumours drifted through Lori's mind. Most of them were idle gossip but one stood out, so grim and unsettling that Lori thought it might hold a fragment of truth. Lorelei's father, disgusted by his daughter's expatriate lifestyle, had once said, 'If she was killed over there, I hope it was an Allied bombing. It would serve her right for betraying everyone back home.'

Doodling on her sketchpad, Lori wrote the word 'betrayal'. She had never weighed the potential of that word before. Lorelei's entire life – her photographs, her sexual liaisons, her escape from Morne Bay – had always been considered a betrayal of the family. But could Lorelei's father have known something else about her?

Lori picked up another one of the print proofs, a portrait of a solitary woman. She stood in front of an open window in a room that overlooked the interior of a Paris courtyard. She wore a long, gauzy kimono, which fell over her shoulders like a folded pair of butterfly wings. Under the kimono she was nude. Her body seemed to have been sculpted out of the same light that streamed across her long thighs, grooved stomach and small, high breasts. One of her legs was raised, her bare foot propped on the wrought-iron guard-rail outside the window. In her right hand she held a silver mirror, which was tilted downwards so that she could study the length of her body. The angle of her head exposed the graceful nape of her neck, and her cropped, curly hair fell across her cheek. A shadow transformed her face into a silhouette.

The back of the print was blank, the woman unidentified, but Lori knew it was a portrait of her great-aunt. For a long time Lori sat looking at the photo.

Suddenly she longed to be in Paris. She wanted to follow her great-aunt's path down the city's leafy boulevards, through its bohemian neighbourhoods, through its labyrinthine night world. She wanted to sit in the cafés – if they still existed – where Lorelei had spent so many afternoons and evenings. She wanted to find the hotel where that photograph had been taken. She wanted to be there in that room, watching her great-aunt. More than anything, she wanted to touch Lorelei just once, to prove that she had been real.

'Where did you go?' she whispered to the woman in the photograph. 'Where on earth did you go?'

8

Manhattan had never felt so exhilarating. In the past Lori had always been frightened of the city's concrete canyons, its gridlocked traffic and brusque crowds. The flocks of stylish women had intimidated her, and the never-ending chorus of car horns assaulted her ears. When Gavin invited her to spend the weekend in his apartment, a flutter of that old apprehension tickled her stomach. But now that she was here, hurrying down the streets with Gavin, Lori felt that she was seeing the city for the first time; not just seeing it, but feeling it, sensing its pulse, falling into its rhythm.

Gavin's pace was faster in New York. He walked with fluid speed, spoke with a harsher clip. His body felt more powerful, as if he had taken on an extra layer of muscle. This new version of him excited Lori. Seeing him like this, a native of this sophisticated urban world, made her ache for him to fuck her. When they passed a teenage couple French-kissing in front of a hot dog stand, Lori threw her arms around Gavin's neck and kissed him just as hungrily. She expected him to be embarrassed, but he pressed his mouth against hers with such force that it took her breath away. The other pedestrians hardly noticed them, except as a roadblock to their progress.

'Do you think anyone would care if we had sex right here?' Lori said when Gavin finally released her. She was panting like a sixteen-year-old, and her panties were drenched.

'Only if we got in their way. Sex, mugging, murder – it's all part of their daily fare.'

'Where are we going first? Central Park? The Empire State Building? I want to do everything a tourist would do.'

'First we're going to meet my editor. Remember?' Gavin laughed.

'Do you think she'll like me? How do I look?'

Lori was wearing a loose black bolero jacket over a cream silk blouse and black leather mini-skirt. A hand-painted scarf around her neck added a splash of colour, looking with its daubs of lavender, green and blue like a strip torn from an Impressionist's canvas. Her hair was twisted up in a sleeker version of her usual French twist, minus the curly tendrils. She wanted to look like a woman who could whip up professional designs and meet the most stringent deadlines. She wanted to look like anything but a country mouse with a cardboard portfolio.

'You look perfect,' Gavin said.

Before the meeting he showed her his loft, a vast expanse of space in a converted warehouse. Giddy with curiosity, Lori wanted to inspect every detail of his home: the books stacked on industrial steel shelves, the complicated stereo system, the black leather furniture and elegant wine rack. But Gavin had other ideas. He led her to a window that overlooked the city. Lori glanced down at the swarm of vehicles that wove through the maze of streets far below.

Gavin wasted no time pulling up Lori's skirt and stroking the soft, sculpted planes of her thighs. He slid two fingers under the hem of her panties and plunged into her moist sheath.

'My, my. You're already wet.'

'You shouldn't have kissed me on the street. It brought out my exhibitionist side.'

'As I remember, it was you who kissed me. I only responded.'

'Well, it was a very passionate response.'

Gavin thrust his fingers in and out of Lori's cunt. She arched her back and pushed her hips forwards. When he rubbed the soft spot beneath her pubic bone, she moaned and threw her head back. In a slow, swirling friction, Gavin's thumb caressed her clitoris. Lori rocked her hips back and forth, a silent entreaty for him to continue.

The cacophony of the traffic, the shadows cast by neighbouring buildings, the gossip of pigeons: all of the city sensations vanished in the bliss of being touched by Gavin. She had never had a lover who could orchestrate her pleasure so skilfully, or bring her to a climax with such confident assurance. She straightened her back so that she could look into his face and see her own desire reflected in his mouth and eyes.

Gavin withdrew his fingers. He placed his fingertips to his mouth, then to Lori's.

'Wait until later,' he whispered.

'But I could come if only –'

'Later,' Gavin repeated. 'Now we have to go and meet Rayne. I want you to think about me while we're talking with her. Imagine my fingers exploring your pussy. Think about my prick turning to stone whenever I look at you. When you see me cross my legs, you'll know I've got a hard-on.'

'You'll be thinking about sex while we talk to Rayne Hughes?'

'Hardly the height of professionalism, I know.'

Lori reached down to test the state of Gavin's crotch. Under his trousers, his penis was standing at full attention. While she rested her hand on his stiff shaft, Lori kissed Gavin's mouth. She could taste her own flavour on his lips. She wondered if Gavin's editor knew him well enough to guess what he would be thinking about, or what he had been doing just before the meeting.

'Do you ever think about me when you're working?'

'I fantasise about you all the time, Lori. I'm as bad as I was when I was eighteen. I'll be checking my watch every two minutes, waiting to get out of Rayne's office. I'll be thinking about getting you in the elevator as soon as I can, backing you up against the wall, yanking those skimpy panties down and shoving my cock into you.'

He grabbed Lori's buttocks and ground his steely member into her. She could hardly breathe. By the time they finally met Rayne, Lori's composure would be shot. She struggled out of Gavin's arms and smoothed her skirt.

'Your editor's going to think we had sex in the taxi. Is my hair messed up now?'

'Your hair is beautiful. Every part of you is beautiful.' Gavin's gaze turned serious as he stood back and took Lori by the shoulders. 'There's something I have to tell you before we meet Rayne.'

'What's wrong? Do you think Rayne's going to object to us working together?'

'No, Lori. I can handle any objections she might have about that. But Rayne has recently raised a few doubts about your great-aunt's history. I wanted to warn you before the meeting that she might bring up those doubts again.'

'What doubts?'

'Before you start doing any serious research into Lorelei Price's life in Paris, you should understand something. You might learn some things that conflict with your impressions of her.'

'Gavin, I know what my great-aunt was like. She was famous for her libido. It's not exactly considered scandalous for a woman to have a healthy sex drive these days.'

'You know about Lorelei, but you don't know everything about her lovers. Some of them weren't the type you'd bring home to your mother. I suspect one of them was involved in her disappearance. She writes about him in her letters – his name is Doran Cross.'

'She hasn't mentioned him in the letters that I've read so far.'

'Well, keep reading. Cross was an erotic photographer who lived in Paris in the 20s and 30s. If you think Lorelei's life was a mystery, try doing a little research into Cross. Sometimes he identified himself as an American, other times as a British citizen. His French and German were so good that he could pass as a native of either country. Just as a clue to how extreme this guy's work was, his photographs made the Surrealists nervous. So did his personality.'

'And this man was Lorelei's lover.'

'Lover and mentor. He was known in Paris as the Enchanter. His reputation with women was legendary. The man was undeniably brilliant, but his taste in photographic subjects was bizarre. So were his sexual predilections.'

'Is that why your editor has doubts about the book? Because of Doran Cross?'

'Actually,' Gavin said, 'Rayne doesn't know about Doran Cross yet. I didn't want to tell her about him until I knew more about his background. The trouble is, I don't like what I've found so far. All I can tell you at this point is that with Cross, Lorelei may have wandered out of her depth.'

'What do you mean?'

Gavin looked at his watch. 'I'll tell you all about him later. We've got to go and meet Rayne. Punctuality is one of her fetishes.'

Before Lori could ask what Rayne's other fetishes were, Gavin had hurried her out of the loft.

Outside the cab window the city passed by like a bizarre carnival, alternately colourful and grim. With each new surprise, Lori's heartbeat accelerated. She longed to join the human chaos outside. This must be how Lorelei Price had felt when she first arrived in Paris, like a mass of exciting contradictions. Nervous and thrilled. Inadequate and extraordinary. Intimidated and aroused.

'I want to stay here forever,' Lori said.

The cab-driver, a bald behemoth, stared at Lori in his rearview mirror. 'You're insane, lady. This place is hell. Me, I'm blowing this popsicle stand. I'm going to live with my mother in Florida.'

Lori buried her face in Gavin's shoulder and laughed.

By the time they reached the building that housed Obelisk Publishing, Lori's rapture had subsided into a case of jangling nerves. She clung to Gavin's hand as he led her through the drab lobby to the elevator. Once they were in, its battered interior smelled sour and musty, and its mustard-yellow walls did nothing to soothe her apprehension.

'Welcome to the glamorous world of publishing,' Gavin said dryly.

'Was this the elevator where you were going to ravish me after the meeting?'

Gavin grinned. 'It has a certain dangerous allure, don't you think?' The elevator wheezed and shuddered, as if in confirmation.

'I'll be happy if we get out of here alive.'

With a groan the elevator released them on the twenty-first floor. Sleek young men and women hustled down the corridor. Lori felt her first pang of real doubt. All of these efficient strangers were dressed in black, from head to toe. Lori pulled the pastel scarf from her neck, balled it up and stuffed it into her pocket.

'Are you all right? You're white as chalk.'

'I'm fine. It's just that everyone here is very . . . young,' Lori said, making a weak attempt to laugh. 'Were they born looking so confident?'

'Most of them are interns or editorial assistants. There's a new crop of them every time I stop by. That look of confidence is actually well-concealed terror.'

'Are you implying that I should be terrified?' Lori asked.

'Not at all. The elevator is the worst part,' Gavin assured her.

Lori didn't believe him for a second. She was out of her element. Her ankles wobbled in her unfamiliar high-heeled shoes, and her fingers felt slippery on her cardboard portfolio. She didn't feel at all ready by the time they'd found Rayne Hughes's office. The door was open, and the room held no visible signs of comfort. It was an airless cubicle, and every available surface was heaped with books. A sliver of light pierced the pile of manuscripts that blocked the office's only window.

'Rayne?' Gavin peered inside.

At first Lori thought that Rayne Hughes was hiding somewhere in this mountain range of books and loose papers. Then she felt a chilly presence in the hallway behind her, and turned to meet the stare of a tall, stunning woman. Lori had never realised that brown eyes could look so cold.

Rayne Hughes was a collage of off-balance parts that somehow melded into beauty. Her eyes were polished beads, her nose a beak, her mouth a broad crimson slash. Her long black hair boasted a jagged part on one side, and its raven gleam was so aggressively artificial that it defied any natural tint to match its glamour. Next to Rayne's elegant asymmetry, Lori felt like a potted petunia wilting in the shadow of a spiky bird of paradise. She extended a limp hand.

'I'm Lori Marwick. I'm a friend of Gavin's.'

Rayne's icy gaze darted from Lori to Gavin. Lori thought she saw the other woman's pale cheek turn pink, but the hint of colour vanished before Lori could identify it as a blush.

'Rayne Hughes.' Rayne ignored Lori's outstretched hand and eased past her into the office. 'I'm afraid I only have one guest chair. Gavin, I assume you'll be standing. Gentleman that you are.'

She's acting professional, not cold, Lori reassured herself. How had Gavin described Rayne? As a 'cautious businesswoman'. Still, a fierce heat flooded Lori's face as she watched Rayne remove a stack of books from the chair and place them with a thud on the floor. Gavin propped his elbow on a book pile that rose to the height of his chest. With his body draped casually against the books, he seemed at ease with Rayne's frosty demeanour.

'Lori and I have a proposition for you,' he began.

Rayne's slash of a mouth lengthened into a sardonic smile. 'I should warn you that I don't do threesomes.'

'Maybe you'll change your mind this time. I want Lori to work with us on the Price biography.'

Rayne's eyebrows rose. 'You need a research assistant?'

'I want a book designer. And a co-author.'

'But Gavin, we didn't –' Lori started to say, before Gavin's warning look silenced her. They had never discussed the possibility of Lori co-authoring the biography.

'Co-author, possibly,' Rayne said with distaste. 'Designer, no. The women photographers series has a unique look and feel. We can't deviate from that for the sake of one book.'

'You can't, or you won't?'

'Both. There's no reason we should change the way this book looks. Lorelei Price is the most obscure photographer we've included so far. We'd be taking a risk by dissociating her from the more well-known artists in the series. And even if we were to do a unique layout, we wouldn't need Miss – Mudwick, is it? Obelisk has its own design department.'

'There is no one at Obelisk who has what Lori's got.'

Rayne's smile was as deadly as a scythe. 'What does she have, exactly?'

'She's a descendant of Lorelei Price. She has Lorelei's blood. She has her name. She has her creativity.'

'Then she probably has the same prejudices that most people have about their ancestors. Family members don't make the most objective biographers. They either want to sling mud or wax sentimental.'

'Lori can bring energy to this project. I don't want Lorelei Price to be remembered as part of a textbook series with arty pretensions. I want this to be a damn good book, not just fodder for a remainder pile in some museum gift shop.'

'Perhaps your friend would be happy to see her ancestor memorialised in a remainder pile. Lorelei Price was a pornographer, after all. If I hadn't insisted that her work had a feminist slant, Obelisk wouldn't have touched her with a ten-foot pole.'

'I don't need your patronising bullshit, Rayne. This is a worthwhile project.'

'And I could scrap it with a flick of my eyelashes. Don't forget that.'

Rayne and Gavin stared each other down. Rayne's mocking smile dissolved as their gazes fused into a beam of anger. Lori wished she could slip out of the office. She fixed her eyes on her cardboard portfolio. Inside were seven mock-ups of page layouts she had designed for Lorelei's biography. How could she show them to this hostile bitch?

Before she knew what she was doing, Lori heard herself speak up.

'Why does erotica have to be validated by a political agenda?' she asked. 'If Lorelei Price is so obscure, why try to sell her work as part of a biography? Wouldn't a book of erotic photographs attract a wider audience? What if there were more emphasis on images and less on text?'

Silence fell.

'Maybe you're right,' Rayne said. 'We could market it as a coffee table book, just in time for Christmas. It would be perfect for doctors' offices. Every fertility specialist in Manhattan would want a copy for the waiting-room.'

'Cut the sarcasm, Rayne. Lori has a point. Obelisk isn't the only publishing house in New York. And you're not the only editor who expressed an interest in Lorelei Price.'

Rayne's face reddened. 'No! I'm just the only one who –' She stopped, took a deep breath, and pressed her fingertips to her temples. 'Look, Gavin, do you think we could talk alone?'

Lori stood up. 'I'll wait outside.'

Gavin followed her into the hallway. He closed Rayne's door.

'Did I make a fool of myself in there?' Lori whispered.

'You were wonderful in there, and I'm with you a hundred per cent. But you have to remember that the Obelisk series has scholarly prestige. This biography would legitimise Lorelei's work. I don't want to throw the opportunity away.'

'Neither do I.'

'Good. I'm glad we agree.' Gavin cupped Lori's chin in his hand and kissed her. 'Why don't you go out and get some fresh air while I talk to Rayne? Do some shopping, have a cup of coffee. Meet me downstairs in the lobby in an hour.'

'An hour?'

'It's going to take a little time to smooth Rayne's feathers. Obelisk is one of the smaller houses, but Rayne has a lot of clout in the industry. Whatever I do, I can't afford to alienate her.'

What about *my* feathers? Lori thought as she rode downstairs in the rickety elevator. Pedestrians jostled her as she walked down the street. She tried to recover the excitement she had felt earlier, but her mind kept wandering back to Rayne Hughes. Her attacks on Lori had seemed more personal than professional, almost as if she were more worried about Lori sleeping with Gavin than working on the book.

The noise and motion of the city were making Lori dizzy. Her feet throbbed in her Italian pumps. She had no desire to shop. She had no desire to sight-see. She had no desire to pay a small fortune for a cup of gritty coffee and a sandwich. She only wanted to kick off the torturous shoes and wade into the refreshing salt waves of Morne Bay.

Less than fifteen minutes had passed since she left Gavin at Obelisk, but Lori decided to go back to Rayne's office. She wasn't in any mood to wait around for Gavin to kiss his editor's perfectly sculpted butt. She already suspected that the anger between Gavin and Rayne was sparked by more than a business dispute, but it wasn't until she heard a muffled moan behind Rayne's door that she knew her intuition had been on target.

The door was closed, but not all the way. A thin crack allowed Lori to hear the unmistakable sounds of hot, juicy rutting. She heard the familiar exhalation of Gavin's breath – concentrated gasps, like a runner building up to the final sprint – and the accompaniment of Rayne's panting sighs. A rhythmic, rocking thud suggested that Gavin was taking Rayne on top of her desk. Lori nudged the door with her finger, opening it just enough to confirm her suspicions. What she saw shocked her more than anything she could have imagined.

Gavin had stripped off his shirt. He stood over Rayne Hughes, who was bent over her desk, her skirt rucked up around her waist and her legs spread wide. Rayne's legs and buttocks were streaked with red welts. As Gavin raised his arm, wielding a folded leather belt over

Rayne's ass, Lori saw where those marks had come from. Rayne shrieked when the belt fell across her cheeks, but her cry was muffled by a gag that had been tied around her sleek head. The leather strap gleamed with the fluids of Rayne's pussy.

'You like that, don't you?' Gavin said. 'You need a good strapping, you disrespectful bitch. Who do you think you are?'

Rayne whimpered a protest, her words incoherent through the gag.

'It's too late to apologise. You need to be put in your place.'

Rayne nodded furiously. Gavin dropped the belt and smacked her right buttock with his palm. She wriggled her hips and spread her legs in a desperate invitation. Her cunt pouted, shaven and glistening. Gavin unzipped his trousers and was soon so lost in the sensation of reaming her that he didn't even hear the door creak as Lori pushed it open by another half-inch.

Lori could see the curve of Rayne's breast behind the shadow of her arm. Gavin grasped the exposed tit and worked the nipple with his thumb and forefinger. Papers flew across the desk as Rayne writhed in response.

Gavin caught his breath and stopped for a moment, delaying his climax. Then he slowed his thrusts, turning his back-and-forth rhythm into a deep, circular grind. Round and round went his hips, with each rotation driving him further into Rayne's cunt. Rayne's scarlet buttocks rose from the desk as she urged her body backwards to meet her lover's thrusts. Gavin froze, threw his head back, and waited for the tide to recede. Lori knew he couldn't hold out much longer. Rayne's pussy was so wet that Gavin's inner thighs were smeared with her juices. He raised his hand to strike her ass again and, with her fleshy cheeks quivering at the blow, he exploded.

The first trickle of moisture felt like an electric spark. A runnel of fluid was wending its way down Lori's thigh. With a start, she realised that her jealousy had given way to a flash flood of lust. She stumbled away from the door, fell back against the wall opposite Rayne's office and she closed her eyes. Images of Gavin's raised belt and Rayne's rosy ass cheeks cascaded through her mind.

'Miss? Are you all right?'

Lori opened her eyes. She could not make out the face of the person who stood in front of her, much less respond to the question. All she could think about was finding a place where she could be alone, a place where she could release the tension that was building inside her.

'The bathroom,' Lori said in a strangled voice. 'Could you tell me where it is?'

'Straight down the hallway. Last door on your right.'

Lori's hand trailed against the wall as she groped her way down the corridor. Maybe it was the sting of betrayal that made the scene in Rayne's office so exciting. Maybe it was the bizarre sight of the aloof and powerful Rayne Hughes being spanked by a masterful man. Lori had hardly recognised Gavin's voice when he told Rayne that she deserved a strapping. Coarse and guttural, his words had sent tremors through Lori's body. With Lori, Gavin had always been tender and considerate, but there was something in the way he gripped her hair and controlled her body that had implied that he was capable of something else altogether.

Locked in one of the stalls in the ladies' room, Lori leaned her forehead against the door to catch her breath. She pulled up her skirt. Her sex emitted a humid musk, and her sex lips were so slippery that her fingertips could hardly gain purchase on her skin. She whimpered as her impatient fingers tangled in the gusset of her panties, then found and rubbed her erect clit, eliciting a quiver of response from her cunt muscles. What she needed was something to fill her, the way Gavin's cock was filling Rayne.

Lori fumbled in her purse until she found what her pussy craved: a substitute cock. The hairbrush's thick, cylindrical plastic handle was the closest thing to a penis that Lori was going to find within the next few minutes. She pushed the brush into herself as far as it would go. First she allowed her inner muscles to get used to the new object and cling to the tubular shape. Then she began to thrust. The brush's bristles pricked her palm, but Lori was so lost in pleasure that she only tightened her grip. With her other hand she rubbed her clit, fingers flying faster and faster.

Lori turned around, leaned against the side of the stall, and tilted her hips so that she could sink the hairbrush even deeper into her channel. Her cunt clung greedily to the plastic handle. She imagined that it was Gavin's prick, and that he was fucking her while the imperious Rayne looked on. More, more – and then a final jab with the hairbrush set her off into a hard, wrenching orgasm that made the whole stall rock. One spasm followed another, and Lori bit her lip to keep from screaming.

Like a sky cleansed by a thunderstorm, Lori's mind felt clear, renewed. No jealousy, no anger, only a calm sense of purpose pervaded Lori's thoughts. She smoothed down her skirt, collected her things and opened the door of the stall.

Rayne Hughes stood at the sink. Preoccupied with her reflection in the mirror, she didn't see Lori at first. The afterglow of sex softened Rayne's angular face, but when she finally noticed Lori, her bliss hardened into triumph. She wheeled around to face her rival.

'Gavin's all yours, honey. Give him ten minutes to recover, and maybe he'll have a hard-on for you, too. If you're lucky, you might even get a taste of his belt.' She smirked and took a moment to scan Lori from head to toe. 'But you're probably not into anything kinky, are you? From the look of you, I'd say you're strictly vanilla.'

Lori said nothing. She washed her hands and reapplied her lip gloss.

'I'm not going to cancel the biography,' Rayne went on, 'but Gavin and I won't be needing your help. I'm sure you'll find another project. Maybe a nice family scrapbook.'

Lori produced a smile as false as her adversary's. 'What a lovely idea, Rayne. Thanks for the suggestion.'

Rayne faltered for a second, then stalked out of the bathroom.

'Maybe you could make a nice family scrapbook,' Lori repeated, mimicking Rayne's acidic sarcasm.

Or maybe Lori could apply her research elsewhere. If she could find out what had happened to Lorelei Price, what was to stop her from publishing the discovery in a book of her own? A sexy book, not a scholarly one. A book that Lorelei Price would have loved. A book that would make Gavin wish he'd never fucked Rayne Hughes today.

Now Lori would go outside and meet Gavin. She would pretend not to see his dishevelled hair and clothes, his smirk of guilty satisfaction. After all, Lori and Gavin had made no vow of eternal commitment, and Lori was hardly a model of monogamy these days. The weekend stretched ahead of her, waiting to be enjoyed. Lori was determined to take in her fill of this pulsating city – and Gavin's pulsating cock.

This might be her last chance to fuck him before she left for Paris.

Alone.

9

Autumn was coming. Long blue shadows had invaded the afternoons, and local girls were browsing through the merchandise at Chimera, preparing to make their debuts at school. Even for vintage shops fall was a peak in the fashion cycle. Melanie would have to act quickly if she wanted to put her plan into action. This morning she had brought her San Francisco shopping bags, with their forbidden cargo, back to the boutique. With or without Lori's permission, she was going to clear some of the dust out of this town's head. Now that she was a partner in the business, she had the right to take some creative initiative.

Regretfully Melanie packed away the items in the summer window display: a collection of women's bathing suits, ranging from a pair of Edwardian bloomers to a bikini from the 60s. Melanie's fingers tingled as she handled the intimate items. She felt the excitement of the women who had worn them; the shyness, the delight and fear of self-exposure. Every time she did something new and daring with the old clothes, Melanie felt she was taking a risk on behalf of their original wearers.

'OK, Mel,' she muttered to herself, 'let's keep this light. Don't get carried away.' First she would let her imagination run free, working out the knots in her idea. Then, before the streets grew crowded and the public was exposed to her evil genius, she would pare down her vision to a palatable window display – with just a touch of spice.

With three mannequins, a shop full of clothes and a

treasure trove of sex toys at her disposal, Melanie set to work. She dressed the blonde mannequin, whom she had named Ingrid, in a leather corset, then draped a 1920s Spanish shawl across her shoulders, tucking it under the mannequin's jutting elbows so that her undergarment was visible. Ingrid's assertive stance made her an ideal dominatrix. Melanie giggled as she placed a coiled whip in her model's hand. She arranged Ingrid's auburn-haired companion, Wendy, at a submissive angle, placing her slightly behind her mistress. Wendy wore nothing but a studded dog collar and a long strand of antique costume pearls, which Melanie wound around Ingrid's wrist. On the floor beside Wendy's feet, Melanie placed the dildo that Lori had found so alarming. Wendy was obviously eager for Ingrid to demonstrate the instrument's use.

'Hmmm. What should I do with you?' Melanie asked the third mannequin, a severe brunette. She would make a good observer, or maybe a dom in training. Melanie dressed her in rubber and made her stand behind Ingrid, so that she could watch the lesson. As a background to her little tableau, Melanie propped an enormous ostrich-feather fan behind her wooden sex fiends. Pleased with the combination of textures and colours, not to mention the outrageous lewdness of her display, Melanie stood back and smiled. What would a passer-by see from the sidewalk? Melanie decided to step outside and take a look.

The scene had already caught the attention of one pedestrian. Head tilted to one side, the man studied the trio of mannequins, his handsome face torn between shock and delight.

'Mr Dupre!' Melanie shrieked, recognising her former drama instructor. She couldn't keep herself from throwing herself on him, and he grunted as she landed in his arms. 'What do you think of my display?'

'Which display are you referring to, Miss Paxton?' the

teacher laughed. His eyes crinkled adorably behind his wire-rimmed glasses. Melanie's heartbeat quickened.

One of the few advantages of spending your adolescence in a small town, Melanie believed, was that you would eventually have the opportunity to fuck all the adults you'd lusted after when you were under-age. The problem was that so many of them lost their allure once you had stopped being jailbait. Mr Dupre was the exception; if anything, he was even more delicious now than when he had been Melanie's teacher.

'Come inside and I'll show you,' Melanie said, beckoning him inside. While his back was turned, she flipped the lock on the door. 'It's been years since I saw you last, Mr Dupre.'

'Please, Melanie, don't remind me how long it's been. And call me Ted.'

Ted Dupre still had the charming habit of removing his wire-frame glasses in the proximity of a pretty female. His eyes were a hazy sea blue, surrounded by the lines of a summer tan. His straw blond hair was as thick as ever, and still cut in the clean preppy style that he had probably worn since college. Grey streaks at his temples only enhanced the blue of his eyes, as well as giving Melanie an intense interest in seeing his pubic hair. But that could wait.

'So what do you think of my vision?' Melanie gestured grandly at the window, as if she'd just daubed the last touch of paint to the ceiling of the Sistine Chapel. 'This isn't my final design, just the first results of a brainstorm. By the time we open it'll look a lot more tame.'

'I'd say your vision is definitely far-sighted. Maybe a bit too far-sighted for this town, but I like it. Yes, I definitely like it. It's provocative, it's daring, and it makes walking down the waterfront a lot more exciting.' His eyes travelled discreetly over Melanie's lush curves. 'I always knew you'd grow up to be a risk-taker.'

'Have I changed a lot since high school?' Melanie spun around on one heel. The launch of her autumn fashion display had put her in the mood to wear fall clothes. She had assembled a pleated plaid skirt – part of some schoolgirl's uniform – a black turtleneck sweater, and knee-high stockings with patent leather shoes. She had tied up her hair in a frisky ponytail, with her bangs hanging slick and heavy above her eyes. Melanie batted her eyelashes and pursed her lips into a petulant little bud. Ted Dupre couldn't seem to lift his gaze from the swell of her breasts under the skin-tight sweater.

'Let's put it this way. When you were a high-school freshman, you dressed like a forty-year-old sex siren. Now you're dressed like a delinquent high-school freshman. Could you please remind me how old you actually are?'

'Don't worry. I'm well over the legal limit.' Melanie smiled. 'Would you like to take a look at our merchandise? You might find something you'd like.'

'I might indeed. I've been meaning to stop by to scout for costumes and props. We're doing *Macbeth* in November.'

'Have you ever thought about setting *Macbeth* in the 1920s? The witches could be sexy flappers instead of ugly crones. They'd look fabulous in hats like this.'

Melanie pulled a black velvet cloche off the hat rack and flounced over to the full-length mirror. She posed and preened, planting her hands on her hips and jutting her chest forwards. Ted stood behind her, drinking in the sight of her plump buttocks under the short skirt. Melanie pulled the band out of her hair, releasing her ponytail. Then she spread her legs and bent over at the waist to pour her hair into the little hat.

In the mirror she could see Ted's mouth fall open. Melanie wore no panties. As the air kissed her bare skin and trimmed bush, her buttocks wriggled with delight.

If she lived to be a hundred, she would never stop enjoying men's reactions when they saw her without underpants. According to Melanie's philosophy of life, panties constrained the cunt and soul.

Melanie stood up, her hair tucked neatly into the cloche. 'How does this look?'

'Try another one.'

Obediently Melanie reached for another hat, then bowed again to gather her hair at the nape. This time she widened her straddle and held the pose longer.

'Higher. Lift your bottom higher.'

A husky command. Forceful. Melanie raised her ass as high as she could, until her hamstrings ached. She couldn't resist leaning down to peek at the teacher from between her parted thighs.

'Like this?'

Ted swallowed. 'Perfect.'

'You'd better come closer. Make sure you get a good look.'

He walked up behind her and took her buttocks in his hands. Then he spread her cheeks, skimming a thumb along the crevice, past her puckered pink bud and all the way down her slippery groove. Melanie let his hand linger there in paradise for a moment before she stood up and turned to face him.

'When I was your student, did you ever want to spank me?'

'Oh, yes. Plenty of times.'

'Was I rude? Lazy? Tardy?'

'You were all of that, and I'm sure you still are. I doubt that anyone's been able to correct you.'

Melanie sauntered cheekily over to the dressing-room and reappeared with the leather riding crop. Now a much better use had presented itself. Melanie trailed the tip of the crop down her throat and across her breasts, and Ted Dupre's eyes followed that leather loop on every inch of its journey.

'Here's your chance to correct me, teacher,' Melanie cooed.

She held out the riding crop. For a few seconds Ted stared at the offering. Then he took the leather instrument and tested its force by slapping it a few times against his palm.

'Your palm is callused,' Melanie remarked. 'Is that from sailing? Or from something else?'

'Are you implying that I have to jerk off to get sexual satisfaction?'

'Why, no.' Melanie blinked. 'I don't even know what "jerk off" means.'

'The hell you don't. Put your hands against the mirror. Spread your legs.'

Melanie squirmed in anticipation. She had always suspected that Ted Dupre had a few kinks under his middle-class, politically correct hide. When she glanced at his reflection in the full-length mirror and saw the protrusion in his trousers, she knew that he was already in love with this role.

Ted flipped up her little plaid skirt. He gave her ass an experimental slap with his hand, his palm as hard as wood.

'Is this going to hurt?' she whimpered.

'Damn straight. I'm going to give you a hiding that will set your plump little cheeks on fire. And that's only the beginning. First you'll get the crop. Then you'll get the rod.'

'Not the rod, teacher! I'm still a virgin!' Melanie ducked her head to hide her grin.

'Do you find this humorous, Miss Paxton? Do you dare to smile when I'm correcting you?'

'No, teacher. I wasn't smiling, I promise.'

The crop landed on Melanie's rump. She squealed. The bite of the leather had surprised her. She braced herself against the mirror and prepared herself for the next stroke. It didn't come. Instead, Ted began to trace a path with the crop from her ankle to her inner thigh. He whisked the crop over her pubic mound, then raised it high and brought it down again, this time with real force. Melanie shrieked. She wheeled around, clutching her bottom with both hands.

'OK, I've learned my lesson. I'll be good from now on.'

'What do you mean? I'm just warming up.'

'I didn't think it would hurt that much.'

His forehead wrinkling, Ted studied the crop in his hands. 'I've never used one of these things – except on a horse. Are you OK?'

Melanie smiled. 'I'm OK.'

Ted let the crop fall to the floor. He took Melanie in his arms and cradled her rump in his hands. 'Poor thing,' he murmured into her ear. 'You don't really enjoy pain, do you?'

'No,' Melanie admitted. 'I love the way the crops and floggers look. And I love handcuffs, and those sexy studded collars. But when it comes to sex, I like to be stroked and kissed and rubbed, not whipped or beaten.'

'You're a creature of pleasure, in other words.'

'That's right.'

'Well, you're still a naughty girl, and you need to be punished.'

Ted took Melanie by the hand, his big, hard hand engulfing her smooth, slender one. He led her into the dressing-room and sat down in a straight-backed antique chair. Then he patted his denim-clad thighs.

'Over my knee,' he said.

'But I told you, I like *pleasure*, not pain,' Melanie whined. The stern tone in her former teacher's voice made her melt, but she wasn't about to let him see that.

'This isn't about your pleasure. It's about your need for discipline. Now get over my knee, young lady.'

Melanie obeyed, arranging her body across Ted's lap so that the taut swell of her belly pressed against his groin. Her former teacher was as hard as oak. She heard him sigh as he raised her skirt, exposing her bare bum to the air. Melanie let her arms hang forwards, her fingers clutching the chair's legs. She really didn't like pain at all.

But the first smack was only a pat, just firm enough to sting. A flurry of swats followed, each harder than the last. To her surprise, Melanie found that her flesh burned pleasantly, and her pussy was tingling in sympathy. She ground her mound into Ted's thigh. The pressure of the coarse denim against her pussy was delicious.

He froze, his hand in mid-air. 'What are you doing, Melanie?'

'Nothing,' she said in a small voice.

He brought his hand down. This time the blow hurt. Melanie wailed.

'You were pleasuring yourself without my permission. You don't have a shred of discipline, do you?'

'No,' she said. Tears burned her eyes.

'I'm going to give you a lesson in self-control today. I want you to count the swats. I'm going to give you fifty, whether you like it or not. Ready?'

Melanie nodded. She counted out loud while Ted spanked her. The counting forced her to concentrate. By the time she had counted to thirty her ass was on fire, and she was gripping the chair so hard that the old wood threatened to split. Her voice wavered as she counted out the final twenty blows. Her whole body reverberated each time he struck her. By the time she got to forty-five, she was crying. By the time she got to fifty, she was coming.

The climax was a complete surprise. A tidal wave of emotion flooded through her as she writhed on Ted's thighs. She didn't know if she was weeping from relief or lust, from humiliation or happiness. Maybe it wasn't only pain that people were seeking when they played with crops and whips, but the huge release that followed. When the orgasm was finally over, Ted eased her into a sitting position on his lap and kissed her tear-slick cheeks.

'Have you learned your lesson?' Ted asked.

'Yes,' Melanie said.

'How do you feel?'

Melanie buried her face in Ted's neck. She thought for a moment. 'I feel different,' she said. 'Almost humble. You can't imagine how bizarre that is.'

'Then the lesson was a success.'

'Yes, but I'll need a refresher course. Some other day, though – I won't be sitting down for a week.'

'Can you kneel?'

From the bulge in his crotch, Melanie guessed what Ted had in mind. She wriggled off his lap, got down on her knees, and unbuttoned his fly. Then she showed him, with her lips and tongue, what a good girl she really was.

The telephone rang soon after Ted Dupre left the shop. Melanie had talked him into buying three bags' worth of merchandise for the drama department, and she was still gloating over the sale when she picked up the receiver. The sound of Lori's voice on the other end altered her mood instantly. Though Lori couldn't be any farther than New York, she sounded worlds away.

'Lori? Where are you?'

'I'm still in the city. I'll be leaving soon. I'll be taking the train and a bus. Can you pick me up at the station?'

'I thought Gavin was going to drive you home.'

'My plans have changed.' Lori's voice had an unfamiliar edge.

'What's wrong?'

'Nothing. I'm on my way back. I just wanted to know if you could pick me up. I'll call you when the bus gets in.'

'Of course I can pick you up. Are you all right?'

'Never been better,' Lori said. Her voice softened as she added, 'There's one more thing, Mel.'

'What?'

'I'm so grateful to have a friend I can rely on. Nothing's more important than trust.'

Unsettled, Melanie hung up the phone. Her confusion lingered through the morning, as she took down her kinky window display and dressed the mannequins in fall fashions that would please the most conservative women in town. By the end of the day, she had sold two expensive tweed suits. That made her feel better – but not much.

Sooner or later, she would find out what had happened in New York.

10

'Do you have a fever, Lori?' Melanie held the back of her hand to Lori's forehead. Lori's cheeks glowed pink, and the light in her eyes was a bit too bright for Melanie's taste. She looked like she was burning with a secret.

'Of course not. I'm just excited. Four more days, and I'll be in Paris.'

'Don't remind me. I'll be spending every waking moment here at the shop for the next few weeks.'

'You'll be fine, Mel.'

'Without you? Not for long.'

Melanie went back to counting out the money from the cash register. Lori hummed as she sorted through a tray of Art Deco jewellery. She slid a ruby baguette ring onto her finger and held it up to the light, watching the gem sparkle.

'What do you think?' Lori asked. 'Does this look like something that Lorelei Price would have worn?'

Lori had already put together several ensembles of clothing from the 1920s and 30s. Plundering her most valuable merchandise, she had set aside a midnight blue bias-cut velvet gown, a black wool coat trimmed with grey squirrel, and a white Schiaparelli trouser skirt that flowed from her hips like water.

'Shouldn't you think more about what Lori Marwick would wear? Autumn in Paris can be unpredictable.'

'I haven't lost my mind, sweetie. I'm packing plenty of warm, practical twenty-first-century clothes.'

'What does Gavin think about you going to Paris without him?'

Lori sighed. 'Gavin doesn't know I'm going.'

'What?' Melanie dropped the handful of change that she'd been counting. Coins spattered across the countertop. 'But the two of you were going to research Lorelei's life together!'

'He can't stop me from doing my own investigation. Besides, I'm taking this trip for personal reasons. Don't worry about Gavin; he's an adult.'

Melanie thought she saw her friend's colour deepen but, before she could get a good look, Lori ducked down behind the counter and began rearranging the jewellery tray in the display case.

'It's not Gavin I'm worried about, it's you. A few weeks ago you were head-over-heels in lust with him. Then the two of you went to see Gavin's editor, and suddenly he's out of the picture. No more dates, no more sex, no more book. Now he's leaving messages every day, but you don't return his calls. What the hell happened?'

Lori shrugged. 'I've been so busy planning for the trip, I haven't had time for anything else.'

'You're leaving something out. What's going on?'

'What's going on is that I finally have a private life. I want to keep this trip under wraps, at least for now.'

Melanie couldn't hold back any longer. 'If you go to Paris and disappear like that great-aunt of yours, I don't know what I'll do,' she cried.

In the beginning Melanie had been delighted by Lori's transformation, but now the changes were coming hard and fast. With all her heart Melanie believed in the benefits of uncharted adventure, but she couldn't shake the fear that Lori was putting herself in danger.

Lori reached across the display case to touch Melanie's arm. 'Is that what this is really about? You think I'm going to disappear?'

Melanie took a deep breath. 'To tell you the truth, I'm afraid.'

'Of what?'

'I'm afraid you're getting obsessed with Lorelei Price. Why do you have to go looking for a dead relative, when there are so many people here who love you?'

'Because I'm learning about myself through Lorelei. Until I started looking into her life, I was frozen in one place. Never changing. Always the same old Lori, who wanted to find one man who would make love to her in the missionary position for the rest of her life. Now I know that sex is a universe of its own, and I haven't even started to explore it. Let me show you something.'

Lori went upstairs to her apartment. A few minutes later she came back down, holding a thick manila folder.

'These are some of Lorelei's photos and letters,' Lori said. 'Gavin loaned them to me. Maybe if you look at them, you'll understand why I feel so strongly about what I'm doing.'

Melanie examined the prints. Although the paper showed the effects of time, the images had lost none of their power. In one photo a woman's lips paid loving court to two engorged cocks, which she held in either hand, her kohl-lined eyes wide with enchantment. In another print, a model sat dreaming in an ornate baroque chair, her head turned thoughtfully over her shoulder, her back facing the camera. She wore thigh-high black stockings and shoes, a white lace chemise and nothing else. Her full, bare bottom was turned towards the camera like a pensive moon. In a third image, two men enjoyed the orifices of a woman who lay spread between them.

The subjects of Lorelei's photos weren't unusual. There was nothing startling or innovative about her technique, no dramatic use of light or experimental post-processing. It was the authenticity of the desire in her subjects' faces that gave the viewer a sense of spying on the lovers, and a longing to be part of the secret paradise they shared.

'Gavin was right about Lorelei Price,' Melanie said. 'She found a way to take pictures of the erotic imagination.'

'Aren't they wonderful? But they aren't all so vanilla. Look at this.'

She gave Melanie another photo.

The woman in the photograph sat in a straight-backed chair. She wore a devastatingly simple black satin evening gown (Melanie's heart lurched as she recognised a Chanel), whose elegance had been ruined forever by a long slash across the bodice. The dress had been cut at the line of the woman's nipples. Her arms were bound behind her back, and her exposed breasts were thrust forwards through the tear in the fabric. Her face – the part that was visible beneath a thin black blindfold – glowed with some private sensation that the viewer couldn't share. Her lips were parted, as if they were waiting to receive a luscious gift. Her long legs tapered down to treacherously high heels, and her ankles were bound to the chair's legs with strips of black satin, probably cut from the dress.

The longer she stared at the picture, the harder it was to look away. Melanie shifted in her chair. Her panties were damp. She didn't know exactly what she was feeling, but her uneasiness was mixed with a strong dose of arousal.

'So what do you think?' Lori asked.

'I think this photo is very . . . powerful. And scary. And a turn-on, all at the same time.' She turned to Lori. 'I can't believe I'm saying this, but this picture was worth cutting up a Chanel for.'

Lori smiled. 'I knew you'd like it.'

'You know, a person could get carried away with this kind of thing. This woman looks like she's lost her identity. Do you know who she is?'

'I don't know for sure, but I think it's Lorelei Price.'

'Then who took the picture?'

'I believe it was one of her lovers. He was a photographer too. This letter describes how they met. If you read it, I think you'll understand.' She gave Melanie a few sheets of typescript. Melanie began to read.

Several nights ago I went to a masquerade ball. There are still lots of parties to attend here in Paris. A girl can forget anything she wants: family, lovers, the threat of war. Wanting to forget all three, I drank too much champagne and danced with enough animals to fill a zoo. In the morning I woke to a fantastic vision in my bed, a heap of magical creatures lying coiled in each other's arms. I saw a tigress, a Hindu goddess, a white stag and a magician, all sleeping soundly.

Little by little I recalled the kaleidoscope chaos of the night before. I remembered the masquerade spilling onto the street. I remembered the white stag rutting against me as I leaned against a lamppost, his cock rooting for my sex through the layers of my gypsy skirts. I remembered the tigress and the goddess dancing in the flames of a street urchin's fire. I remembered the magician leering at me through his mask as he handed me a glass of elixir – not champagne, but a more potent liquor that sent me spinning like a pinwheel.

Those four revellers must have followed me back to my studio and tumbled into my bed. Now they lay drowsing in the aftermath of the masquerade's spell. I slid out from the heap of arms and legs, crept out of bed and set up my camera to capture the scene.

Suddenly I realised that one of the subjects in my tableau was awake. The magician's eyes were open. He wore a black mask, through which his fierce gaze burned. His mouth was moist and full, its colour so deep that his lips would have looked feminine if not for the stern lines of his chin and jaw. The folds of his cape spread across a bare chest, as smooth and hairless and pale as a slab of marble. His black tights revealed the contours of a very impressive tool.

'Don't waste your time,' he said. 'The light is wrong. Wait a quarter of an hour, and the sun will cross-light your sleepers perfectly.'

His cockiness annoyed me. I often use the dawn to good effect; the soft light suits my temperament, and the early morning is perfect for catching the shards of dreams. I assured the magician fellow that I knew what I was doing, then continued setting up my camera.

Stealthy as a panther, the magician slid off my bed. With a grip both steely and soft, he grabbed my wrist.

'Do as I say,' he whispered. 'Trust me.'

Before I could protest, the magician touched my cheek. His hand travelled along the curve of my throat and down my chest. It was a painfully slow journey. By the time he reached my breast, my nipples ached.

'Look at me,' he said.

I refused to look at the saucy son of a bitch. Then he stripped off his mask, and the unexpected motion made me look up. Not only did I see him, but I recognised him.

The magician was Doran Cross, one of the most notorious photographers in Paris. I use the word 'notorious' in its darkest sense. No one knows who Cross really is. Some say he is an American expatriate; others claim that he is British. He speaks many languages so fluently that he might belong to any country, but he shows no loyalty to any nation.

The Surrealists were quick to embrace him and give him a name of their own; they call him the Enchanter. Now they regard him with a mixture of fascination and fear. He is a master of midnight dreams. Everyone in Paris knows his work, but even in this carnival of hedonism, no one will admit to being aroused by it. His imagination runs like a subterranean river beneath our daily lives. Evil rumours haunt him. He is accused of trading his soul for genius.

'You're Doran Cross,' I said.

A fleeting smile crossed his face. 'My admirers call me the Enchanter.'

'I'm not one of your admirers.'

'But you will be. I'm also offering to take you as my student.'

I laughed. 'I don't need a teacher. I'm doing perfectly well on my own.'

But I was tempted. I thought of all the things he could show me – orgies in the bedrooms of aristocrats, secret rituals in the Bois de Boulogne, the most exclusive *maisons closes* in the city.

'I've seen your work,' he went on. 'It isn't bad. But I can improve you. I've never taken a pupil. You're the only photographer in Paris who comes close to what I'm doing.'

'No,' I said.

'Understand this – unless you study with me, you'll never be more than an amateur. You'll produce the kind of shots that are printed on naughty postcards that bourgeois gentlemen hide from their wives. Silly pictures of women with floppy breasts and empty eyes.'

Doran stared me down. I saw that his eyes weren't black but the deepest brown, a russet darker than clotted blood. His features were so sharply sculpted that they might have been carved from ice. He was an angel of the night, a director of nocturnal impulses. My heart pounded.

Before I could speak again, Doran kissed me. His

mouth was cold, but his tongue was scalding hot. He cupped my breasts in his palms. I moaned, anticipating pleasure, but his fingers pinched my nipples so that I cried out in pain. Those dual bolts of agony on top of my arousal took me to such a peak that I almost came. My knees buckled, but Doran wouldn't let go. Through the pain, I saw what he would demand of me: trials of my body, mind and will. Finally he released my nipples. I gasped in gratitude. Then he pulled his rigid member out of his tights.

If I couldn't be a slave to Doran Cross's mind, I could submit to him for the sake of that cock. Long and broad, it curved like a ruby sword to touch his belly. A drop of fluid, glittering like a diamond, crested the slit.

'I can show you more than the secrets of my art,' he said. He was gentle now, his voice pure seduction. I imagined how it would be to be filled by him daily, to become his in every sense. Where would this man take me? If I followed him to the far borders of his desires, how would I find my way back?

Cross clasped my head in both hands. His fingers massaged the nape of my neck, as if he were kneading the hide of a favourite animal. Then I realised what he wanted from me, and I lowered myself to my knees. Face to face with his beautiful prick, I thought I would faint. His balls hung heavy, soft, ripe – I longed to lick him there, in the most sensitive part of his body. There he would be as vulnerable as I was.

The droplet of liquid fell from his glans and splashed onto the floor.

'Taste it,' he said.

To my shame, I found myself crouching on the floorboards. My tongue lapped at the fallen fluid as if it were the last drop of water in a desert.

'Lie on your back,' he demanded.

I did as I was told. The floorboards felt cold and gritty through the gauze of my gypsy frock. Cross stood above me. I could see the underside of his cock, the ruddy ridge. I felt like a drowning woman, looking up through the water at the prow of a ship that could save or destroy me.

'Pleasure yourself,' he ordered.

I pulled my skirt above my waist. When Doran saw that I was as blonde below as above, he gave a soft groan of pleasure. I spread my lips and strummed at my clit. He stroked his cock at a slow, restrained pace, but I noted that his hand trembled. A sheaf of glossy, blood-black hair fell across his glistening brow, and his full mouth was heavy with desire.

My clit had risen from its little hood, and a rivulet of moisture had drenched my sex. I parted my thighs even further and he spread his legs slightly in turn, bracing himself. I rolled my hips in time to the movements of my hand and sank my middle finger into my channel. Cross's cock grew in his hand as I plunged my finger deeper into my cunt. Which one of us is the magician now? I thought with satisfaction.

Heat spread through my body as I realised that I was going to come. The tension on Doran Cross's face resembled pain as he closed his eyes and held very still, restraining his climax. I did not bother to contain mine, but let it wash through me in warm waves. My back arched and my pelvis rose from the floor, my hands roving across my body – belly, breasts, hips, waist – as I luxuriated in the sensation.

Holding back his cries, Cross bit his lip so hard that blood beaded on his mouth. This was the act he had intended to humiliate me with, this spraying of his seed as I lay below him. But I was the one who had made him bite through his own skin. His semen fell down on me in white ribbons, like flags of surrender.

Doran lay beside me on the floor. He held me as the sounds of a Paris morning filled the room. The revellers on my bed still hadn't moved; whatever potion they had drunk the night before had sealed their sleep. I got up off the floor and went back to my camera. Doran Cross stood behind me as I photographed the sleepers, his hands encircling my waist, murmuring suggestions about light and angle. Later we developed the plates together in my tiny makeshift darkroom. The result of the morning was a series of images straight from a fairy tale, a reproduction of the magic hush that filled my studio that morning as the stag, tigress and goddess lay intertwined in my sheets.

I want to see what he can teach me. I will let Doran Cross lead me through his world. I'm not afraid of him – his control over me will never be complete. No matter where Cross takes me, I will always belong to myself first.

Melanie set the photocopied letter down on the counter, then picked up the photo of the woman in the slashed satin dress.

'I don't believe that the woman in this picture is the same woman who wrote that letter,' Melanie said. 'Lorelei Price was strong enough to go to France alone and establish a career taking sexy pictures, at a time when decent women weren't expected to think about sex at all. Then she met this other photographer, this "Enchanter" guy, and she sacrificed everything for him?'

'Maybe.'

'Oh, come on. It doesn't make sense.'

'That's why I'm going to Paris. To find out what really happened.' Lori glanced at the ormolu clock that sat on a shelf behind the cash register. 'It's almost five. You'd better take that deposit to the bank.'

Melanie closed the cash drawer and gave her friend a hug.

'Don't forget to write down the name and address of that hotel,' Melanie said, 'or you'll never hear the end of it when you get back.'

'I will,' Lori promised.

'You damn well *better* come back,' Melanie added under her breath as she left the shop and locked the door behind her. 'Or I'll go to France and drag you back myself.'

11

Melanie didn't recognise the black BMW that pulled up along the sidewalk as she was leaving Chimera, but she definitely knew the driver who climbed out of the car. Gavin MacLellan's silhouette was as sleek and impeccable as his automobile. Even in the autumn twilight Melanie could see the purposeful set of his shoulders, the hard angle of his jaw.

'Gavin!'

'Hello, Melanie.' He sounded relieved to hear the friendly tone of her voice, as if he had anticipated a colder response. 'Is Lori home?'

'She's home,' Melanie admitted. 'But I don't think she wants to see you.'

'I'm sure she doesn't.'

Gavin looked up at the second-floor window of Lori's house. Melanie's eyes followed his gaze. Lori's shadow passed across the curtains, and the sheer fabric shifted. Then the lights went out.

'I'm afraid that proves you right,' Melanie sighed.

'I'm not usually the type of man who bangs on a woman's door and demands an audience. But I'll make an exception this time.'

'Wait!' Melanie grabbed his arm. 'Could we go somewhere and talk first?'

'I just drove all the way up here from New York. I want to see Lori.'

'Look, Gavin, if you pound on her door now, she won't open it. Why don't you wait an hour or so? Then you can come back and catch her off guard.'

Gavin's jaw relaxed. Melanie tilted her head back, clasped her hands behind her back and lifted her breasts in a pose of flirtatious supplication. A shameless trick, but it was for a good cause.

'Please? It's still early. Don't you have time for one quick drink?'

'Maybe one,' Gavin relented. 'But I'm not leaving town before I talk to her. If she won't speak to me on the phone, she'll damn well talk to me in person.'

Gavin opened the passenger door of the BMW and Melanie slipped in. She could not hold back a sigh of sensual satisfaction at the buttery depth of the leather seats, the clean masculine odour of the car's interior. As Gavin drove, she stole glances at his profile. Once – maybe twice – she shot a look at his crotch. Melanie loved watching men drive. Gavin's hands moved expertly on the steering wheel as he guided the car through the narrow, sharply turning streets to the harbour. Lori was so lucky; she had felt those hands all over her bare skin.

Stop it! Melanie ordered herself. Lori was in love with Gavin, even if she didn't want to acknowledge it. And Gavin was clearly crazy about Lori. Melanie couldn't change that. She didn't want to change that . . . except when she caught the drift of Gavin's scent: a mix of leather, soap and summer-bronzed skin.

They stopped at the Dockside. The bar was almost deserted. Gavin ordered Scotch on the rocks, and Melanie ordered an Irish coffee with extra whipped cream. Gavin chose the same table where he had first met Lori, under the gaudy fisherman's net.

When they sat down, Gavin's shoulders appeared to loosen, but his eyes were no less troubled. He tipped his drink back and forth, watching the golden liquid curl in thick waves around the ice cubes. Melanie dipped her spoon in her whipped cream, then licked the utensil clean. Gavin didn't even notice the kittenish flicker of her tongue. The man must be hopelessly in love.

And lovelorn men were incredibly suggestible. If Melanie made the right moves, she could soothe her fears about Lori without spoiling her Paris adventure.

'You know, Gavin, I had an ulterior motive for asking you to have a drink with me.'

'What's that?'

'I wanted to talk to you about Lori.'

Gavin's eyes flashed. 'Do you know what's going on? Ever since New York . . .' his voice drifted off.

'New York?'

'Something happened that weekend. I made a stupid mistake. It didn't even occur to me that Lori knew about it until after she was gone. I should have suspected that something was wrong when she went home a day early.'

Melanie propped her elbows on the table and rested her chin on her hands. 'Want to talk about it?'

'Well, Friday we met with my editor. To put it bluntly, it was a disaster. Rayne Hughes didn't want Lori's help on the book, and she told her so in no uncertain terms.'

Melanie winced.

'But Lori seemed to accept Rayne's decision, and I thought she enjoyed the rest of the weekend. Either I have the sensitivity of a brick, or she put on a damn good act, because I didn't have a clue that she was so upset. All she told me was that she was worried about leaving the shop for so long, and she wanted to go home earlier than she had planned. Why would she hide her feelings from me?'

'I wish I could tell you.' Melanie dug a small cave in her whipped cream and sipped at her whisky-laced coffee.

'I never meant to hurt her. Now I can't get close enough to ask her to forgive me. All I want to do is explain why I did such a stupid thing.'

'Did this "stupid thing" have something to do with your editor?'

'Rayne Hughes and I have been lovers on and off for years. Professionally, Rayne and I are good together. Personally, we can't be in the same room without doing one of two things: fighting or tearing off each other's clothes.'

'Wow.'

'Exactly. We've always had explosive sex. The problem is that the sex couldn't make up for our differences. We couldn't live together without tearing each other apart, so we decided to separate. After that, things went much more smoothly. The physical attraction seemed to die down, until Rayne met Lori.'

'Nothing revives those sparks like a little competition,' Melanie said with a mandarin smile.

'I asked Lori to leave the office so I could talk to Rayne. I wanted to calm her down, convince her to let Lori work on the Price project. Rayne wouldn't budge. She's a brilliant editor, but she was letting her jealousy cloud her judgment. We started to fight, and I turned around to close the door so the whole building wouldn't hear us shouting. When I turned back to Rayne, she had ripped her blouse open. Literally. The silk was torn. She was standing there in her black lace bra. Then she sat down on the desk and spread her legs. She wasn't wearing stockings. All I could see was miles of creamy skin – and more. She wasn't wearing panties. I lost control. It was like someone flipped a switch, and we went from fighting to, well, our other favourite form of communication.' Gavin took a long sip of his Scotch, draining the glass in one swallow.

'And you think Lori found out?'

'I'm sure she did. She must have come back sooner than I expected. She either heard us, or saw us, or both.' Gavin slammed his glass down on the table. 'Why didn't she tell me? Why couldn't she just have it out with me, call me a bastard to my face? I can't take this silent treatment anymore.'

'So you drove all the way up here to talk to her,' Melanie said. 'Look, if it's any consolation, I don't think what you did was so terrible. You and Lori hadn't made any commitment to each other. She knows that. And I don't think a committed relationship is what she wants right now. This whole Lorelei Price thing has opened her up in a way I've never seen. She wants to explore. Experiment.'

'Fine. But does she have to freeze me out in the process?'

'Something's going on inside Lori. I don't know what it is and, to be honest, I don't like it much, either. Don't get me wrong, I was thrilled that the two of you got together. No one wants her to blossom more than I do. But I think she's got obsessed with finding out what happened to Lorelei, and until she works out this obsession, she's cutting herself off from people who care about her.'

'What's it going to take for her to get over this?'

Melanie took a swig of her drink. Betraying one's best friend required fortification. 'It's going to take a trip to Paris.'

'But that's perfect! I'd love to take her there. In fact, we talked about Paris a lot that weekend. She asked me all kinds of questions about hotels in Montparnasse; about the galleries, the restaurants, the clubs. I wanted to show her everything myself. I thought we'd solve the mystery of Lorelei Price together.'

'Gavin,' Melanie said as gently as she could, 'Lori is already planning her trip to Paris. She's leaving in a few days.'

'You mean she's going by herself?'

'That's right.'

Gavin's dark eyes filled with pain. 'Why would she do that? We were going to do the research together. I'm the one who gave her Lorelei's prints and letters. I can't believe she's taking off on her own!'

'I'm afraid it's your fault, Gavin. You gave Lori a new set of wings, and now she's using them.'

'Right. She's using them to fly out of my life.'

'She'll come back. I know she will. Especially if you let her go this time. Let her work this through by herself.'

Gavin rubbed his forehead. 'I don't know if I can do that.'

'Well,' Melanie said with an artful lift of her shoulders, 'there's a way you could let her go and still keep an eye on her. You could secretly follow her to France.'

'Are you joking? That would only make things worse. If Lori found out, she'd think I was a psychotic stalker. Besides, I'm not ready to give up my dignity to follow her around like some lovesick puppy.'

'Of course. You wouldn't want to interfere with Lori's adventure. All women need to go a little crazy now and then. Take foolish risks. You know what I mean?'

Gavin scowled. 'I know exactly what you mean.'

'So are you going back to Lori's house tonight?' she asked.

'No. I'll let her come to me when she's ready. If she's ever ready. If she needs to pursue Lorelei Price on her own, I can't stop her. Tonight I'll drive up to my house, and in the morning I'll head back to New York.'

'I think that's for the best. Everything will look better tomorrow, after you've had a good night's sleep.'

After you've had a good, long time to think about Lori running wild in Paris, Melanie said to herself.

'Let me drive you home,' Gavin said.

'Don't bother. I'll be fine walking.'

Melanie got up and gave him a kiss on the cheek. She let her lips linger for a few seconds longer than she should have. He smelled of rich, bitter honey. If only she dared to touch his skin with her tongue, nudge his shoulder with her breasts, subtly offer her body as a salve for his pain . . . then she would be a different sort of woman. The sort she didn't like.

Some sacrifices were cruel. Tonight Melanie would have to satisfy herself. The buzz of her vibrator was going to shake the Eastern seaboard.

She had seen him.

Lori kicked herself free of the pile of quilts and blankets. On this frosty October night, her body burned with restless energy. Earlier that evening, when she passed the kitchen window and saw Gavin's BMW on the street below, Lori had had to summon every ounce of willpower to stop herself from running downstairs. Had he noticed the flicker of movement behind the curtains as she jumped away from the window?

Even if she weren't still haunted by the image of Gavin's hips bucking between Rayne Hughes's thighs, Lori would have kept her distance from him. When she made the decision to go to Paris, she had started a journey that she had to complete by herself. It was obvious that Melanie felt left out too, and more than a little hurt by her friend's secrecy. Lori hadn't meant to be cruel. She simply needed time and space to nurture her plan.

Over three weeks had passed since the disastrous meeting at Obelisk. Lori's days had been filled with travel arrangements and impromptu French lessons. All of this chaos was underscored by an uneasy feeling that the trip was going to ruin her financially. She was a small-town shop owner, not an international jetsetter. What did she think she was doing, running off to France?

Now Gavin had shown up, adding to her tension. Lori sat up in bed, tucked her knees against her chest and rocked back and forth, but the soothing motion couldn't distract her from the ache spreading through her lower body. A keen sensation, something between regret and lust, uncoiled inside her core and crept upwards to her taut nipples. Moisture welled between her thighs. She was hot – so hot.

Lori jumped out of bed, struggled out of her flannel nightgown and went over to the window. Naked, she pulled back the curtain and pressed her palms against the chilly pane. She arched her back and leaned forwards, until her breasts touched the icy glass. The cold made her gasp. In the meagre light of the new moon, she could see nothing outside but the implacable storefronts on the street below. There was no black BMW gliding by to offer her a second chance.

Lori backed away from the glass as a memory of Gavin assailed her mind. It was of the morning after the first night they had made love. Gavin lay naked on his bed in the glass house, sprawling against a pile of feather pillows, his arms spread across their soft mass. Against the white linen, his skin was nut brown, and his long, loose hair fell in sable waves over his shoulders. One bare leg was bent at the knee, revealing a damp nest of black curls and pink flesh in the crevice between his thighs. Out of the nest rose his cock, lolling half-erect against his other thigh. Lazily he reached down to grasp it. Under his fingers, long familiar with his body, the shaft grew turgid, and a slow grin spread across Gavin's face. Lori remembered that look of leonine triumph. She remembered it so clearly that it made her want to scream with frustration.

Lori began to fondle the folds of her cunt, unconsciously at first, then with sensual deliberation. She'd been so busy these past few weeks that she hadn't even taken the time to make herself come; now her neglected body demanded satisfaction. The window was a glass stage, allowing anyone on the street below to see her, but she didn't care. She wished that Gavin was standing behind her, ready to mount her while the whole town watched.

Then a new image came to Lori: Gavin gripping a handful of her hair as he used his belt across her ass. She imagined him punishing her the way he had punished Rayne, smacking her flesh until her cheeks were fiery-red globes. She heard his masterful voice calling her a bitch, telling her that she was getting what she deserved. Lori had never dreamed that she could want such hard treatment, but now that she had witnessed it, she couldn't forget. Lori had always been independent and, in her own quiet way, strong. Watching Gavin with Rayne had awakened desires that she was almost afraid to acknowledge.

The burning in her cunt had heightened into a delicious tingle. Lori's body tensed. Standing, she could feel her clit rising erect from its tiny hood like a miniature cock. She tweaked the little nub as hard as she could without causing pain – once, twice, and then the climax took her. Hard, short spasms tore through her body. She filled herself with four fingers, wishing she could take her whole fist.

'Damn you, Gavin.'

Lori smacked the window-sill with her palm. Why did he have to appear under her window tonight? She had been so close to forgetting.

Maybe Melanie was right: Lori was flirting with madness. Ever since she had started planning her trip to Paris, unfamiliar emotions seized her at strange times. Lust, sorrow, rage, joy: emotions much stronger than anything she used to experience.

Lori's frustration fled as quickly as it had come, leaving her exhausted. As she plummeted into sleep, a thought crossed her mind that might have come straight from one of Lorelei Price's letters. If she followed this path to its farthest limits, to Paris and maybe beyond, how would Lori find her way back?

12

Before she left for Paris, Lori had an important source of information to track down at home. She hadn't told Melanie that she was going to visit the son of Justin Maxwell, the professor and photographer who had bribed Lorelei Price to leave the States. If Melanie knew that Lori was going off to harass an elderly man for clues about her great-aunt, she'd be convinced beyond a doubt that Lori had gone off the deep end.

William Maxwell lived in the college town of Sommerhill and, as his father had been, he was a professor at the small, exclusive institution. The flame-splashed autumn countryside was glorious enough to banish any ghosts, but Lori hoped to find at least one spirit in William Maxwell's memory.

Though she was a lifelong resident of New England, Lori was not immune to the restrained beauty of Sommerhill. The steeples and spires of Beardsley College graced the smoky blue sky, and low hills washed with yellow and red formed an intimate backdrop to the eighteenth-century campus buildings. This was the town where Lorelei Price went to college. This was where she fell in love with photography – and with Justin Maxwell, the man who convinced her that her eye was made for a camera, not a canvas.

William Maxwell lived in a residential neighbourhood south of the campus. Lori parked her car at a distance from the house and walked down the street. Children swooped by on bicycles, and young mothers paraded down the sidewalk with strollers. The sun was warm, but its light fell at a rueful autumn angle.

Lori hoped that Maxwell wasn't spending this Saturday with his family. How would she introduce herself to him? *Hi, I'm Lori. The grand-niece of your father's lover, Lorelei Price.* Maybe Maxwell would catch the family resemblance before Lori had a chance to identify herself.

Maybe he would slam the door in her face.

Maxwell's house was a prim white Cape Cod with an impeccable sweep of lawn. Lori forced herself to take one step after another until she was standing at the door, staring at her own distorted reflection in the gleaming brass door-knocker. She was raising her hand to lift the knocker when the door opened. A tall, lean man stood in the doorway.

So much for the doddering old professor she had envisioned. Lori guessed that Maxwell was in his fifties, but he held himself with the athletic ease of a younger man. His nickel-blue eyes and thick grey hair made a striking contrast with his skin, which had a salt-beaten tan that spoke of many summers of ocean sailing. A trim goatee covered his square chin, and the top buttons of his faded blue Oxford shirt were open to reveal a muscular throat. He wore wire-rimmed glasses, which he removed carefully, as if to see his visitor in a different light. When he saw Lori clearly, his sun-chapped lips curved in delight. Her stomach tightened as those startling blue eyes assessed her figure.

'I saw you walking up to the house,' William Maxwell said, 'and I couldn't wait for you to knock. Are you going to come in, or may I stand here and admire you for the rest of the afternoon?'

Lori tried to remember how she had planned to introduce herself, but the words caught in her throat. Through some mad sense of déjà-vu, she believed that this meeting had taken place before. She believed that William

Maxwell resembled his father as strongly as Lori resembled her great-aunt, and that the vibrations of attraction between them had been just as intense.

'I'd like to come inside, Professor Maxwell,' Lori managed to say.

'Call me William, and I'll let you come anywhere you like.'

Maxwell smiled, his face taking on the wild allure of a grinning wolf. He stepped back, and with a gesture of mock gallantry ushered Lori into his house.

'Why don't we go out to the back yard?' he suggested. 'It's a sin to be inside on an afternoon like this. Me, I've been sinning all morning – grading papers in my stuffy office.'

'You teach English at Beardsley, don't you?' Lori asked. She followed William through the house and out to the back yard. He led her to a wrought-iron table, brushed the leaves off one of the chairs and motioned for her to sit down, then took the seat across from her.

'I do, indeed. How did you know?'

'I did a little research. I know who you are, and who your father was.'

William tipped his head to one side, scrutinising Lori in the shaft of sunlight that fell across the table. 'Really,' he said. 'Tell me more. Would you like a drink?'

Lori gave a shaky laugh. 'That might be a good idea. Maybe it would help me work up the nerve to tell you why I'm here.'

'Frankly, I don't care why you're here. The fact that you *are* here is reason to celebrate,' William said. He grinned again.

Dangerous. This was a dangerously flirtatious man, continuing the family tradition of breaking hearts. Lori felt her self-possession returning. She might be nervous, but she was no love-struck college sophomore. William Maxwell got up and went into the house. While he was gone, Lori steeled herself against the seduction that was sure to come. By the time he returned with two tall glasses in his hands, Lori had convinced herself that the professor wasn't very attractive at all.

'It's a bit early for cocktails,' Maxwell said, 'but this seems to be turning into a special occasion.'

Lori took a sip of the drink, which turned out to be a very potent Vodka Collins. 'I guess I've aroused your curiosity,' she said.

'You've aroused something a lot stronger than my curiosity. But now that you mention it, I don't remember catching your name.'

'My name is Lori Marwick. That's short for Lorelei.'

'Ah. So that's it.' William leaned back in his chair. Only a trace of flirtation remained in his smile. 'I wondered if I'd ever cross paths with anyone from her family.'

'You know who I am?'

'Of course. It's obvious now that you're related to Lorelei Price. You look so much like her.'

'She was my great-aunt. How do you know what she looked like?'

'It wasn't hard to find photos of her in the Beardsley archives. She was all over the campus. Performing in plays, singing in musicals. Seducing her professors.'

'She didn't seduce your father!' Lori protested. 'She was your father's student. He was the one to blame.'

'Not according to my mother. She almost lost her husband to Lorelei Price, and she never really got him back. I wasn't even born when the affair ended, but my father's memory of Lorelei was so vivid that she might as well have been living with us.'

Lori stood up. Her face was hot. 'I'd better go.'

'No. Please sit down.' Maxwell reached out and took Lori's wrist. 'Tell me what you want to know.'

Lori sat down again. 'I want to know what happened to her.'

'So did my father. It was a lost cause.'

'You mean he never found out?'

William shook his head. 'He carried on his own investigations behind my mother's back, but he never learned what finally happened to Lorelei. He was obsessed with her long after her family sent her into exile.'

'Wait a second – Lorelei's family didn't send her away. She went to France because your father paid her to leave the country!'

'You've obviously learned the Price version of history. My father couldn't have afforded to send Lorelei to Paris. He was a college professor. We lived in a state of what is politely known as "genteel" poverty.'

'Whereas Lorelei's father owned a prosperous shipping business,' Lori said. The truth was slowly taking shape. 'He could easily have afforded it.'

'Now you're getting the idea. Unfortunately, Lorelei Price wasn't as bright as you. Or she was too much in love to see the truth. She believed everything her father told her. She believed that her lover was paying for her to go to France, on the condition that she never communicate with him again.'

'Everyone else in my family believed that, too,' Lori murmured. 'Including me. I feel like I should apologise. I've always had the impression that Justin Maxwell was cruel, manipulative. A cad.'

William took Lori's hand again and squeezed her fingers. 'My father loved Lorelei. He would never have sent her away. He would have married her, if he could have found a way to do it. And I'm the one who should apologise.'

'For what?'

'For implying that Lorelei was some cheap tramp who

seduced my father. The attraction between my father and Lorelei was mutual, right from the beginning. She was a miracle of a woman: beautiful, sexual, gifted, full of life. If she hadn't gone to France, my father would have carried on with her until he died.'

'I wish I knew what happened to Lorelei,' Lori cried. 'Why aren't there any records? Why doesn't anyone know?'

Maxwell sighed. He pulled his glasses out of his shirt pocket and toyed pensively with the earpieces. 'I can't answer those questions for you. But I can tell you one rumour that you've probably never heard.'

'What's that?'

'After the war the enlisted men who'd been injured in Europe started coming home. One of them had lost his leg in France. Decent fellow, a family man. It seems that when this man was in Paris, he heard about an American photographer who had become involved with a collaborationist.'

'The Enchanter,' Lori murmured. Doran Cross, the man who spoke many languages but seemed to hold allegiance to no particular country. Lorelei's father had believed that his daughter had betrayed someone. Was it only her own family? Or was the scope much larger?

'I beg your pardon?'

'Nothing,' Lori said. 'Please go ahead.'

'Apparently the American photographer had an affair with this man who was an active Nazi collaborator. In other words, he wasn't just passively accepting the Reich's occupation of France; he was working with the Nazi party.'

'Did Lorelei's father believe she was a traitor, too?'

'It was a chilling connection to make, but her father couldn't afford to ignore the rumour. He paid a large amount of money to stifle it.'

'I can't believe that! His daughter was in danger, and all he did was throw money around to stop a rumour?'

'Arthur Price was in the shipping industry. He profited from the war. How would it look to have a daughter who collaborated with the enemy? His reputation would have been destroyed.'

'There's no proof that she did anything of the kind.'

'You're right. But you have to remember that the political climate at the time was intensely patriotic. Between her love life and her risqué photography, Lorelei did a lot of damage to her father's reputation while she was living in the States. If the community thought she'd been associating with a collaborationist, Arthur Price would have been ruined.'

'Where did you learn all this?'

'From my father. As I told you, he did his own investigations. Look, Lori, I'm not presenting all this as hard fact. All I know for sure is that Arthur Price took the rumour seriously enough to buy the soldier's silence.'

'Do you think it was true?'

'I think you should accept that possibility.'

'I don't want to accept possibilities. I want to know the truth.'

Maxwell set his glasses down on the table. He leaned forwards and rested his hands on Lori's knees. His fingers felt warm, strong and hard through the fabric of her jeans. Though Lori wasn't looking at him, she could feel his eyes probing her face. When she raised her eyes to meet his, she shivered at the intensity she saw there.

'The truth is that you have your own life,' William Maxwell said. 'Your own body, your own beauty.'

Before Lori could reply, William silenced her with his mouth. She found herself responding to the kiss, accepting his rough lips, his graceful tongue. The kiss, like their initial meeting, felt like a repetition of a past encounter.

The knowledge that she was reliving Lorelei's passion heightened Lori's excitement. Here was one form of truth she could learn – the truth of the flesh.

She moaned as William's skilled fingers fondled her breasts, tugging at her nipples. Their kiss deepened, Lori sucking softly at William's tongue in a suggestion of pleasures to follow. He took her hand and guided it downwards to touch the evidence of his arousal. His erection felt reassuringly strong and solid, like his hands. This must be what Lorelei Price had loved about Justin Maxwell – his steady presence, his confident intelligence. Lori could sense that strength coursing through William's body, in the insistent thrum of his heart. He would be a self-assured lover, effortlessly taking the lead. As moisture flooded her pussy, Lori suddenly saw how erotic it could be to submit to an older dominant man.

Then William broke the kiss. He stroked Lori's hair, her cheek. His fingers paused beside her ears, then lingered on the gold filigree earrings. The earrings that had belonged to Lorelei Price.

'What's the matter?' Lori asked. 'Why did you stop?'

'I don't want to take advantage of you. As much as I'd like to flatter myself that you're burning with lust for me, I know you're looking for something else.'

Lori looked down at her lap. 'I probably shouldn't have come.'

'I'm glad you did. You've given me an hour of stimulating conversation and the best kiss I've had in years. But there's one thing you should know before you leave.'

'What's that?'

'Discovering the truth about your great-aunt will be extremely difficult. If you do find out what happened to her, you'll have to be prepared for the worst. It's very likely that Lorelei was never able to reconcile her chosen life with her family history. And it's possible that she died in violent circumstances.'

Lori thought about the letters, with their descriptions of Lorelei's adventures. For a moment Lori considered telling William about the unmailed correspondence. The letters had been addressed to William's father; shouldn't William have a chance to read them?

No, Lori decided. The letters had been written to arouse a lover's jealousy, a punishment that Justin Maxwell had never truly deserved. Maybe Lorelei never mailed the letters because in her deepest heart, she hadn't believed that Justin deserved it either.

Lori rose from her chair, then bent over and kissed Maxwell's cheek. 'Thank you for telling me what you know,' she said. 'Now I'm off to do my own investigation. The day after tomorrow, I'm going to Paris. Wish me luck?'

William smiled. 'Good luck, Lori. If you don't find out anything about your great-aunt, I hope you discover something about yourself.'

He showed Lori to the door and watched her walk across the lawn. When she was almost out of earshot, he called out something that sounded like 'Drive carefully'. Lori smiled. Now he was acting more like a father than a lover.

She kicked at a pillow of lemon-yellow leaves that someone had raked off the sidewalk. A tremor of excitement ran through her. Leaves were falling on the streets of Paris, too – and soon she would be there to see them.

It wasn't until she was driving away from Sommerhill that Lori realised she had misheard the professor's last words. William Maxwell had not called out, 'Drive carefully.' He had simply said, 'Be careful.'

13

Lori's first morning in Paris came as slowly as a childhood Christmas. With her eyes wide open and her hands clasping the blankets around her chin, she lay motionless, as if perfect stillness could make the dawn come faster.

Finally a pencil-thin line of pale sunlight rimmed the heavy drapes in her hotel room. Lori stretched languidly. She was going to make herself wait, tantalise herself with the surprises that awaited her.

Paris wasn't what she'd expected. At first she had been dismayed by the severe contours of the contemporary Parisian architecture, the cavalcade of foreign languages, the rush and press of people who so clearly belonged to the twenty-first century. This was not Lorelei Price's Paris, but a modern cosmopolis. The chaos, vibrant as it was, seemed hardly real to her. She believed that she could find the older city hiding behind the new if only she could locate the right trap door or secret hallway.

Where is the Paris of the 30s? she wanted to ask the taxi driver who drove her from Charles de Gaulle airport to Montparnasse. But the driver was too concerned with earning his fare to help her find a vanished city. Marking Lori as a tourist, he had given her his own tour of Paris, complete with terrifying traffic manoeuvres and rambling narration. The fare left her reeling. As she fumbled through her money, trying to figure out the driver's tip, Lori vowed that she would be making her way by subway or on foot from now on.

She wasn't going to be a typical tourist in Paris. She had more interest in seeing old hotels and cafés than in seeing Versailles or the Luxembourg Gardens. She wanted to see Le Dôme, of course, and the former Hôtel des Écoles, which was now the Hôtel Lenox. Lorelei Price had stayed in the Hôtel des Écoles when she first came to Paris, having heard that it was the recent residence of Man Ray. Lori yearned to stay in one of those historic places herself, but they were out of her price range. Instead she had arranged to stay in a cheaper hotel nearby.

Her room was cramped, with drab décor, but when she opened the drapes to look outside on her first morning in the city, Lori caught her breath in delight. The tall double windows opened inwards, and when Lori leaned out to peer over the wrought-iron railing, she found herself looking down into a small, intimate courtyard paved with stone. Slender evergreen trees provided graceful accents in the corners of the courtyard, while the windows opposite were frilled with the foliage of long hanging plants. The yard was just big enough for two outdoor tables. A paperback book had been left face-down on one of the chairs, as if someone expected to return to this quiet hideaway and continue their reading at any moment. Lori smiled. There was something about that square of timeless, private space that struck her as quintessentially European.

It also struck her as familiar. Lori left the window and searched through her suitcase, removing the folder of Lorelei's prints. She had meant to mail the materials back to Gavin before she left the States, but in the end she couldn't bear to leave the country without them. She pulled out the photograph of Lorelei Price on a Paris balcony. Her great-aunt stood in front of a railing very much like the one in Lori's room. The window looked out on an intersection of grey walls that obviously formed the borders of a courtyard. Could the room in the photo be located in this old hotel?

Gavin would be able to help her, if he were here. Lori could still remember the intense light in his eyes when he talked about Lorelei Price. He would show Lori the distinguishing characteristics of the room in the photo, and guide her to the right places to find out exactly where the photo had been taken.

Lori shut the folder. She wasn't going to let painful memories spoil this trip. When she got back to the States, she would try to mend things with Gavin. At the moment there was nothing she could do but enjoy Paris.

Lori ate a light breakfast of coffee and a croissant in the hotel's small dining-room. She was too timid to leave the solicitous atmosphere of that anglophone shelter and sample the treats in one of the nearby pâtisseries. Most of the hotel staff spoke English, or accepted her clumsy French with polite indifference, but stepping out onto the street was like plunging into swift, unfamiliar waters.

Yet once she ventured outside, Lori's fear gave way to curiosity and pleasure. Clutching an umbrella in one hand and a city map in the other, she set out walking through the raw, rainy morning. With childish glee, she soon realised that the map actually worked, and that she was successfully, if slowly, navigating the bohemian neighbourhood of Montparnasse.

The first stop on her itinerary was the home of Geneviève Pommier, daughter of the woman who had found Lorelei's letters after she disappeared from Paris. Mlle Pommier lived in the fifteenth arrondissement, a neighbourhood not far from the one where Lori was staying. She was a critical source of information, and Lori was terrified of meeting her. She had no idea what Mlle

Pommier would think of an American woman who spoke rusty French and claimed to be a descendent of Lorelei Price. Lori figured that the woman would either ask for money in exchange for clues, or refuse to talk to her altogether.

After two hours of foot travel and several pleas for help from brusque Parisians, Lori finally managed to find Geneviève Pommier's residence. Lori would have been enchanted by the charming townhouse if she hadn't been so exhausted and nervous. Her heart hammered as she knocked on the door. After several seconds it opened, revealing the flat, suspicious gaze of a woman in her sixties. The woman's round face was set with small, sharp features and surrounded by a frizz of gunmetal grey hair.

'Madame Pommier? Hello. I am a relative of Lorelei Price,' Lori began in halting French. 'I am looking for information about her. I would be interested in anything you could tell me. Any photographs –'

At the word 'photographs', Mlle Pommier retreated like a hedgehog into its burrow, all but closing the door. 'I have no photographs for sale,' she said in clipped English.

'I don't want to buy anything. I only want to see photographs from your collection. Anything that you'd be willing to show me,' Lori pleaded. 'It's important to me. I've come all the way to France from the United States just to find out what happened to Lorelei Price.'

'No. I will not show anything. Go to the gallery if you want to see.'

'The gallery? You mean Lorelei Price's photos are on exhibition?' Lori's hopes rose.

The door slammed in her face. Lori stared, stunned, at the varnished wood. She hadn't expected to be treated like visiting royalty, but she had never expected such rudeness either.

Miraculously the door opened again, and a wrinkled hand darted out, holding a business card on which was printed the name of an art gallery in Montparnasse.

'You want to see photos? Go to the Galerie Saskia.' The door closed again, this time without the emphatic thud. Thus ended Lori's meeting with Geneviève Pommier. If not for the card that she held in her hand, Lori would have been completely crushed.

The rain was coming down in slanting, silvery sheets, and the sidewalks gleamed. Lori was glad she had decided not to wear one of her vintage ensembles. Instead, she had chosen clothing straight out of Morne Bay: an Irish fisherman's sweater, sensible green raincoat, jeans and boots. The outfit wasn't glamourous, but it was suitable for browsing in a gallery. Lori checked the address of the Galerie Saskia, and after comparing it to her Métro map, determined that the place was located on a street not far from her hotel.

Once she found the street, Lori searched in vain for the gallery. The address, as far as she could tell, did not exist. Wet, weary and cold, she trudged up and down the sidewalks. She was about to give up and head for a warmly lit brasserie across the street when a hand touched her elbow.

'Are you looking for the Galerie Saskia?'

It was a male voice, speaking English with a French accent. Lori turned to see a man standing behind her. He wore a charcoal trenchcoat, and his dark blond hair was beaded with rain. His features were narrow, lupine, and stubble covered his lean jaws like smoke; Lori had never seen a three-day beard look so sexy. His eyes were pewter blue behind light wire-framed glasses.

'I was watching you from across the street,' he explained, pointing to the brasserie. 'It was clear that you were lost.'

'How did you know I was looking for the gallery?'

Something about this man was both exciting and unnerving. Under the low, warm tone of his voice, Lori sensed a current of intensity. Though he had touched her elbow only lightly, she still felt the pressure of his fingers, as if he were continuing the contact with his mind.

'Americans can never find the Saskia. It's well hidden.'

'How could you tell I'm American?'

He smiled. 'How could I not?'

Lori's spirits, already sagging after her confrontation with Geneviève Pommier, sank even further. She had wanted so much to fit into Paris life, yet here she was bumbling around in the rain, so obviously an American tourist that a total stranger could identify her nationality from across the street.

'I lived and worked in the States for many years,' the stranger added kindly.

'Could you show me where the gallery is?'

'Of course. I will give you a tour, if you like. I know the Saskia well.'

'I wouldn't want to trouble you.'

'I insist.'

Lori's cheeks warmed. She had never been the object of such a direct, focused stare. She felt pinned by the stranger's steely eyes. Just as she was about to look away, he smiled and bent forwards at the waist in a mock-gallant bow.

'I am Jean-Michel Lacoste, at your service. Won't you allow me to guide you?'

Lori hesitated. The angular intensity of Jean-Michel's face, the rich detours that his accent made around the English consonants, his scent of tobacco and rain, stirred her senses. Her desire and her sense of caution were equally aroused by this man, who seemed to hide a forceful will under his elegant detachment. Lori's love of fine clothing made up her mind – how could a man wearing such an impeccably designed trenchcoat be unworthy of her trust? She took Jean-Michel's arm.

'You weren't far,' he said, leading her into a narrow alley. 'This is where the Americans go wrong. They don't expect a secret entry; they believe that all doors should be open to them.'

The alley opened onto a wider passageway. Lori caught her breath. The passage was thick with shining golden leaves, like the trail through a dense forest. Lighted windows glimmered through the foliage. Jean-Michel took her under a stone archway to the gallery's recessed door.

'Before we go in,' he said, 'tell me why you wanted to come here.'

The question caught Lori off guard. 'To see – well, to see the gallery, of course.'

'Why this gallery? Why not another one?'

'I wanted to find my great-aunt's photographs,' Lori went on. 'Her name was Lorelei Price.'

'Lorelei Price? You can't be serious.' Jean-Michel's eyes were illuminated, for the first time, with something more than casual curiosity.

'Oh, yes. I'm very serious.'

'Do you know her work?'

'I know some of it, but I want to know more. I tried to see the woman who owns the photographs, but she wouldn't talk to me. She sent me here.'

'Of course. Geneviève Pommier doesn't talk to anyone unless there's a significant amount of money involved. I'm surprised she took the trouble to refer you to the Saskia. You must have impressed her.'

'I doubt that very much,' Lori said. 'Does that mean Lorelei's photos are here?'

'Some of them are here. The more important question is, do you really want to see them?'

'I wouldn't have come all the way to Paris if I didn't.'

'I understand.' Jean-Michel placed his hand on the ancient handle of the door. 'Are you sure you're ready?'

Lori nodded.

'After you, then,' Jean-Michel said, and ushered her inside.

The corridor's inner wall was lined with windows, through which she could see the rain-soaked autumn trees of a hidden garden. Black-and-white photographs of subtly posed nudes hung along the outer wall of the L-shaped corridor that led into the gallery. Compared to what Lori had seen of her great-aunt's work, these images were conservative, even quaint.

'I assume these photos aren't Lorelei's,' Lori said.

'Absolutely not. My grandmother could display these in her kitchen. As you'll see, the Galerie Saskia has two faces. Not unlike a woman.'

'Or a man,' Lori countered.

Jean-Michel glanced at Lori and smiled. 'When we know each other better, we will see which one of us has the more deceptive mask.'

When we know each other better. Lori's skin tingled. She had known forceful men before – Gavin was one of them – but they were open with it, expressing their desires as energetically as they pursued them. She had never been the subject of such quiet, artful manipulation before. When Jean-Michel placed his hand on her back, she trembled. He gave no indication that he noticed her discomfort, but she knew he was the kind of man who noticed everything. He would save his observation for the time when he could extract the most value from it.

In the gallery's main exhibition room, two other couples stood studying the photographs. The visitors shuffled their feet and chatted idly. They gave the impression that they were not enjoying the exhibits but distracting themselves as they waited for something more exciting. The subjects of the photos were young, slender women.

Light and shadow made love along the swanlike curves of their bodies; their lips and nipples were harmless enticements, like meringue kisses.

The rhythmic click of a pair of high heels announced the entrance of an alarmingly elegant Amazon. The creature's asymmetrical beauty, a look that the French might call *jolie-laide*, reminded Lori painfully of Rayne Hughes. The woman's short auburn hair surrounded her face in a cap of glossy petals. Her green eyes were too large, her nose uneven, her mouth an overblown, sensuous mistake, but the whole was stunning. Her slim body, poured into a black leather dress, exuded an aggressive, almost feral odour. She had the longest legs that Lori had ever seen and, even on this chilly day, she wore no stockings.

The Amazon dismissed the other visitors with a disdainful glance, then bypassed them to stalk directly to Jean-Michel.

'Danielle,' he murmured, as she kissed him on one cheek then the other.

Jean-Michel and Danielle exchanged a few words in rapid French. Lori caught none of it, except for a few references to her great-aunt's name. The Amazon displayed no emotional reaction to Lori as Jean-Michel introduced them, but Lori saw a glint of interest in those jade eyes. Was it the curiosity of a competitor, or the roving hunger of a predator?

'Would you like to take her upstairs now?' Danielle asked Jean-Michel in English.

'Is there anywhere else worth going in this place?'

The other visitors looked on in envy as Danielle led Jean-Michel and Lori through the room and up a dark, narrow staircase. The presence of another woman should have reassured her, but the severely elegant Danielle wasn't a great source of comfort. Lori could tell, the moment Danielle leaned her catlike body against Jean-

Michel, that she had been his lover. To her surprise, Lori felt a small burst of jealousy.

The hallway at the top of the stairs looked like the interior of a typical office building. A bulletin board studded with newspaper clippings hung on the wall, and a potted tree stood wilting in a shadowy corner. Danielle reached into the collar of her low-cut leather bodice and pulled out a key, then opened one of the doors and flipped a switch. Rows of track lights came to life along the ceiling.

'I'll wait here,' Danielle said in English, arranging her long limbs against the wall.

Jean-Michel entered the room, but Lori held back at the threshold. She didn't like the fact that Danielle was waiting outside, like some kind of lookout. In sophisticated Paris, where sexual expression fitted seamlessly into cultural life, why should Danielle be acting like a furtive bootleg pornographer?

'Come,' Jean-Michel said. 'Come, come.' He circled Lori's waist with his arm. 'Don't look at the floor, Lori. Look at the walls. Here is what you've come so far to see.'

The high-ceilinged room was long and narrow, with no windows. Jean-Michel released Lori. She walked tentatively around the room. She could see what the photos contained but, now that she was here with this mysterious and compelling man, she felt their power with an immediacy that she had never expected.

'Danielle, close the door,' Jean-Michel said.

Danielle obeyed. Lori moved slowly from one print to the next, feeling her way through the charged silence. A dark, unsettling symphony of images surrounded her. These pictures were the icons of a cult she had never known existed. She noticed that some of the contemporary prints were signed with Jean-Michel's name. So that was why the Frenchman was at home in this private exhibition room – he was part of the underground world portrayed in the photographs.

'Get closer,' Jean-Michel urged. 'See if there's anything that inspires you.'

'Inspiration isn't the word I would choose,' Lori said.

'What, then? How would you describe what you are seeing?'

A woman knelt on the floor, one cheek resting against a Persian carpet and her hands bound behind her back. A man raised a lash above her exposed buttocks. His face was in shadow, but hers was clear: her lips were pursed in a pout of anticipation, as if she both feared and craved the contact of the lash. The crop was a blur in the air; the leather must have struck her flesh right after the shutter fell. Lori could almost taste the pain on her own skin. Once a woman had tasted that pain, could she come to savour it? To need it?

The next photo stopped Lori in her tracks. A half-nude woman was splayed open like a trapped bird, squatting over a vase that held a single white rose. The petals of the flower skimmed her vulva, which had been shaved so that its lips were twins of the white bud. The lower half of the photo was cast in a milky-white light, but the upper half was all shadows. The woman wore a black corset. Her arms were extended above her head, bound at the wrists, the rope affixed to a chain hanging from an unseen point above. Her face, with its classical features, had the translucent pallor of Grecian marble. She was a study in stark contrast, poised on the fine edge between anguish and delight. Her head was thrown back, pale curls tumbling over her shoulders and her eyebrows delicately furrowed. Behind her, in the shadows, stood a larger figure. Lori couldn't make out any details of his identity, only the black mass of a compact, powerful male form.

The man's hand rested on the woman's shoulder. Her

face was half turned, as if she were about to kiss her lover's wrist. His right hand rested around her neck, in a gesture that was half caress, half appropriation.

Lori turned away from the photo, shielding her face as if scalded. Jean-Michel murmured words of concern, but she couldn't hear him through the fog of confusion and disbelief that engulfed her.

The woman in the photo was her great-aunt. With everything she knew about Lorelei Price, Lori wasn't startled to find her in this gallery. Nor was she surprised to find Lorelei posing with a powerful, anonymous man.

What she hadn't expected to see was the ring on the man's finger, a heavy military emblem of an eagle. Lori knew enough about European history to recognise that insignia for what it was.

The eagle, in that form, was a cherished symbol of the Nazi party.

14

'I'd heard the rumours that Lorelei's lover was a collaborationist. But seeing that ring ... it was like being punched in the stomach. I guess she had fallen in much deeper than I realised. I feel so ashamed. Why did I come here chasing Lorelei? Why couldn't I have been content with my life as it was?'

Lori buried her face in her hands. A cup of coffee sat on the table in front of her, but its delicious scent seemed to come from a distant world, a world of simple pleasures that she might never be able to experience again.

'Because you were looking for something more than contentment,' Jean-Michel said.

They were sitting in the brasserie across from the Galerie Saskia. Jean-Michel had tried to order a light meal for Lori, but she couldn't have swallowed food even if she wanted to.

'You can't suppress the horrors of the past,' Jean-Michel went on. 'You have to face them, live through them. You had a choice between living with your great-aunt as a family memory, and understanding her life. You chose to understand. Did you think it would be easy?'

'Of course not. But I didn't think it would tear me apart!' Lori cried.

The other patrons turned to look at Lori, a red-faced American, noisy and shrill. They probably assumed that she was fighting with her lover, not doing battle with the past. For a moment Lori wished that Jean-Michel really had hurt her in some tangible way. On one level she did feel angry with him, for so casually handing her the key to Lorelei's secret life. But he didn't seem disturbed by Lori's anguish. His eyes, as he gazed at her, were two grey-blue analytical stones.

Jean-Michel had personal knowledge of the clandestine games that were illustrated in those photographs. Lori had proof of that.

'You're right,' Lori said. She sat up straight in her chair. 'I did come to Paris to understand. So help me.'

'Help you how?'

Lori realised now what made Jean-Michel different from other men. It was not only his European mannerisms, his air of owning a heritage of centuries of self-possession, but also the subdued tone of his voice. It would rarely rise above a certain pitch, she realised, unless he were moved to passion. Its soft timbre never varied, yet his words retained all the hypnotic power of a cobra seducing a lamb.

Lori took a sip of potent coffee before answering.

'Help me understand why Lorelei became what she was.'

'What makes you think I can do that?'

'I saw your name on several photographs in the gallery upstairs.'

'So?'

'So, you took some of the photos in that exhibition, the same kind of photographs that Lorelei's lover took. I want you to put me in my great-aunt's place. Make me understand.'

Jean-Michel's lips formed a thin, oblique smile. He balanced his chin in his hand, as if literally weighing Lori's proposition.

'Lori,' he said, 'do you know how I recognised you as an American?'

'How?'

'American women look very young to me. They look – what is the word – not innocent, something else.'

'Naïve?' Lori said sharply. 'You think because I was shocked by what I saw in that gallery that I'm naïve?'

'No. That's not the word I was looking for. "Guileless", that's it. No intention to harm or deceive.'

Lori pushed her chair back. 'Thank you for spending your day with me, Jean-Michel. You did me a great favour. Now it's time that I got back to my "guileless" little vacation.'

She tried to toss her hair back, but the damp curls caught under her purse strap and she yelped at the pain. Jean-Michel stood up. With a touch as soft and deliberate as his voice, he untangled her hair, lifted its weight away from her neck and straightened her strap. Lori could feel his breath against the nape of her neck. Her body tensed.

'I don't take your proposition lightly,' he said. 'When I saw you, I had a more simple kind of seduction in mind. Now I can see how sensitive you are. It's one thing to show you pictures. It's quite another to show you total submission.'

Jean-Michel moved his hands to her waist. His grip on her flesh was cold, assertive, yet Lori could feel some of the same tenderness that she heard in his voice.

Just as she was about to sink back against Jean-Michel, she realised that he was no longer there. She turned, dazed, to see him pushing his way through the crowded brasserie. He didn't even glance over his shoulder as he left the building, but he did pause in the doorway. Not long enough for Lori to catch up to him, but long enough for her to begin to follow.

The moment she stepped out of the brasserie, Lori was engulfed by a tour group of American high-school students. Like a wave, the teenagers pushed Lori down the street; she couldn't have followed Jean-Michel even if she wanted to. In spite of the strong coffee that Lori had drunk earlier, she felt exhausted. Her anonymous hotel room beckoned. On her first full day in Paris, Lori wanted nothing more than to pass out.

Back in her room, lying fully clothed on her bed, Lori plunged into sleep. She dreamed that she was standing on the stage of a dark, smoke-veiled nightclub. The tips of burning cigarettes pierced the gloom like tiny red rosebuds. Jazz played in the background, the sexy growl of a saxophone. She was fully exposed, the centre of hushed attention.

Though she could make out the painted lips and marcelled hair of a few women in the audience, Lori knew that the crowd was made up mostly of men. She could sense them, tense and impatient. The rhythm of their pulses mingled with the beat of the drums in the band, so that she couldn't tell if she were dancing to music or to the throbbing of a few dozen erections.

Somewhere in the anonymous audience, watching her with angry desire, was Gavin MacLellan. Gavin was not the director of this show, and he knew it. All he could do was watch. The man dictating her movements stood behind her in the shadows. His instructions issued softly from his full, dark lips: the lips of Doran Cross.

'Open yourself for the crowd,' he whispered. 'Let them see you. Turn your velvet box inside out.'

Lori swayed back and forth until she caught the liquid rhythm of the music. She spread her legs and tilted her hips forwards, her striptease turning into a slow simulation of sex. The man in the shadows ordered her to spread herself open for the audience. To tease herself. To fuck herself.

And then she knew that she was no longer exposing her own body, but being exposed for someone in the darkness, someone who had been chosen by the man standing behind her. Her fingers shook as she pulled them across her body, displaying thighs, breasts, belly, framing her mons. The game was making her wet, but thoughts of her future were making her tremble. She had given herself to many men, but she had never been offered to one as a gift.

The word *sacrifice* flickered across her mind, like a panicked bird flying across the stage. The drums grew louder.

Not drums, but knuckles rapping on wood. Lori struggled out of her dream. She looked around, disoriented. Sounds of the city drifted through her open window. Paris. She made her way groggily to the door.

'The gentleman asked me to bring this to your room,' said the bellhop standing in the hallway.

From the expectant look on the young man's face, Lori guessed that this 'gentleman' had not only requested the personal delivery, but had paid for it, and that Lori was supposed to add a contribution of her own. She dug a crumpled bill out of her pocket, handed it to the bellhop, and took the box. When she opened it, she wondered if this gift had somehow followed her out of her dream.

The garment, wrapped in a layer of tissue, looked like a pornographic caricature of the classic little black dress. The brief tunic, with its thin satin straps, could only have been purchased by a man who had studied the curves of Lori's body. The cloth would shimmer on her small breasts, making them appear to move like water. The hem would fall precisely at the point where the silky recesses of her thighs turned into sleek muscle. In this simple shift, her legs would look endless.

Considering that she had been bundled in a sweater, jeans and a raincoat, Lori wondered how Jean-Michel had sized up her body so perfectly. The gift was from Jean-Michel; Lori had no doubt about that. Guileless, she might be. Stupid, she was not.

Folded up in the tissue lay another scrap of fabric: a pair of matching panties, a web of black lace held together by a satin gusset. Lori would never have guessed that Jean-Michel would choose such a feminine gift. She would have expected a leather thong, maybe a lace corset, but not these ethereal wisps. Maybe this was part of the game, the first stage of initiation. First he would ply her with presents that suited Lori's taste. Then, little by little, he would replace her tastes with his own.

At the bottom of the box lay a note. Lori opened the stiff, creamy card.

> Come see me tonight. If you have changed your mind, please keep this gift as a memento of our meeting today.
>
> JM Lacoste

Lori dropped the card. Part of her wanted to throw the box in the garbage, pack up her things and fly straight back to the United States. Part of her wanted to try on the slip and panties, just to see if they fitted as well as Jean-Michel had thought they would.

This was a dare. Only a woman who was bold enough to wear that scrap of cloth in public on a chilly Parisian night would be brave enough to join Jean-Michel in his game. And unless she played that game, Lori would never understand what had happened to her great-aunt. Through research, she might come to comprehend Lorelei Price with her mind, but she would never understand her with her flesh.

Lori yanked her sweater over her head and unbuttoned her jeans. She unclasped her bra, and hesitated only a second before peeling off her underwear. Should she wear the lacy cobweb that Jean-Michel had given her? Or should she wear nothing at all?

15

Wrapped in her vintage coat, Lori stood on the street in front of her hotel. She had checked the address on Jean-Michel's note in her Paris guidebook. Lori knew enough about the city to recognise this as one of the city's more exclusive arrondissements. A taxi shot down the rainy street, its driver oblivious to Lori. If Jean-Michel were well-off enough to live in a prosperous neighbourhood, why had he left her at the mercy of Parisian taxi drivers? Maybe this small humiliation was part of his game.

A black Citroën rounded the corner and stopped in front of Lori. She peered inside. A woman sat behind the wheel. Sleek hair, cold eyes, a face too asymmetrical for conventional beauty – the driver was Danielle, from the Galerie Saskia. She lowered the window on the passenger side and called out to Lori.

'Get in. He's waiting.'

Lori took a few steps closer to the car. The movement sent a draught blowing up against her bare legs, and she clutched the lapels of her coat. Danielle's lips were smiling, but her eyes had a gleam of scorn. No doubt she thought Lori was a prude. 'Strictly vanilla' was the phrase Rayne Hughes had used.

Lori took a deep breath, opened the car door and slid inside. The cab smelled of cigarette smoke and Danielle's perfume. Danielle reached over, grasped the hem of Lori's coat and unceremoniously flipped it up, as if she were confirming a purchase at the market. When she saw the scallop of black lace at the top of Lori's bare thigh, she nodded in approval.

'Good. You wore his gift. He'll be pleased.'

Danielle placed her hand on Lori's thigh. Lori flinched.

'You aren't used to being controlled, are you? Even in small ways.'

'Controlled?' Lori repeated. 'Is that what's going to happen to me?'

'That's what you want, isn't it? By agreeing to be Jean-Michel's student, you've already given up a small part of your autonomy. That's why I touched you, because whether you realise it or not, you've given me permission.'

'Are you part of the game?'

'I am part of Jean-Michel's life. For me, this is much more than a game.'

Danielle pressed down on the gas pedal, and the little car shot forwards. As the vehicle hurtled through the bumpy narrow streets, Lori clung to the door handle. The Frenchwoman drove with reckless skill, averting collisions with a masterful turn of the wrist. A hundred doubts rocketed through Lori's mind, but she was afraid of distracting Danielle with questions. When the car stopped, Lori could see that they had entered a very different social sphere. The street was quiet, its gracious buildings aloof in the darkness. An aura of privilege charged the air.

Danielle turned to Lori.

'Are you ready?'

Without warning, the Frenchwoman grasped Lori's face in both hands and searched her eyes, as if she were measuring Lori's resilience. Lori refused to back down. As she returned Danielle's stare, the other woman's expression softened.

'Maybe you will be stronger than I thought,' Danielle said.

She guided Lori into the building and up a staircase, then unlocked a door at the top of the stairs and motioned for Lori to step inside. The dim confines of the stairway hadn't prepared Lori for the interior of Jean-Michel's flat. The nightscape of Paris glittered through tall windows, and ornate crown mouldings graced the high ceilings. Oriental rugs lay across the parquet floors. Formal antique *bergeres*, upholstered in brocade, stood alongside daring avant-garde chairs and stark glass tables, while gilded eighteenth-century statuettes contrasted with Cubist paintings on the walls. The precious works of art merged into an eclectic symphony of styles, paying tribute to Jean-Michel's exquisite taste. Yet there was something disturbing about the profusion of rare objects. The sheer number of beautiful things revealed a voracious need to possess.

'Jean-Michel is quite a collector, isn't he?' Lori asked uneasily.

'Yes, he is,' Danielle said.

'Where did he get all these gorgeous pieces?'

Danielle gave Lori an odd look. 'Most of them have belonged to his family for generations.'

'Of course.' Lori blushed and tugged at the sash of her coat. She felt like a flea-market haggler who'd just asked the price of the mirrors at Versailles. 'Is Jean-Michel here?'

'He's in his studio. We'll see him later. First, I have to get you ready.'

'Ready for what?'

'I'm going to prepare you for your shoot. Jean-Michel has given me instructions.'

'You mean I'm going to be photographed?'

'For Jean-Michel, everything begins with the image. Come with me.'

Lori followed Danielle down a hallway and into a small chamber that looked like a cross between a dressing-room and a beauty salon. The floor was covered with large black-and-white tiles. Full-length mirrors had been set up in a semi-octagon. In one corner stood a shampoo basin and a table, on which sat an array of hairdressing tools. This was nothing like what Lori had imagined. She had pictured herself sharing a romantic meal, complete with wine and candlelight, with the mysterious Jean-Michel Lacoste. Instead she was standing in some kind of private barbershop.

'Take off your coat,' Danielle said, holding out her taloned hand. Lori hesitated, but obeyed. Shivering in her black slip, she had never felt so exposed. Danielle tossed the coat onto a chair, then moved Lori across the floor as if she were a wooden mannequin and positioned her in the centre of the mirrors. Then she dived into Lori's hair and yanked out the pins. Lori's curls tumbled down her back.

'Jean-Michel was right. All of it must go.'

'All of what?'

'Your hair.'

Lori stared at herself. Her reflection attacked her from all sides. Her long blonde hair looked unkempt, wild, like a child's defence against womanhood. Standing behind Lori, Danielle placed her hands on Lori's hips.

'You've come this far,' Danielle murmured. 'Don't stop now.'

Lori let Danielle wrap a plastic smock around her shoulders. Her legs wobbled as she walked over to the shampoo bowl and climbed into the reclining chair. She leaned her head back against the basin and closed her eyes. Warm water fell across her forehead, and Danielle massaged her scalp with expert fingers. The Frenchwoman's closeness – her smell of smoke and perspiration and perfume, the heat of her breasts – was soothing and arousing at the same time.

Danielle's breathing quickened as she leaned closer to Lori, her firm waist pressing against Lori's arm. These signs that Danielle shared Lori's pleasure restored some of Lori's sense of control. It was Lori, after all, who had decided to come here tonight. She had allowed Danielle to lead her into Jean-Michel's private domain. Danielle was right: Lori had come too far to stop.

Danielle dried Lori's hair with a thick white towel, then took her over to a high stool which faced a waist-high counter. No mirror this time – Lori was facing a black expanse of wall. She would not be allowed to see her transformation. She held her breath as Danielle's heavy shears sliced into her hair. One by one the curls fell to the floor, forming a shiny heap on the tiles. Years of Lori's life had gone into growing that hair.

Lorelei Price had cut her hair when she came to Paris. Bobbing her golden locks was one of the first things she'd done when she arrived in the city. *I've cut my hair*, she wrote in a letter to her lover. In that short phrase, Lorelei seemed to convey the wonder, dismay and defiance that her grand-niece was feeling now, so many years later.

Danielle finished her work with professional speed. Lori's head felt as light as a hollow eggshell, and she reached up to touch her shorn neck. Although she couldn't yet see the results of Danielle's work, she could feel the skilful lines of her new bobbed style. Danielle rubbed gel into Lori's hair, then combed the curls with her fingers while she waved the dryer over Lori's head. When she was finished, she helped Lori out of the chair and took her back to the semicircle of mirrors. Then she whisked off the protective cloak, leaving Lori standing in her black lingerie.

Lori gasped. Her hair flowed back in short waves from her face, revealing her striking bone structure to perfection. Without the mass of hair, the graceful length of her neck and the elegant lines of her shoulders were exposed. The cut made her look mature, sophisticated, timeless. Lori's eyes filled with tears.

'It's beautiful,' Lori said. 'But such a loss ...'

Danielle took Lori by the shoulders and gave her a stern shake. 'Loss is part of submission. We all give up something important, some part of our identity. Look.'

Danielle lifted her skirt. She wore garters and sheer black stockings, with no panties underneath. Her mons was shaved, her cleft as bare as a shell. From the apex of that rosy cleft dangled a delicate gold chain, which was linked on either side to a piercing in each labia.

'Get closer,' Danielle urged. She pushed Lori's shoulders. 'Look at what's been done to me.'

Lori knelt on the floor. Danielle parted her lower lips so that Lori could see the intricate weaving of metal through flesh. The Frenchwoman's vulva was strung with golden thread. The strands were loosely woven, but there was no possibility of penetration, except by the weaver. Directly below Danielle's vagina dangled a tiny golden padlock and a pair of miniscule bells.

'Does Jean-Michel have the key?' Lori asked. She couldn't take her eyes off this marvel of erotic cruelty. Hardly aware of doing so, she lifted her hand and touched the lock with her finger. The bells tinkled.

'Yes. But he rarely uses it. He prefers to leave me locked, to use my other openings when he needs them.'

'Why did you let him do this to you?'

'Why did you let me cut your hair?' Danielle asked.

A bright light flashed. A shutter clicked. From the doorway, Jean-Michel had been watching the two women. In his hands he held a camera.

Startled back into self-consciousness, Lori rounded her shoulders defensively. Jean-Michel's eyes explored her body, but his gaze was as objective and unrevealing as the lens of a camera. When they had first met, Lori had been covered from head to toe. Now she felt shorn and naked; she had no idea whether Jean-Michel approved of the way she looked.

Why do you crave his approval? asked her inner critic. *Are you already dependent on a stranger's whims?*

'The hair is perfect,' Jean-Michel said to Danielle. 'But I want more of her exposed.'

Danielle took hold of the thin straps of Lori's slip and pulled them down over her shoulders, then cupped Lori's breasts for Jean-Michel's inspection. He lifted the camera. The shutter clicked. Lori saw no sign that he was aroused, or even impressed, by what he saw.

'Now, lick Danielle's cunt,' Jean-Michel ordered Lori. 'Explore her. Go ahead.'

Lori followed his instructions. The sight of the other woman's delicately mutilated labia caused her a pang of sympathetic pain; at the same time, she wondered how it would feel to have her own flesh held captive to a man's desires. She grazed the mesh of golden chains with her lips, tasting the mingled flavours of metal and musk. Danielle sighed. Her long fingers caressed the newly cropped curls at the back of Lori's neck, then crept down to cradle Lori's breasts, kneading the nipples. Lori gripped the tiny lock between her teeth and tugged. Danielle's sighs turned into moans. Her fingernails dug into Lori's flesh as her hips tilted forwards to meet Lori's mouth. Lori was barely aware of Jean-Michel's flash going off. The sudden illuminations were like lightning, a backdrop to the storm of sensations moving through her body. The taste of gold and cunt, the pain of Danielle's talons, the awareness of her own nudity and the heaviness of her own arousal ... it was all as strange and exciting as a dream.

'*Arrêtez*,' Jean-Michel said. 'That's enough for now. Danielle, bring her into the other room. It's time to start the game.'

Danielle helped Lori to her feet, and Lori followed the Frenchwoman into Jean-Michel's studio.

* * *

'Champagne.'

Jean-Michel handed Lori and Danielle crystal flutes filled with sparkling liquid. Lori sipped the crisp, dry drink and looked at her surroundings.

The studio was cluttered with tripods and umbrellas and other equipment that Lori couldn't identify. In the centre of the floor sat a low platform, surrounded by panels like the ones Lori had seen in fashion shoots. A white futon lay on the floor. Heaps of pillows circled the mattress, covered in white cotton painted with black Chinese characters.

'Take your clothes off, Danielle.'

Danielle stepped up onto the platform, slithered out of her dress with all the practised ease of a professional model, and draped her nude limbs across the futon.

'First you'll be the eye behind the camera,' Jean-Michel said. He beckoned Lori over to a camera that sat on a tripod facing the platform. 'You'll see what it's like to be the one manipulating the scene.'

Lori hesitated. 'But I don't know anything about photography.'

'You don't have to know. For now, you only have to see.'

Jean-Michel showed her the basics of working the camera. Then he unbuttoned his shirt and went over to the platform to stand above Danielle. His upper body was lean but muscular, the pectoral curves shadowed by smoky fur. Bare-chested, without his glasses, he was even more attractive than Lori had realised. As Danielle rose to her knees and began to work at the buttons on his fly with her long, nimble fingers, Lori's mouth went dry. The camera sat in front of her, waiting, while Danielle proceeded to free Jean-Michel's stiffened cock.

Again Lori felt like she was in a dream, this time a performance nightmare. Would she be punished if she couldn't use the equipment properly? She had never handled anything more sophisticated than a simple point-and-click 35 millimetre camera.

'Use your eyes,' Jean-Michel murmured. 'Trust yourself.' His head fell back as Danielle's painted lips engulfed his shaft. He murmured approvingly and grabbed handfuls of her short hair.

Lori wasn't so sure she could be trusted not to break anything, but at least she could identify the lens on the camera. She bent down to peer through it, and immediately noticed the way the studio lights fell across the curves and planes of Jean-Michel's torso, turning his body into an erotic landscape. Danielle's cheeks hollowed as she sucked him; her face offered its own study in light and shadow. Seen through the lens, her angular face was more glamorous, more mysterious. The lovers began to move together in a sinuous dance, Jean-Michel's hips rocking slowly as Danielle's head glided back and forth to meet his thrusts.

Lori pressed a button on the side of the camera. The high-speed shutter whirred, capturing frame after frame. She was in control now. As little as she knew, she was still able to shape this scene, recreate it, capture it.

Jean-Michel's back arched. He threw his head back. Danielle focused her attention on the engorged crown of his cock and let her hand attend to the slippery shaft.

'I want you to pull out of her mouth when you come,' Lori said. 'Pull your cock out and come across Danielle's face and breasts.'

To Lori's delight, Jean-Michel pulled his cock roughly from Danielle's mouth. Danielle's green eyes widened, but she played along, lifting her chest and pressing her breasts together as Jean-Michel brought himself to the last stage of his climax. Her nipples, a surprising shade of cinnamon, were soon peaked with white pearls, her breasts ribboned with cream. Jean-Michel gritted his teeth, directing the final spurts at Danielle's mouth and cheeks. Lori couldn't help smiling at the sight of the Parisian woman's disdainful face streaked with come, like a woman in the pages of a porno magazine.

'Rub his come into your nipples,' Lori said to her female model. Danielle obeyed, keeping her eyes on Lori as she followed her instructions, coaxing her nubs into peaks. Lori could swear she saw a new respect behind that green glare.

'Now lick your fingers clean. Enjoy the way he tastes.'

Danielle's fingers disappeared between her succulent lips. Watching that mouth, Lori grew wet. The camera augmented her arousal, transmitted it to her models. Through the lens she was participating in their love-making, their excitement, even their degradation. She wished she could stand here all night, directing their bodies, but Jean-Michel was zipping up his trousers and preparing to reclaim his role. As she stepped away from the tripod, Lori realised that she was shaking from head to toe. She'd never felt a rush quite like this one: directing a sex scene, photographing the results. No wonder men like Jean-Michel loved sexual power.

'Enough,' Jean-Michel said, resuming his place behind the camera. 'You've seen what it's like to be in my position. Now go over to Danielle. She's waiting.'

As Lori approached the platform, Danielle's eyes glowed. Lithe as a white leopard, she stretched across the futon.

Lori knelt beside her. Danielle raised her arms over her head, making her breasts rise. Lori touched one of the cinnamon nipples.

'No!' Jean-Michel's order made Lori jump. 'Tonight I want to photograph your pleasure, Lori. Danielle's turn will come later. Danielle, you will make love to Lori. Lori, you are not allowed to touch Danielle. I want to capture the way your face changes when you climax.'

The women changed places. Lori lay down on her back

among the pillows. From under the pile of cushions Danielle produced a black scarf and a long strip of soft leather. She tied the scarf around Lori's eyes, shielding her from the lights, then told Lori to raise her arms over her head, so that she could tie her wrists with the leather.

Danielle's lips descended over one of Lori's nipples. The Frenchwoman's lips suckled lightly at first, then more intensely, her teeth chafing the nub. Her hands never stopped exploring Lori's body. Wherever those long fingers travelled, they left trails of fire. In the background, Jean-Michel's shutter clicked again and again, becoming a backbeat for Danielle's roving hands. By the time her fingers entered Lori's pussy, Lori was so wet that she could hear her lower lips part. The ball of Danielle's thumb found Lori's clitoris, then pressed until Lori cried out.

'Danielle. Come here.'

Danielle rose from the futon. Lori could have wept with frustrated desire. She heard the sound of Danielle's feet padding across the floor, then murmured French as she consulted with Jean-Michel.

Footsteps crossed the floor, fading into silence. Lori waited, her clit still throbbing.

'Jean-Michel?'

Lori turned her head from side to side, trying to detect any sound or motion around her. Minutes passed. Her arousal dissolved into uneasiness, then panic. Her shoulders ached from the unnatural position, and her hands tingled.

'Hello!' she called. 'Please! Come back.'

The footsteps returned, pausing in front of the futon. Through the blindfold Lori could barely make out the dark mass of someone standing above her.

'Who's there?'

Lori felt the weight of a body lowering itself onto the

mattress. With her hands tied, she couldn't touch her lover, but she thought she recognised the spicy smell of Jean-Michel's cologne. Her cunt twinged in expectation. She raised her knees and parted her thighs.

Jean-Michel lowered himself onto her. Fully clothed again, he unzipped his trousers and rubbed his hard member against her sex. The scratchy wool of his sweater abraded her belly and breasts, making her nipples painfully erect. Lori lifted her hips, forcing his cockhead to slip downwards through her wet notch. Then he plunged inside her, his shaft long and hard, and she was bucking up to meet him as the friction of his prick made her burn from the inside. His breathing was ragged but controlled, his thrusting precise. He quickened his motions as her muscles tensed. As her cunt clenched in preparation for orgasm, her cries almost drowned out the click of the shutter. Moments before she reached her peak, Jean-Michel whipped off the blindfold.

In the rush of light and air, Lori realised that her lover was not Jean-Michel. The person looking down on her, cheeks flushed with excited satisfaction, was Danielle. She wore Jean-Michel's clothing, Jean-Michel's cologne. With her slicked-back hair, she could be either male or female.

Shock and pleasure, confusion and fear converged in one sensation that hit Lori like a thunderbolt. Danielle thrust harder, driving her faux cock into the hilt. She bent down to bite Lori's nipple, sending her even higher. As the waves subsided, she kissed Lori on the lips, then nibbled at her swollen breasts as Lori caught her breath. The strap-on cock was still lodged inside her. Smaller orgasms rode through her like wavelets, each one setting off the next, until Lori was so lost in pleasure that she had no idea where she was or what she was doing. Being fucked by a woman had turned her inside out.

The shutter never stopped clicking.

'This was your first lesson, Lori,' Jean-Michel said. He poured fresh glasses of champagne and carried them over to Lori and Danielle, who lay recovering in each other's arms. 'All of your assumptions are about to be turned upside-down. The faster you learn to release those assumptions, the sooner you'll understand your great-aunt's sexual cravings. Do you understand?'

Danielle helped Lori sit up, and held the champagne flute to Lori's lips. Lori sipped gratefully. She was too dazed to answer Jean-Michel's question, and his smug, secretive smile suggested that he didn't expect her to reply.

16

Gavin sat in his darkened house, watching a harvest moon rise over Morne Bay. A bottle of Glenlivet sat beside him on the floor, and a Satie piano arrangement played on the stereo. The haunting notes of *Gymnopédie*, usually too ethereal for Gavin's taste, were ideal for his mood tonight. The music reminded him of rainy autumn days in Paris.

His objective mind understood why Lori had gone to France without him, but his heart felt battered. He had betrayed Lori and been betrayed by her but, in his wounded state, he couldn't tell which hurt more.

Gavin poured another finger of whisky. As he set the bottle on the floor, his eye caught the gleam of a tiny object wedged in a corner. He got up, crossed the room, and bent down to touch the glittering thing, then pried it out of the corner and cradled it in his palm.

It was a bead from Lori's dress.

She had been incredible that night. So sophisticated, so lovely, yet so hot and passionate and wild. He held his hand up to the light and let the bead roll back and forth in his palm. Lori had transformed herself from a practical, down-to-earth businesswoman into a devastating beauty. He hardened now, remembering her eager mouth. Gavin had never had a lover who was so generous and greedy at the same time. He thought about Lori's slim, tanned legs spread wide for his tongue, her honey-blonde pubic curls damp with arousal, and at the heart of those curls the slippery pink folds . . .

Light flooded the room. Gavin jumped to his feet. The

glare didn't come from inside the house, but from the security lamps he had installed around the property. Outside, tyres crunched on the gravel drive.

Lori?

Gavin could still see her, standing frozen in the scrutiny of his lamps. For a second he almost believed that when he opened the front door he would find her there again, standing beside her jeep and trembling like a deer.

Instead of a muddy jeep, a brand new silver Jaguar occupied the driveway. Stepping out of the Jag was not Lori Marwick draped in vintage beads but Rayne Hughes poured into black leather. Proving that she truly was cold-blooded, Rayne barely shivered in her tight dress whose neckline plunged almost to her navel. Only a leather bolero jacket stood between her pampered alabaster skin and the no-nonsense chill of the New England night.

'Gorgeous car,' Gavin said, keeping his eyes on the silver automobile instead of Rayne's cleavage. 'Something tells me that you're the only literary editor in New York who's driving a new Jag this fall.'

'Daddy gave it to me,' Rayne said with a flip of her hand. 'It's another pay-off for my shitty childhood.'

She took her time crossing the driveway, letting her hips roll and her thighs flash. Every twitch of her short skirt revealed the tops of her black silk stockings. The friction of her thighs seemed to generate a scent of musk. He wouldn't be at all surprised if she had been playing with herself as she drove. Nothing excited Rayne like a powerful, expensive car – nothing except a powerful wealthy man with a hard cock and a firm hand.

Rayne's eyes flickered to Gavin's groin. Her lips curled. She shook her hair over her shoulders, giving him an unobstructed view of her flawless white chest.

To his irritation, Gavin realised that his hard-on

hadn't subsided. Rayne's arrival had simply redirected his cock's attention from fantasy to reality.

'God, these lights are blinding,' Rayne said. 'Can't you turn them off?'

Rayne wouldn't have complained if she could have seen how the stark beams flattered her glossy hair and heavily painted eyes and lips. Her efforts to look like a high-priced call girl were even more successful than she realised.

'Why are you here, Rayne?'

'I needed a break from the city, and I wanted to take my new baby for a drive.'

'And?'

Rayne held out a business envelope. 'You left a few things in my office the day you showed up with that friend of yours. What was her name? Laura Mudwit?'

'Lori Marwick.'

'Oh, yes. Anyway, when we were getting hot and heavy on top of my desk, a few cards fell out of your jacket. I thought they might be important.'

'So important that you waited almost a month to give them to me?'

'I didn't have reliable transportation.' Rayne gazed lovingly at her Jaguar. In other words, Gavin thought, she didn't have the right vehicle to make a dramatic entrance into his driveway. It must have taken her three weeks' worth of effort to wheedle that Jag out of her father.

'You could have relied on the postal system,' he said. 'A stamp would have cost a lot less than the gas you put in that car.'

'True. But then I wouldn't have the pleasure of seeing you, would I? Besides, you haven't been returning any of my calls. How could I trust you to open a letter from me?'

'That's a pathetic excuse,' Gavin said, but he felt a pang of pity for Rayne. Under the sleek surface of this sexy ball-breaker he saw the ghost of a spoiled, emotionally starved little girl. Rayne wasn't the only one who hadn't had her calls returned since that day in her office. He was embarrassed to think of the number of messages he'd left on Lori's answering machine in the past few weeks.

'Maybe I'm more desperate than you think.'

Rayne looked up at Gavin through thickly mascaraed lashes.

'You might as well come in,' Gavin sighed.

He led Rayne into the house, turned on the lights and pulled a bottle of Merlot out of the wine rack. Rayne selected a wine-glass from a kitchen shelf and found a corkscrew in a drawer.

'Make yourself comfortable,' Gavin said dryly.

'I already am.'

While Rayne opened the wine, Gavin looked through the business cards she had given him. He found a few casual contacts from the architectural conference in San Francisco, and a card from an outstanding Moroccan restaurant. None of the cards was important enough to drive all the way to Morne Bay, or even to justify the cost of postage. Except for one.

Gavin studied the card from the Galerie Saskia, turning it over and over in his fingers. Rayne glanced over and caught him looking at it. She strolled across the kitchen, sipping her wine.

'Funny,' she said. 'I've been to Paris more times than I can count, but never visited that gallery. Next time I'll have to spend more time in Montparnasse. The proprietress has an unbelievably sexy voice.'

'You talked to Danielle? Why the hell would you do that?'

Gavin glared at Rayne. She lowered her eyes and lifted her glass to her lips.

'Curiosity. Some might say it was an invasion of privacy, but I thought I was justified.'

'How?'

'I've got a lot at stake with this book, Gavin. Namely my reputation. With any other author, I'd be a lot more demanding about little details like sources, disclosure, permissions, etc. I've given you slack because I know you. And, to a certain extent, I even trust you.'

'Thanks.' Gavin slammed his palm down on the counter. 'I'm flattered.'

'Don't get pissy with me. All I did was call the gallery to make sure that you'd gotten permission to use any of the Price photos in the book.'

'I'm not sloppy about permissions, and you damn well know it.'

'No, I have to admit you're not. Danielle said you were meticulous. But that was hardly the most interesting thing she said.' Rayne put her wine-glass down, clasped her hands behind her back and stepped over to the window to look at the moonlit bay. 'Lovely view,' she said.

'Stop being a tease. What did Danielle tell you?'

'Well, it seems you might have some unexpected competition.'

'What are you talking about?'

'That friend of yours, Lori, is doing her own research. She came by the gallery and asked to see the Price photographs. She was with a man, apparently, who introduced her as a relative of Lorelei Price. Lori just loves to drop that name, doesn't she? Apparently it gives her a borrowed cachet.'

Gavin tried not to grind his teeth. 'Lori was with a man?'

'Yes, a man. A homo sapiens with a penis.'

'Oh, for God's sake, Rayne.'

'I doubt Lori was with this guy for *God's* sake. Danielle told me his name – Jean-Michel Lacoste. Again, I was curious, so I did a little research. Turns out he's a freelance photojournalist. Not very widely published, though. Probably because it's just a cover for his real vocation.'

'Which is?'

'Fetish photography. He's very well known in the BDSM community, if "community" is the right term for it. Does private photo shoots for wealthy clients for obscene amounts of money.'

'Nice research. You should be writing books of your own. Your work could make some juicy fiction.'

'Oh, I haven't even gotten to the juicy part yet. Jean-Michel comes from a very wealthy family.'

'So?'

'So, without their influence, Jean-Michel would have been mixed up in more than one little scandal. Seems he led a few bored, well-to-do housewives on a tour of his private underworld. Straight sex just didn't cut it for Lacoste. Neither did run-of-the-mill bondage. He wanted to make these women into complete submissives – change their looks, remake their personalities, even wipe out their old identities. Apparently he's quite good at it.'

Pain shot through Gavin's skull. He had been gritting his teeth so hard his jaws ached. He had encountered a man like Lacoste in his research on Lorelei Price: Lorelei's lover Doran Cross. The Enchanter. Authoritarian, sexually compelling, profoundly manipulative, he had taken Lorelei's talent and warped it to his own purposes. Kinky images bombarded Gavin's imagination: Lori blindfolded and gagged, her wrists cuffed; Lori being teased with whips and flogs; Lori being forced through a series of sexual tests, each more painful and humiliating than the last.

But none of these exotic images enraged him as much as the idea of Lori lying naked under another man, her eyes alight with lust, her body open to take him inside her.

'So this bastard thinks he's some kind of Svengali,' Gavin said.

'Well, he *is* very seductive, they say. To some women, he's apparently irresistible.' Tracing the contours of her neckline with one finger, Rayne approached Gavin.

'I've got to get to Paris,' he muttered.

She placed her hands on his shoulders, gazed into his eyes and moistened her lower lip with her tongue. One limber leg rose to stroke the inside of his thigh, her knee lingering at his crotch. 'Paris? Why would you go there, when you've got so much right here in front of you?'

Though Gavin's mind was thousands of miles away, his body was responding to Rayne. Feeling his stiffness, she replaced her knee with her hand and began to massage his penis.

'I know what you're thinking, Gavin. You want to play white knight, go rushing to the rescue of your golden-haired lady. Trust me, she won't appreciate it. You'll charge into Lacoste's studio and find Lori on all fours wearing nothing but a dog collar, being fucked by him and loving every minute. You'll spoil her vacation. She'll never forgive you.'

'Stop it!'

Gavin pushed Rayne away. It was all he could do not to slap her porcelain cheek. Still, he had to give her credit for warning him about Lacoste. While Rayne collected herself, Gavin began to pace. The anxiety that had been building inside him for the past week was swelling into full-blown panic. First thing in the morning, he would call his travel agent and make arrangements to fly to Paris. In three days he had a critical project presentation but he couldn't afford to wait that long. He'd get one of his partners to cover for him, claim it was a family emergency.

'You're overreacting,' Rayne said, pouting. She sat down in one of Gavin's deep leather chairs, crossed one leg over the other, and swung her ankle back and forth. If she were a cat, she would be twitching her tail. 'It's not as if Danielle saw Lacoste leading Lori around in handcuffs. She said he gave her a tour of the gallery. That's all.'

'You don't know what's in that gallery.'

'Actually, I do. Danielle was very helpful. She confirmed my worst suspicions about Lorelei Price. Next time I'm in Paris, I'll definitely be stopping by the Galerie Saskia. I can't wait to see the artsy pics of Lorelei Price playing sex slave to a Nazi officer.'

'Rayne –'

Rayne turned the chair on its casters so that she sat facing Gavin. She parted her thighs and sank lower into the chair, until her skirt rode up around her hips. Idly she ran her finger back and forth across the lace hem of her smoke-coloured stockings.

'When were you going to tell me the truth about Lorelei Price? Five minutes before your deadline?'

'A photo isn't the truth. It's only a glimpse through a window.'

'In this case, that glimpse is incriminating enough. You're going to have to search long and hard to find a publisher who will print a tribute to a Nazi whore.'

'Are you saying that you don't want to handle the book? Be straight with me. I've had enough of your games.'

'Have you?'

Rayne smiled and slowly lifted her skirt. Gavin's cock

reacted like a charmed snake as the leather rose, exposing Rayne's thighs all the way up to the crotch. She had shaved her vulva, something that used to drive him insane. Even after she moved out of his apartment, he would sometimes masturbate to the memory of the first time she did that for him. She had come to his office to meet him for lunch, dressed in a severe navy-blue business suit. While his secretary's back was turned, she had raised her index finger to her lips, then lifted the skirt. Underneath, her bare cleft glistened with moisture. She was already soaked. He had gotten so painfully hard that he had had to shuffle out of the office like a stunned adolescent, his attaché case shielding his crotch.

Gavin closed his eyes and took a deep breath. He could fuck Rayne tonight, no problem. His prick was already leaping for her like a puppy dog, and his cramped muscles would benefit from a work-out. All he had to do was shut down his conscience, which had no business nagging at him anyway. He owed nothing to Lori. As Melanie had reminded him, Lori had made no commitment to Gavin, nor he to her. Rayne could be right about Lori and this photographer. If she wanted to discover risky pleasures, indulge dangerous cravings, she couldn't have found a better tour guide than someone like Jean-Michel Lacoste.

But the fact remained that Gavin was worried about Lori. And he was worried about Lori's research. If she found out about Doran Cross's background, could she hold up against the truth?

'Come over here, love.' Rayne raised one leg, fully baring her pink gateway. 'Let me help you calm down. I know you need it.'

'You're right,' Gavin said. 'I do need it. But I need Lori more.'

'More than this?'

Rayne lowered herself to the floor, her long legs folded

underneath her, her arms outstretched and her forehead pressed to the ground. Her black hair was swept forwards, baring the snow-white pillar of her neck. Her buttocks formed a black leather valentine, ripe for whipping. The ritual was achingly familiar. In that supplicating position, she used to beg Gavin to forgive her for her sharp tongue, her abrasive manner. He would punish her, bringing them both the release that they craved.

'Take off your clothes. I want you naked,' he said.

He turned his back so that he wouldn't see the glitter of victory in Rayne's eyes as she slithered out of her leather sheath. She stripped quickly, as if he might change his mind, although that wasn't about to happen. Gavin's need had its own momentum; he was going to spank the living hell out of Rayne whether she liked it or not. No fancy floggers or paddles, either; he wanted to feel the palm of his hand against her flesh, to feel her skin go from cool to hot as he delivered the blows she so richly deserved.

When he turned around, Rayne was standing with her hands clasped behind her back. Her head was lowered, but he could tell by the curve of her cheek that she was smirking. She had arranged her legs in a coy pose, one in front of the other, to show off her thigh-high stockings and fuck-me pumps.

'What do you think you're doing?'

Rayne whimpered in confusion.

'Didn't I say completely naked? Shoes and stockings off. Now!'

Rayne kicked off her shoes and struggled out of her stockings. Her haste came from fear this time. No longer smiling, she lifted her face to look at Gavin.

'Is that better, sir?' she asked.

Gavin looked her up and down. Standing in her bare feet, her legs quivering, Rayne appeared authentically submissive. Gavin wished that he could wipe away her thick mask of makeup, but he couldn't wait that long.

'Keep your eyes down,' he said. 'Don't look at me or speak unless I give you permission. You've forgotten your training, haven't you?'

In wordless agreement, Rayne lowered her face. Gavin took her hand and led her over to the sofa, then sat down and patted his thigh. Rayne arranged her body across his legs, her rump tilted upwards, and her head drooping towards the floor. Throughout her youth Rayne had studied ballet; now she could assume the most humiliating positions with an ease that any dancer would envy. His groin throbbed under the weight of her hips, but she knew better than to taunt him by rubbing against his erection. She held herself still, waiting for him to begin.

Suddenly Gavin imagined that Rayne's pale, voluptuous body had been replaced with another one, slim and still tanned from summer days beside the water. He felt Lori lying across his lap, tentative and shy, torn between guarding her natural dignity and giving in to the pleasure of being spanked. He rubbed Rayne's buttocks, but instead of her chilly skin he felt Lori's warm flesh.

'Sir? Please.'

Rayne turned her head to look up at him. She wanted this so much that her voice broke on the word 'please'. Gavin came back to reality. He started the punishment with a few mild swats, but soon he was spanking Rayne with resounding smacks that made her cry for mercy. He had never spanked her this hard; her cheeks were nearly violet. She had earned the punishment, for trying to lure him away from a woman he really loved, and for coming here tonight to pour salt over the wound she had made.

But even as she shrieked, Gavin felt Rayne's mound burrowing into his thigh, not with her usual insistent grind but with a subtle, steady pressure that would soon bring her to orgasm. Gavin wanted to come, too, so much so that he groaned in frustration, but he held back. God, he loved to watch her get aroused, to see her glacial composure melt into radiant abandon.

Seconds before her climax, Rayne arched like the figurehead on the prow of a ship. She spread her legs and cried out, an incoherent plea. Gavin plunged three of his fingers into the hot swamp between her thighs and fucked her to her peak. Her body stiffened into a quivering arc. Her lips opened. A moment of silence, then Rayne screamed. The glass walls shivered.

Spent, Rayne drooped across Gavin's thighs. He had been grinding his teeth to keep from exploding; now he released a shuddering breath, as he settled back into the cushions and pulled Rayne's limp body onto the sofa beside him. She nestled her head against his shoulder. Hot tears soaked through his sleeve. He had gotten used to her weeping; it was part of the routine. First the punishment, then the catharsis, then a long, deep sleep. In the morning she would wake up, her energies renewed, and be the same relentless bitch he had known for years.

After her sobs had ebbed into sniffles, Gavin stood up and lifted Rayne off the sofa. Her body felt lighter than he remembered; she must have lost weight since he ended their relationship. The thought gave him a pang of guilt. Though he knew he would probably regret it, he carried her into his bedroom, lay her down on his bed, and covered her with quilts.

'I'm the only woman who's ever satisfied you this way,' Rayne murmured as she drifted off. Soon light snores rose from the sleeping bundle.

As much as he hated to admit it, Rayne was right. She had coaxed Gavin's sadistic impulses into desires more powerful than he'd ever imagined. She had nursed their erotic symbiosis into a bond that might have lasted a lifetime, if Rayne had been able to free herself from her fears. She loved kink, she loved pain, and she adored wearing the fetish clothes that Gavin bought for her at edgy boutiques in the Village. But when push came to shove, she couldn't give up control to Gavin. In his heart, Gavin knew that she would never submit completely to any man.

Gavin walked back to the living-room and resumed his post in front of the window. His erection had never died down, and his balls ached from putting off his orgasm. He unzipped his fly and stood looking out at the bay as he stroked his prick, remembering the way Lori had begged him to fuck her in front of the window. She had been insatiable that night, wanting his cock in her mouth, in her pussy, in her ass. When he came inside her, the explosions had been so strong that they had nearly blown him out of his skull –

Come spewed in a liquid arc. Gavin growled with each spasm, not so much from pleasure as from the urge to bellow in frustration. He could find women to sleep with any night of the week, have hot, no-strings sex whenever he wanted it. With Lori he wanted so much more that he couldn't even foresee the extent of his need.

Gavin stayed awake until well after midnight, planning his strategy for getting to Paris. Just before dawn he went back to the bedroom and lay down – fully clothed, so that Rayne wouldn't get any ideas. When she woke, he would hustle her into her Jaguar and send her back to New York, so that he could get on with the business of finding Lori.

17

After the photo shoot Danielle drove Lori back to her hotel. The tension between the two women had vanished. Lori felt at ease with the striking gallery owner, who filled her in on Jean-Michel's idiosyncrasies as the Citroën roared through the city back to Montparnasse.

'Whatever happens between you and Jean-Michel,' Danielle advised, 'don't expect to stay in his home, or even share his bed for a night. None of his other submissives ever stay with him.'

'His *other* submissives? How many are there?'

'For now he has me, and one other woman in Paris. He's had more in the past. I help him maintain them.'

'How do you do that?'

'I style their hair and makeup, buy their clothes, take them gifts, relate his instructions. I drive them to and from his apartment. I model with them, if he wants me to. Sometimes I'm ordered to punish them, if Jean-Michel is travelling or has an appointment. I make love to them for his pleasure – and for my own.' She glanced at Lori out of the corner of her eye. 'You don't understand, do you?'

Lori shook her head.

'I'm an independent woman, Lori, a business owner, like you. In the past, I never allowed anyone to control me. Four years ago I met Jean-Michel, when I was showing some of his work at my gallery. After the opening-night reception, he took me out for a late dinner, and he told me that he wanted to own me.'

'What did you say to that?'

'Nothing at first,' Danielle laughed. 'I choked on my

wine. After I could breathe again, I told him I would consider his proposal.'

'Without knowing what it involved?'

'Oh, I knew. I didn't know the details, and I didn't know how far he would go, but when he said that he wanted to own me, I felt . . .' Danielle raked her auburn hair with her fingers as she searched for the right English phrase. 'The bolt of thunder, you call it? *Le coup de tonnerre*, we say in French. I got so wet, I soaked my underpants. I knew that I wanted to belong to him, even though I'd never belonged to anyone but myself.'

'That's what I need to understand,' Lori said. 'That feeling that turns you into someone else.'

Danielle stopped the car in front of the hotel. 'But, little one, that feeling doesn't turn you into someone else. It shows you who you really are.'

'Where does it come from?' Lori persisted.

Danielle raised her hands, palms upwards, in a helpless gesture. 'I don't know. We could ask a psychiatrist. We could ask a priest. We could ask our parents what happened to us when we were small. Believe me, I tried to analyse my needs in the beginning. But that didn't change them.'

'What are your needs?'

'To submit. To feel pain. I need to be disciplined by someone strong, and sometimes I need to make love to someone very soft.'

She gave Lori a kiss. Danielle's lips and tongue were a warm, juicy pulp that tasted salty and musky, sour and sweet. Lori wondered how she could ever have found the Frenchwoman so forbidding. Under Danielle's icy shell was a woman both gentle and passionate, who could deliver a caress as delicate as a moth's wing, or fuck as forcefully as a man.

'That's enough for tonight,' Danielle said, stroking Lori's breast. 'Tomorrow, Jean-Michel will show you more. He'll come for you at eight o'clock. Be ready. He's always on time.'

'Eight o'clock? Why so early?'

'Because it's what he wants.' Danielle's fingers turned into pincers, grasping Lori's nipple and squeezing until she yelped. 'Jean-Michel is very serious about this, Lori. Don't underestimate him.' She patted Lori on the cheek. 'Get some sleep, little one. I'll see you tomorrow.'

As she got ready for bed, Lori tried to recall if she had ever had the level of submissive response that Danielle described. Curiosity – she had certainly felt that – and arousal, and desire. But had she ever felt anything close to that bolt of thunder?

She remembered an evening by the bay, the first night she met Gavin. She recalled a firm hand on the nape of her neck, a rock-solid cock pressing against her belly. A deep voice, husky and assertive, ordering Lori to take her hair down. A long, hard kiss that left her wobbling like a newborn foal.

Before she knew what she was doing, Lori had pulled her calling card out of her wallet and was dialling a number across the ocean. Right about now, the sun would be rising over the sea, the first light crossing Gavin's face as he lay in his bed. Somehow Lori knew he was staying there, in the glass house in Morne Bay. She had a feeling that ever since he appeared that night below her window, he hadn't been back to New York.

After a few moments of transatlantic static, the telephone rang. Lori's heart sank as she counted five rings, then six and seven. Just as she was about to hang up, she heard a click, followed by muffled sounds of disorder.

'Hello?'

His voice. Even blurred with sleep, Gavin's voice was like lightning in Lori's body, plunging straight through her heart then leaping down to her cunt.

'Hello,' he said again, alert now. Lori could see him,

propped on one elbow, his hair hanging loose over his shoulders. She opened her mouth to speak, but her throat was so tight that only a thin whisper came out. Then Lori heard a voice in the background, so close to the telephone that the speaker had to be curled up against Gavin's body.

'Gavin? Who the hell is calling at this hour?'

The voice was thick and smoky and profoundly annoyed, the voice of a woman unused to being woken at dawn.

It was Rayne Hughes. In Gavin's bed.

Lori hung up the phone. So much for dark princes and bolts of thunder.

'Fuck the fairy tales,' Lori said out loud.

She switched off the bedside lamp and lay in the darkness, thinking about the things Danielle had told her that night. Lori had had enough of love, with its soft, squishy centre. From now on she was going to seek out the razor-sharp edges of desire.

Jean-Michel arrived at eight o'clock the next morning, as Danielle had promised. Lori was just sitting up in bed when she heard his knock. She groaned, kicked off the covers, and combed her curls with her fingers. Opening the door, she found her tutor impatiently checking his Swiss watch. Dressed in a black Italian suit with a black shirt and tie, his dark blond hair combed back from his forehead, Jean-Michel was the best eye-opener that Lori could have had.

'Wow,' she said. It was all she could manage.

Without so much as a greeting, he stepped past Lori into the room, closed the door and locked it.

'What's this?' he asked, scowling at Lori's Boston Celtics T-shirt. 'You're not ready?'

'Jean-Michel, I'm not in the mood for the game. Not yet. Give me some time to wake up.'

'Your mood doesn't matter, little one. Go and get ready,' he ordered. His tone was even, but his eyes were stone hard. '*Vite, vite.* We are meeting someone for breakfast in an hour.'

Lori was too tired to fight with him. She sighed and padded into the bathroom. Jean-Michel blocked the door when she tried to close it.

'The door stays open,' he said.

'What?'

'Leave the door open. When I'm with you, you won't close any doors unless I give you permission.'

'But Jean-Michel, I need some privacy,' Lori laughed. 'I have to wash and use the toilet.'

He shook his head. 'Privacy is for independent women. An owned woman is always subject to her master's eyes. If I owned you, I could demand to see you naked at any time. Take that shirt off. Go on.'

Lori obeyed.

'Give it to me.'

Reluctantly Lori handed over the T-shirt. Melanie had given her the oversized garment years ago; the basketball team's logo had faded, and the seams were torn, but Lori still wore it to bed almost every night. Jean-Michel held the shirt for a moment, his nose wrinkling in distaste, before balling it up and throwing it on the floor.

'A beautiful woman shouldn't wear a rag like that. You might as well drape a garbage sack over the Venus de Milo.' He looked around the small hotel room, taking in the frayed chenille bedspread, the striped wallpaper, the clashing floral pattern of the draperies. 'If you were mine,' he mused, 'I would never let you stay in this place. Not even for one night.'

Lori thought she heard a wistful note in his voice when he said the word 'mine', but Jean-Michel didn't give her any time to think about what it meant. Tapping his foot in its polished leather shoe, he stood outside the door while she ran a soapy sponge over her skin. Her bladder ached, but she couldn't stand the thought of being watched while she peed. Lori had lived alone for so many years that she wasn't used to casual intimacy with another person, much less Jean-Michel's intense scrutiny.

She tried to ignore Jean-Michel's reflection in the mirror as he stood behind her, supervising her preparations. But it was hard to pretend that he wasn't there, when her body kept reminding her of how attractive he was. She couldn't help stealing peeks at his stern, sensual mouth. Every time she looked at those lips, her pulse accelerated.

After self-consciously applying makeup and combing her hair, Lori announced that she was ready to get dressed.

'You haven't finished,' Jean-Michel said, pointing at the tiny closet that held the commode. 'Do what you need to do.'

'I can't. I'm sorry, I just can't.'

'Do it, little one,' he ordered. 'Now.'

Lori felt tears gathering in her eyes as she sat down on the toilet. Jean-Michel stood in the doorway, towering over her. Lori stared at her knees. She tried to relax enough to obey him, but every muscle in her body was clenched. She could feel Jean-Michel's impatient stare boring into her vulnerable flesh. His disapproval made her sob in frustration.

'Don't cry,' he said in a softer tone. He bent down and lifted her face, then kissed her cheeks, forehead and mouth, and tweaked her nipples. As she responded to his caresses, his murmured encouragement, Lori's clenched muscles let go. The rushing cascade felt as keen and sweet as an orgasm.

'Very good, little one.' He stroked the underside of her chin as he looked into her eyes. 'You see how it feels to give up control? If I owned you, you would get used to this, and more.'

Lori nodded. The flush hadn't left her cheeks. She had never felt as naked as she did now. Feeling equally humiliated and aroused, she followed Jean-Michel out of the bathroom. He made sounds of scorn, with the occasional grunt of appreciation, as he rifled through the clothes in her armoire.

'This will do for today,' he said. The Schiaperelli trouser suit soared across the room like a white bird, floating onto Lori's bed. Lori stepped into the suit and studied herself in the mirror. Her bobbed hair complemented the garment; she might have been a fashion plate from the 30s.

'You have good instincts,' Jean-Michel said. He stood behind her, his geometric black suit contrasting with the fluid lines of her white trousers. 'That kind of taste can't be taught. You must have inherited it from your beautiful ancestor.'

'Did my great-aunt let Doran Cross do all these things to her?' Lori asked.

'Oh, yes,' Jean-Michel said, 'and that was just the beginning.' He ran his finger along Lori's jawline, then down her throat. 'She wore a collar for him. You'll wear one for me. A simple strip of black velvet, with a diamond here.' His finger came to rest in the hollow of her neck and he leaned his cheek into the dip of her shoulder. His skin felt surprisingly warm for a man with such a cool temperament.

'A diamond?' Lori said, with an awkward laugh. 'Isn't that a bit much for a game?'

Jean-Michel stepped away from her. 'I take this game very seriously.'

'You'd better tell me the rules, then.'

'Ultimately, there's only one rule: you will obey me. If

you are late, if you're unwilling to do anything I ask, if you contradict me or show disrespect, I will punish you. If you absolutely refuse to do as I say, then the game is over.'

'So you could ask me to do anything, and I'd have to obey you?'

'In the time we have together, I won't be able to push you as far as I'd like to. If we were entering into a longer relationship, we would negotiate, and arrive at a contract. But in three weeks' time, I can only give you a sample of the life that Lorelei Price lived. That's what you asked for, isn't it?'

'Yes,' Lori said.

'You'll have to trust me enough to follow my orders. I don't know your limits, but I do know your level of experience. I know the kind of woman that you are.'

'Guileless, you said.'

Jean-Michel smiled. 'You have a good heart, that's true. I don't believe you have the potential for evil. But after last night, I know that you're far more complex than I thought. And much more daring. You amazed me, Lori.'

The admiration in his voice made Lori glow with pleasure. So much for vanilla. If Rayne Hughes could see Lori now, she'd see a very different version of the country mouse she had met in New York.

But Lori had no desire to see Rayne again, or Gavin for that matter. By now Rayne and Gavin were probably living together, having hot and heavy sex five times a night and twice before breakfast. Rayne was probably the type of woman who got tired of a man once she'd snatched him out of someone else's hands. As soon as she had finished gloating over her conquest, she'd discard her prize and move on to someone else.

Lori hadn't entertained such petty thoughts since the

age of fourteen, but the image of Gavin getting dumped by Rayne made her smile.

Lori was still smiling as she followed Jean-Michel down to the lobby. The concierge and a cluster of hotel guests gaped at the sight of them: the blonde in white silk and sweeping beige cashmere, the man in his black Armani. Lori tried to duck her head, but Jean-Michel pressed his hand against the back of her neck to keep her erect.

'Look straight ahead,' he said. 'Don't be ashamed of your beauty. You'll lower your eyes when you talk to me, but with everyone else you'll maintain your composure.'

A silver Mercedes was parked outside. Before he let Lori climb into his car, Jean-Michel insisted on photographing her in various poses along the street: standing beside the stone wall of the hotel, sitting at a wrought iron table outside a café, leaning against a lamppost. A few early-morning pedestrians and shopkeepers glanced at Lori, studying her face as if to discover where they might have seen her before. At first Lori was embarrassed by their curiosity, but gradually she began to relax, and even to enjoy being the object of their stares.

'You've taken more pictures of me in the past twenty-four hours than I've had taken in my entire life,' Lori said when they were in the car. 'Were you collecting souvenirs back there, or just trying to embarrass me?'

'A little of both,' Jean-Michel said. He gave Lori one of his rare grins. 'I want you to get used to being inspected by others. Other men – and women – will be looking at you a great deal over the next few days. You'll have to learn how to respond.'

'How's that?'

'As if you were my property,' Jean-Michel said. 'You'll respond to any praise with a graceful neutrality. You'll feel pride at being a credit to me, but no sense of personal gratification.'

Jean-Michel rested his hand on Lori's leg. She felt very uneasy, and not only because of his one-handed driving. Obeying his instructions was one thing, but did he really think he could tell her how to feel?

'Don't be afraid,' he said, squeezing her knee. 'I'm taking you to visit a woman who has been living this life for years. When you meet her, I think you'll understand.'

They took a Byzantine route through the city, bypassing familiar landmarks and driving through streets that became increasingly obscure and secluded.

'Jean-Michel, are we still in Paris?' Lori joked nervously.

'Close enough,' Jean-Michel said. 'But not too close. We're going to one of the distant banlieues. With the route I take, it would be next to impossible for anyone to follow me here.'

'Why so much secrecy?'

'You'll see, soon enough.'

Jean-Michel stopped the car in an alley behind a nondescript townhouse on a drab suburban street. He took a set of keys out of his pocket and opened the gate that led to the inside of the building, then used a second key to open the inner door. Instead of proceeding through the foyer, Jean-Michel stopped short. When she saw what stood in their way, Lori caught her breath.

Kneeling on a woven straw mat was a naked woman. She held her arms behind her head, and her eyes were cast down on the floor. Her chestnut-brown hair was pulled tightly back from her face, but the severe style did nothing to diminish her exquisite looks; if anything, a more elaborate style would have been a useless distraction. Even kneeling, she was clearly very tall, with endless arms and a swan's neck that was only slightly lined Lori guessed her to be several years older than herself Her age augmented her beauty, bringing a serenity and repose to her perfect features.

Something about the woman struck a chord in Lori's memory. At first she thought it was the classical symmetry of her features that made her seem familiar. But when Jean-Michel ordered the woman to stand up, and Lori saw her stunning blue-green eyes, the colour of polished New Mexican turquoise, Lori knew exactly where she'd seen that face. For a brief time in the 1980s, those extraordinary eyes had illuminated countless news-stands on the covers of fashion magazines like *Vogue* and *Harper's Bazaar*.

'My God,' Lori stammered. 'You're Ilse Wilde.'

Fifteen years ago, Ilse Wilde had been one of the top models in the world. The name 'Wilde' was a perfect match for her reputation. She used to wear her hair in a bleached white mohawk, like the punk rockers whose limousines she was always tumbling out of, and she had been as famous for her drunken displays of nudity as for her beauty. Her career had been spectacular but short. One minute she was the hottest face in the industry, the next, she had all but vanished from the public eye. After a few heavily publicised bouts with rehab, followed by repeated failures to revive her modelling career, she disappeared altogether.

And now here she was, standing right in front of Lori, wearing nothing but a black velvet collar with a baguette diamond in the centre.

'Bring us our breakfast, little one,' Jean-Michel told the former model.

'Yes, monsieur.'

The 'little one,' who topped Jean-Michel by at least two inches, turned silently and left the room. She still had the willowy build of a fashion model, but her signature mohawk had been replaced by a heavy, gleaming braid that was tied in a loop at the nape of her long neck.

'She didn't even notice me,' Lori said. She couldn't help feeling snubbed.

'Yes, she did. It's just that you responded to the person she used to be. Ilse isn't a wild child anymore. She hardly remembers that part of her life.'

'When did you meet her?'

'I photographed her in the early 80s, before she became famous. We did some fantastic work together in New York. She loved to dress up in leather and chains, and she's always been a natural submissive.'

'Submissive? In those days? You've got to be kidding.'

Jean-Michel smiled. 'Outrageous behaviour can mask a deeply submissive personality. Ilse went overboard trying to hide who she really was. When she finally stopped abusing herself, she was able to see her true nature, and to love it.'

'So how did she end up here with you?'

'Five years ago, her former master released her. When I found out she was available, I was overjoyed. I'd been coveting her since the day I met her. Now she's mine.' Jean-Michel took Lori by the arm. 'Come on. She's waiting for us.'

Lori caught her breath when she entered the room. The lushly romantic interior had nothing in common with the bleak suburb outside. Like Jean-Michel's home, this apartment held countless beautiful objects, but there was a unity to the décor that put Lori immediately at ease. She wished that she could spend days here, memorising details: the antique tapestries, the textures of wood and velvet and satin. A pair of French doors opened onto an interior courtyard, which was resplendent with fall foliage. Veils of gauze were draped across the framework of a large wooden sculpture. Chrysanthemums cascaded in furry golden profusion from Ming vases. The scents of black coffee and fresh bread rose from a lacquered Chinese table in the centre of the room. Ilse knelt on the floor beside the table, pouring coffee into porcelain cups. Jean-Michel and Lori sat down in a pair of chairs, and Ilse served them breakfast. There were steaming croissants and creamy white butter, dusky autumn grapes and gooey French cheese.

Under any other circumstances, Lori would have loved to sit in this cavern of sensual treasures and stuff herself with fruit and cheese and croissants, but with Ilse Wilde kneeling naked at her feet, she could barely nibble at the food. Questions swarmed in her mind. How had Ilse decided to get into this lifestyle? What did she do all day? Was she always naked? Did she ever miss being a celebrity?

Judging by the serenity of Ilse's face, and the radiance of her apricot skin, Lori would have said that Ilse didn't miss her old life at all. When she modelled, she had been scarecrow-thin; now she was still slender, but her breasts were fuller, her thighs and belly more rounded. Her pubic mound had been shaved as smooth as a seashell. Lori had glanced at Ilse's pussy when the former model had been kneeling down on the floor, and had caught the glint of gold. A padlock identical to the one Danielle wore hung from her cunt-lips.

'Ilse committed a serious violation last week,' Jean-Michel said to Lori, as if Ilse weren't there. 'I loaned her to a friend of mine for the evening, and he told me that she refused to suck his cock in a restaurant. What do you say to that, Lori?'

Lori, caught chewing, said nothing. She would have had no idea what to say anyway, even if her mouth weren't full of croissant. Ilse's cheeks had gone bright pink. She stared at the floor.

'Well? What do you think of a slave who disobeys her master?' Jean-Michel pressed.

'I can understand how Ilse felt,' Lori admitted. 'I would have been embarrassed too.'

'But there's a difference between you and Ilse. You are an independent woman. Outside of this game we're playing, you control your own sexuality. Ilse is an owned slave; she doesn't have the luxury of shame. She signed a contract agreeing to let herself be used sexually by me or my friends in any way we want, anywhere we choose. My friend took Ilse to a very exclusive restaurant, a place where the staff and clientele are absolutely discreet, so that he could enjoy her in public without having to worry about his reputation. But Ilse wouldn't serve him. Why not, Ilse?'

Ilse mumbled something.

'What's that?' Jean-Michel asked. He set his plate and cup on the table and rose from his chair. He walked over to Ilse, stood behind her, gripped the loop of braided hair and pulled her head erect. She winced, but didn't cry out.

'Speak clearly,' he said. 'Tell my guest why you disobeyed.'

'I had too much wine,' Ilse said. 'He ordered me to drink, then I felt dizzy. I couldn't have done what he wanted me to do next; I would have been sick.'

'What sort of wine was it?'

'A Bordeaux.'

'Did you enjoy it?'

Ilse closed her eyes. Tears glinted on her long lashes. She shook her head.

'Why not?' he asked, in mock surprise.

'Because I broke a rule,' Ilse whispered.

'Ilse isn't supposed to drink or use drugs,' Jean-Michel explained to Lori. 'It's part of her contract. Her body is my property. She is not to harm it in any way. Because of her history, I don't even allow her to use medications that contain alcohol. Yet the other night, she drank wine. What do you think of that?'

'It was the wrong thing to do,' Lori said. 'But if your friend told her to drink, wasn't she obliged to do it?'

'Ah. There's the rub.' Jean-Michel released Ilse's braid. 'Ilse found herself in a dilemma. She had to choose between obeying her master and obeying a man whom she was supposed to serve for the evening. Under the terms of our contract, Ilse was supposed to do everything this man asked her to do, unless it contradicted her master's orders. Sucking another man's cock falls within the realm of the rules I've established for Ilse. Drinking doesn't. That seems simple enough, doesn't it?'

Lori had to agree. In this case, the violation seemed clear, but she could imagine that the rules could become twisted, treacherous. A woman could get lost in a labyrinth like that.

'I told Ilse that I would punish her when the time was right,' Jean-Michel said. 'Drinking is a violation that's worthy of release, but I've chosen not to let Ilse go. This is the first time she's broken that rule, so I'm giving her a second chance. But I'm going to punish her today. Lori, you'll help me.'

'How?'

Ilse glanced up at Lori, and for a moment the women's eyes met. In that flicker, Lori saw an unmistakable gleam. Ilse wasn't trembling with dread. She was shaking with excitement.

Under her confusion, Lori felt anticipation mounting.

'First, you'll choose the instrument that I punish her with. Go over to that armoire and pick something out. Choose carefully. If I think you're being tender-hearted, I'll punish you, too – and the choice of tools will be mine.'

Lori walked over to a tall, gracefully carved antique

cabinet. Its polished doors glowed like mahogany mirrors, revealing decades of loving attention. But the contents of the stately antique were anything but traditional. As soon as she opened the twin doors, the rich, spicy scent of leather engulfed her. Inside that armoire hung the most astonishing array of instruments that Lori had ever seen: crops and whips, floggers and paddles, even a bridle and a dainty saddle. And the leather was only the beginning. Feather ticklers and fur cuffs, clips and clamps and black satin masks hung on their own rack inside the miraculous cabinet.

'Ilse takes good care of her things,' Jean-Michel said. 'And I reward her by buying her the best. Pick whatever you want, Lori; we're waiting.'

Lori didn't know where to start. She couldn't even name half of the implements, much less identify their purpose. What if she chose something that caused horrible pain? She couldn't stand to watch Ilse's flawless skin being marked. On the other hand, if she picked something totally harmless, Jean-Michel would be angry, and Ilse would think she was a coward. If only Melanie were here, she'd know exactly what to choose.

The thought of her best friend gave Lori a surge of confidence. She settled on a slender, flexible leather paddle that looked menacing enough to please Jean-Michel, but didn't seem capable of leaving permanent marks on Ilse. On the spur of the moment she chose a striking domino mask, with glittering sequinned ovals where the eyes should be. If Ilse had to suffer, she might as well look glamorous while she was doing it. As Lori was closing the doors, something sparkly caught her eye. It was an unusual pair of ruby and diamond pendant earrings, held together by a delicate chain.

'What about these?' Lori showed the items to Jean-Michel. He smiled.

'Very creative choices. We'll put them to good use.' He

yanked Ilse's braid, pulling her to her feet. 'Get the frame ready,' he said. The tone he used with Ilse was harsh, dark. Lori had only had a taste of that voice herself. It made her quiver.

Ilse crossed the room to the veiled structure that Lori had noticed when she came in. She had assumed that it was some kind of sculpture or spare furniture, but when Ilse pulled away the drape of shimmering gauze Lori saw that the structure was a simple wooden frame, about ten feet tall. A pair of leather manacles dangled from chains on either side bar, with two more attached to either side of the base of the frame.

Jean-Michel demonstrated how the frame worked. By turning a wheel at its base, the wrist manacles could be moved up or down along the frame's interior grooves, depending on how high the arms were to be raised. When the manacles reached the desired height, he pressed a lever with his foot, and the grooves locked into place to hold them tight.

'I had this built especially for Ilse,' Jean-Michel explained, stroking the wood with loving pride. He showed Lori how high the manacles had to be elevated in order to accommodate Ilse's height and her long arms. 'At the highest level, Ilse's arms are lifted so high that she stands on tiptoe. But I rarely take my little one to that extreme.'

Ilse took her place in the centre of the frame, and Jean-Michel restrained her wrists and ankles. He was gentle but firm, positioning her precisely the way he wanted. Watching him manipulate Ilse's body and listening to his commands, Lori felt a strange sense of envy. The structure of Ilse's life was suddenly apparent: a life that was carefully monitored and controlled, bound by rules that enmeshed her like hundreds of invisible strands. Alternately pampered and punished, she was the absolute object of Jean-Michel's desire.

Lori had never been the absolute object of anyone's desire. Not yet.

'My little one is ready. Put on the mask and clamps,' Jean-Michel said.

Lori approached Ilse, who stood with her arms manacled above her head and her legs spread wide, her ankles restrained. Feeling shy, Lori held out the mask as if to ask the other woman's permission, but Ilse lowered her head so willingly that Lori's hesitation dissolved. She pulled the mask over Ilse's sleek hair and secured the band. Then she applied the ruby clips to Ilse's earlobes, with the pretty gold chain dangling against her throat.

Ilse made a choking sound. Lori thought she'd hurt her somehow, but the stifled choke turned into an explosion of laughter. When Jean-Michel saw what Lori had done, he burst out laughing too.

'What's the matter?' Lori asked. 'Did I put them on the wrong way?'

'You put them on the right way,' Jean-Michel said. 'But in the wrong place.'

Still chuckling, he removed the clips from Ilse's ears. Then, to Lori's shock, he applied them to the woman's pale nipples. The pain of the clamps wiped any trace of amusement from Ilse's face. She whimpered as Jean-Michel twisted the tiny screws at the side of each clamp. He picked up the chain that connected the two clamps and handed it to Lori.

'You'll hold this while I punish her,' he instructed. 'And as I beat her, you'll tug on the chain. Don't be gentle, either. Make no mistake; she'll be disappointed if you don't give her what she craves.'

Lori stood in front of Ilse. Jean-Michel took off his jacket and threw it over a chair, then he stripped off his tie, loosened his collar, rolled up his sleeves and got into position behind her. He slapped the paddle against his palm a few times, as if warming it up. Behind the sequinned mask, Ilse's face was a gorgeous mystery. Holding the chain clamped to Ilse's tender flesh, Lori had a sense of what it must be like to be in Jean-Michel's place, wielding total power over a woman. She tightened her grip experimentally. Ilse's nipples stretched into long points, and her beautiful mouth twisted.

The strength of her own response took Lori by surprise. She had never deliberately hurt another person in her life, but inflicting pain on Ilse was shockingly exciting. Then Jean-Michel struck the first blow with the paddle, and as Ilse's body arched forwards in response to the smack, Lori gave the chain a good, hard pull.

Ilse's shriek resounded through the townhouse. Lori almost came from the delicious rush of power and the shared experience of Ilse's pain. She could feel the impact of the leather on her own skin each time the paddle fell, and the excruciating bite of the clamps on her own nipples. With each blow, the ruby ornaments swung furiously. Between Ilse's thighs, a long drop of clear liquid hung suspended, clinging to the little gold padlock.

'Harder,' hissed Ilse.

It was the first word Ilse had spoken to Lori. At first Lori didn't believe what she was hearing, but when Ilse ground her teeth and repeated her plea, Lori realised that Jean-Michel had been right. If Lori didn't give Ilse what she wanted, she would be dissatisfied – and so would Jean-Michel.

Lori pulled the chain until Ilse's nipples were stretched to an impossible length. Ilse threw her head back and gave a deep moan, which escalated into a scream when Jean-Michel struck her ass with all his might.

'You may come, little one,' Jean-Michel said. 'I know you've been holding back.'

Ilse fell forwards, as if in a swan dive, her arms behind her, bearing her weight. Her face, in agony, was as gorgeous as an angel's, but the groans and squeals coming from her mouth were bestial. Ilse was coming, and with all her heart Lori wanted to be there with her, at that pinnacle of pain and pleasure. When Ilse's spasms subsided, and her head slumped down onto her chest, Lori released the golden chain. She wished she could kiss Ilse's poor nipples, but she had a feeling that Jean-Michel wouldn't approve of such tenderness.

Jean-Michel put the paddle down. His face was flushed with exertion, and the bulge in his trousers said all that needed to be said about his state of mind. He left the room and came back wiping his face and throat with a towel.

'Come over here,' he said to Lori. 'Take a look at my handiwork.'

Lori stepped around to the opposite side of the frame. Jean-Michel pointed to Ilse's inert body. Her ass cheeks, formerly the colour of white peaches, were criss-crossed with red stripes. Lori cringed at the sight of the marks, but was relieved that at least she hadn't chosen a tool that would draw blood. Jean-Michel unbuckled the manacles and lifted Ilse away from the frame. As soon as she was free, Ilse lowered herself to her knees, still trembling violently.

'What do you say now, Ilse?'

'Thank you for punishing me, sir,' the woman gasped.

'Did you learn your lesson?'

Ilse gave an emphatic nod.

'Are you sure about that?' Jean Michel released the clamps on her nipples. Ilse squealed in pain. 'They hurt even more when they come off,' he explained to Lori.

Jean-Michel was standing so close that Lori could hear his pounding blood; she could see and smell the fresh sweat beading on his throat and pooling in the hollows of his collarbone. She didn't have to look below his waist to know that he was rock hard. Lori wished he would fuck her, right there in front of Ilse.

'Did Ilse's pain excite you?' he asked.

'Yes,' Lori gulped.

Jean-Michel took her sex in his hand, squeezing her hot, slippery flesh right through the Schiaperelli trousers. She could feel her wetness saturating the old silk, but she didn't care. She ground herself against Jean-Michel's palm and let him see just how excited she was.

'Take your clothes off,' he ordered, addressing her now in the masterful voice he had used with Ilse. Lori got her legs tangled in the white trousers as she rushed to obey, and almost fell over as she hopped around on one leg, but Ilse didn't laugh. No amusement or envy crossed the former model's face. She seemed content to kneel quietly, her eyes lowered to the floor, as her master watched another woman strip.

Didn't Ilse ever feel jealous? Lori wondered, as she stood naked in front of her and Jean-Michel. Was she ever allowed to have a bad mood?

'Ilse, go and get Lori's gift,' Jean-Michel said.

Ilse rose. Her motions weren't quite as fluid as they'd been before her beating, but she still walked with grace and composure.

'If you were mine, I'd shave you,' Jean-Michel said to Lori. He took hold of her pussy again, handling the folds with a connoisseur's touch. 'But it would be a shame to get rid of this lovely blonde bush.'

That blonde bush was glazed with Lori's juices. She was so turned on that when Jean-Michel's index finger skimmed her clit, her body quaked from head to toe.

'Don't come yet,' he teased. 'Not until I give you permission.'

'But I need to come *now*.'

'Not yet.' He brushed her clitoris again. 'Greedy little slut.'

'Please!' Lori couldn't believe she was hearing herself

beg, but at this point she would have gotten down on the floor and grovelled for release.

'All right, then. Come.'

He drove the heel of his hand into Lori's mound, and the floodgates opened. As the orgasm rushed through her, Jean-Michel held her face with his other hand and made her look at him. Through the blurred waves of her pleasure, she saw the satisfaction in his eyes. And there was something more, an odd light that she was way too far gone to identify. By the time she was coming down, the light had vanished.

Jean-Michel held her in his arms and stroked her back. 'You've done very well this morning, Lori. You may feel proud of yourself. Ilse, give me Lori's present.'

Lori turned around. Ilse had come back into the room. She gave Jean-Michel a flat grey box.

Lori knew what was inside before Jean-Michel opened the lid. The diamond sparkled with the inner fire unique to fine, impeccably cut gems. Jean-Michel lifted the black velvet band from its nest and held the diamond in his palm, turning it from side to side, dazzling Lori with its prismatic brilliance.

'No,' Lori said. 'I could never accept a gift like that.'

It was one thing to play a game of being owned, but she wasn't going to let herself be bought. She thought Jean-Michel would be offended by her refusal, but he only nodded.

'I understand. I don't expect you to keep it. But I would like you to wear it for me while you're here in Paris. Try it on.'

He fastened the collar around Lori's neck. She expected the glorious gem to feel like ice, but it felt warm and vibrant, alive with its own value.

'What do you think?' Jean-Michel asked. 'How does it feel?'

'It feels wonderful,' Lori admitted. 'But it makes me nervous to be wearing something around my neck that's worth more than everything I own.'

'You'll wear it as long as the game lasts. When the game is over, you'll give it back to me,' Jean-Michel said with a shrug. 'Simple enough, isn't it?'

'Yes,' Lori agreed reluctantly. 'I suppose it is.'

But Lori suspected that this game was about as simple as the multi-faceted diamond.

The harem bells over the door at Chimera tinkled so often these days that Melanie was starting to hear them in her sleep. She had never officially announced the opening of The Alcove, as she called her selection of erotic merchandise. One day, after Lori had been gone long enough for Melanie to overcome her twinges of conscience, she simply set up her offerings in a corner at the back of the shop, hung a paisley sarong over the nook, and posted a sign that read: 'For Our Customers 18 and Over Only'.

Morne Bay's residents trickled in like ants scouting a sugar spill: first curious, then ecstatic about their discovery, then eager to tell their friends about Chimera's display of 'bedroom accessories'. Of course, respectable townspeople couldn't just saunter into the shop and pick up a vibrator or an edition of the Kama Sutra. They had to buy a blouse or a necklace as well, to disguise the nature of their mission. So much the better – profits were skyrocketing, and Melanie's supply of toys was running low. She spent her evenings on the internet, surfing through online sex stores. But Melanie preferred to shop in the flesh, and she knew that she was going to have to make some purchasing expeditions soon. Any travel would have to wait until Lori returned, and Melanie was starting to worry that her friend had got lost in Paris.

Except for one excited phone call, Melanie hadn't

heard from Lori since she left for France. When she wasn't worrying about her friend, Melanie was doing her best to keep her brainchild from growing into a monster. Yesterday she had placed an advertisement in Morne Bay's newspaper, seeking temporary sales help, and today she was interviewing a couple of girls who responded to the ad four hours after the paper rolled off the presses. They were social outsiders in Morne Bay, as Melanie had been at that age, eighteen-year-old fashionistas who would probably work at Chimera for a month or two before flying off to New York or San Francisco.

'So when can you start?' she asked the girls, who had introduced themselves as Luna and Pagan. Melanie knew that their given names were Beth and Jennifer, but she liked the fact that they had forged unique identities for themselves. She was also intrigued by the metal lacework that crossed Luna's cheek, linking her nose rings with her ear piercings; and she adored Pagan's combat boots, which were painted with iridescent glitter as if she'd just stomped through fairyland.

'Tomorrow,' said Luna.

'Today,' blurted Pagan.

The girls looked at each other and giggled. 'We can't wait to start selling the bondage gear,' Pagan explained.

'But you're interested in the clothes as well. Right?'

'Definitely. We love the clothes. We *wear* the clothes. See?' Luna twirled around, displaying the quilted floor-length skirt of a 1960s maxi dress that she had, indeed, bought at Chimera.

'All right, ladies,' Melanie said. 'Be here at eight tomorrow morning. Do you have any questions?'

'Just one thing,' Pagan asked hesitantly. 'Do you think the shop's going to be open for a while?'

An icy lump formed in the pit of Melanie's stomach. 'Of course the shop will be open. We're doing better than ever.'

'Well, that's just it,' Luna said. 'Most of the town is crazy about The Alcove, but there are a few people who aren't.'

'And those people are saying that they're going to close Chimera down.'

Melanie breathed deeply. She tried to ignore the images that were flashing through her mind: Chimera being stormed by an angry mob, Lori coming back home to find her shop dark and empty, Lori hunting down Melanie, Lori strangling Melanie . . .

'Who's saying that?' Melanie asked.

'Well, Maggie Hanover, for one,' Luna said.

'Mostly Maggie,' Pagan interjected.

'But she runs the town council.'

'And those prudes do whatever she says.'

Melanie happened to know that most of the council members had purchased items from The Alcove, and the ones who hadn't bought anything had been into the shop to sniff around. She had expected disapproval, even outrage from some of the townspeople. But she hadn't prepared herself for any serious opposition; she had been too busy trying to keep up with the sales.

'Listen,' Melanie said, with more assurance than she felt, 'no one is going to close Chimera down. But I'm glad you warned me about Maggie. Why don't the two of you come in at noon tomorrow instead of eight? Give me some time to work things out.'

Melanie could tell by the girls' drooping faces that they were skeptical. As soon as they left the shop, she locked the door, dug her address book out of her purse and found a critical phone number. Paul Weathers, whom Melanie had dated one summer before he came out of the closet, had just installed a pair of French doors in Maggie Hanover's bedroom. If he weren't such a brilliant carpenter, Paul could have made a living as a blackmailer; he was that good at gathering dirt.

'Paul, it's Melanie. I'm in trouble.' Melanie wasted no ime when he answered his cell phone. 'I need facts.'

'What's in it for me? Maybe a vibrating anal plug from hat Alcove of yours?'

'If you give me the right information, you can have ınything you want from The Alcove for the rest of your ife.'

'What do you need to know?'

'I need to know everything about Maggie Hanover. Ier childhood secrets. Her teenage sex fantasies. I need o know what kind of books she hides under her bed.'

Paul thought for a moment. 'To tell you the truth, Aaggie doesn't have a lot of secrets. There's not a single lirty novel under that Laura Ashley dust ruffle. The voman is as boring as she looks.'

'That can't be true, Paul. Everyone has a secret erotic ife. Sometimes you just need the right equation to ınlock the door.'

'Well . . . I did find something very odd in one of her lresser drawers. I was looking for some spare nails at he time,' he added hastily.

'Whatever. Just tell me.'

By the time Paul had finished describing what he had ound, Melanie was smiling like a Persian cat, and Paul vas on his way over to the shop to choose his reward rom The Alcove.

'he next morning Chimera was closed to all customers out one. Melanie was worried that Maggie Hanover vouldn't accept her invitation to a private viewing of 'he Alcove, but at nine o'clock Maggie appeared wearing ın oatmeal gabardine suit, her grandmother's pearls and . quizzical smile. True to her uppercrust breeding, Mag- ;ie wouldn't get confrontational unless she were backed ıp by a crowd of villagers brandishing torches.

'I'm so glad you could come. Welcome to Chimera.' As

soon as Maggie stepped inside, Melanie turned the dead-bolt lock.

'Charming little place.' Maggie's eyes travelled around the room, taking in the racks of dresses, the shelves of antique linens and the autumn bouquets of dried leaves and berries.

'But you haven't seen the best part.' Melanie took Maggie's hand, leading her to the back of the shop. 'We just started offering a new selection of exotic gift items. We wanted to add a little spice, a touch of fantasy to our inventory.'

Melanie opened the curtain with a flourish, revealing the shelves of shiny new toys. A rainbow array of glass dildos stood beside a selection of classic erotic books. A display of vintage Mardi Gras masks framed a selection of gags, nipple clamps and fur handcuffs. Crops, floggers, paddles and ticklers hung on an antique coat rack. Melanie caught her breath whenever she looked at her Aladdin's cavern of treasures, and she couldn't help but notice that her guest wasn't breathing regularly either.

Maggie Hanover was really quite attractive, Melanie thought, studying her from the corner of her eye. If she didn't have such stodgy taste in clothes, she'd be a knockout. Her hair was a natural cornsilk blonde, her eyes were clear blue, and a delicious rosy stain was spreading across her cheeks.

'I realise that some people in town might not approve of our latest addition,' Melanie said, 'so I wanted to give you a chance to take a look in private, before you make a final judgment. Go ahead and explore; I'll be right back.'

While Maggie stood frozen in front of The Alcove, clutching her handbag as if it were a lifeline to decency, Melanie changed her clothes in one of the dressing stalls. When she came out fifteen minutes later, Maggie was reaching for a shimmering glass dildo. As soon as she heard Melanie's footsteps, she snatched her hand away.

'Really, this isn't to my taste,' Maggie started to say. Then she saw what Melanie was wearing, and her mouth formed a mute O.

Melanie had changed into a red satin cheong-sam gown with a mandarin collar, a jewel of a dress from the 1940s. The fitted bodice and sheath skirt, embroidered with dragons, accentuated her curves. She had twisted her hair into a high knot, held in place by a pair of lacquered sticks. Her face was half concealed by a black sequinned mask that extended into feathery wings. Maggie Hanover couldn't take her eyes off Melanie's shoes – open-toed sandals with stiletto heels – until she saw what Melanie held in her hands.

'Maybe this is more to your taste,' Melanie said, holding the whip out for Maggie's inspection. The whip was purely decorative, fit for nothing more than a costume party, but its effect was even more powerful than Melanie had expected.

'What *is* that?'

Fear and delight mingled in Maggie's voice. Her eyes glowed; her lips glistened. The dull crust of her adult shell was crumbling, and a shining, secret self was poking its way out. Only a very old erotic fantasy could cause a metamorphosis like that.

'This is something you've wanted for a long time,' Melanie said. 'Get down on your knees and look closely.'

Quivering, Maggie knelt. She gaped at the coiled whip as if it were a gorgeous, deadly snake.

'Kiss it.'

Maggie pursed her mouth shut. At first Melanie was afraid she might have gone too far. Then the blonde tentatively pressed her lips to the whip's braided handle. While Melanie stroked her hair, Maggie sucked the handle as if it were hard candy. 'You're a very good girl, aren't you, Maggie?' Melanie purred.

Maggie's face was slack with adoration. 'Yes, miss.'

'You will call me Mistress Q,' said Melanie. 'And when I summon you, you'll come to the shop or to my home. You'll do whatever I ask and, in return, I'll show you pleasures you never dared to hope for.'

'Oh, yes.'

'I'm what you always wanted. I'm the woman you used to dream about. Aren't I?'

'Yes, Mistress Q,' Maggie whispered. The feral scent of arousal seeped through her lilac bath powder.

Melanie smiled. She could easily get into the dom role; being on the top side of a power exchange was an amazing rush. 'I won't let you come now,' Melanie said, 'but I want you to come later, when you're by yourself, and think of me. Will you do that?'

She didn't have to ask. Maggie would be rubbing the slick V of her white cotton panties as she drove home in her Volvo sedan. She'd be hitting her climax by the time she pulled into her driveway, and all the while she would be thinking of Melanie, who looked just like a character in a faded comic book she had hidden in her dresser for years: the Mysterious Mistress Q. Within a week or two, Melanie predicted, she would have the head of the town council eating out of the palm of her hand.

Melanie had too much respect for the power of sex to play blackmail games with her customers. The Alcove held magic, and Melanie wasn't about to abuse it. But she couldn't help wishing that she'd used a hidden camera to prove that she'd had Maggie Hanover on her knees – and to show Lori that she never had to worry about the future of Chimera.

18

Lori's original plans for Paris had been thrown out the window; her days were now organised by Jean-Michel. In the mornings he came to her hotel room to help her dress. Each day he brought her new clothing, garments he had picked out himself. Her vintage dresses and costume jewellery gathered dust in the armoire; Jean-Michel refused to see her in anything but his own selections.

'I want you to be what I see,' he explained. 'As long as we're playing the game, I will define you.'

She hardly recognised the woman he was constructing: a sex object clad in elaborately laced corsets, ruched velvet skirts and fantastical shoes with cruelly high heels. Dressed like his personal call girl, Lori accompanied Jean-Michel to restaurants, museums and some of the most exclusive underground clubs in Paris. She was never allowed to wear panties, so that Jean-Michel could enjoy her at any time. She loved the feeling of being nude under the sexy clothing, but the clothes and collar felt more like props than natural expressions of herself. Still, she couldn't help basking in all the attention. She had never been the object of such pampering, or the recipient of such an avalanche of gifts. When it was time to go back to the States, she would return all of Jean-Michel's jewellery and clothes, but for now, Lori decided to enjoy herself to the hilt.

Lori wished that she could tell Melanie about Jean-Michel. She daydreamed about sitting in a Paris café with her friend, sipping wine and confiding in her about all the strange and wonderful changes that were taking place. She imagined Melanie's brown eyes sparkling with curiosity as she listened to Lori's adventures. The costumes, the jewellery, the kinky toys, the exotic sex ... Melanie would either die of envy, or try to have her friend committed to an institution.

Lori couldn't believe how much Jean-Michel expected her to learn in such a short time. She had to memorise twelve submissive positions and practise them naked while Jean-Michel watched, correcting every move and shooting photos. The positions demanded flexibility and stamina; Lori was grateful that Melanie had forced her to take a yoga class last summer. Each pose gave Jean-Michel access to one or more of her openings, which she had to keep clean and shaven at all times. He didn't make her shave her mound completely, but he did require her to keep the outer folds of her cunt and the area around her anus free of hair. Danielle, who was as skilful with a razor as she was with her tongue and fingers, helped Lori with this task. The Frenchwoman also tutored her in the proper mannerisms: keeping her eyes lowered, her voice low, her gait graceful, and her posture erect but demure.

'I feel like I've gone back in time,' Lori complained. 'Back to the eighteenth century. Does Jean-Michel really expect his women to act like this?'

'His women *want* to act like this,' Danielle reminded her sternly. 'At least when they're around him.'

Then there were the training sessions. Every day Jean-Michel pushed Lori to another extreme. Just when she thought he had taken her to her ultimate limits, he nudged her a bit farther. He blindfolded Lori and tied her to his bed for hours while he teased and tortured her eager body with feathers, fur and hot wax. He made her wear lightly clamped nipple ornaments under her clothes so that she would always be on the borderline between arousal and discomfort. He subjected her to long endurance tests in his private dungeon, where she was tied to an X-frame or a bench and punished in dozens of delectable ways. Lori learned to accept pain in small increments, until she developed a taste and then a hunger for the sensations of the lash, the flogger and the paddle.

In quieter moments Lori had to clean the same instruments that were applied to her flesh. Before long, the scent of the wax she used to condition the leather was enough to get her juices flowing, and the preparatory smack of a paddle across Jean-Michel's palm could bring her to the brink of orgasm.

Of all the tests Jean-Michel put her through, public exposure was the most difficult. He was fond of taking Lori to popular tourist sites and photographing her while she exposed her bare ass or pussy, or played with herself like a wild slut. If she felt hesitant or frightened, Danielle was always there to help her along, the Frenchwoman's sexual confidence acting like an opiate, easing Lori's doubts and fears.

One afternoon Jean-Michel ordered Lori to make herself come in front of a group of tourists in the Bois de Boulogne, where Lorelei Price had taken some of her notorious photos of society women. Lori balked at first, but Danielle urged her on in a lewd whisper, arousing her with dirty words and threats.

'Rub your pretty pink twat for your master, little one,' Danielle hissed, 'or he'll spank you to within an inch of your life.'

And unbelievably, Lori found herself climaxing in front of a group of senior citizens who might have attended the Methodist church in Morne Bay. Before the poor tourists could recover their wits, Jean-Michel whisked Lori and Danielle away in his Mercedes. He promised to reward them for their performance with dinner at his favourite private club.

The club was located in an industrial building that looked about as exclusive as a meat-packing plant. But like so many of the places to which Jean-Michel had taken Lori, its anonymous interior hid marvellous secrets. Before they could proceed through the anteroom, Jean-Michel had to check in with a guard, a beefy man whose bald skull and golden earring reminded Lori of a pirate. The guard hailed Jean-Michel as if he were a long-lost brother, slapping him on the back and kissing him noisily on both cheeks. He handed Jean-Michel a purple velvet sack that jingled when Jean-Michel slipped it into his pocket. Lori guessed that the sack was stuffed with coins or tokens of some kind. The men chatted in French, the pirate eyeing Lori with a combination of suspicion and lust as they talked.

'Is she in your service?' he asked Jean-Michel. 'I can't let her in if she's not.'

'Of course, Nico,' Jean-Michel said. 'And you already know Danielle.'

Danielle and Nico exchanged frosty looks. Then the pirate begrudgingly unlatched a velvet rope that hung across the entry to the club, and allowed Jean-Michel and his guests to enter.

As soon as they stepped through the twin doors, Lori was enveloped by an aura of prosperity as tangible as cologne – men's cologne. The place was obviously designed for masculine tastes and masculine pleasures, boasting deep plush carpets, sturdy oak furniture, gaming and billiard tables, and a wall-size television that was broadcasting a football match. The odours of cigar smoke, whisky and beer pervaded the atmosphere, the drinks supplied from a mahogany bar with polished brass fixtures that swept around the back wall. Nude women, each more beautiful than the last, strolled by like deer in a testosterone forest, carrying trays loaded with ashtrays, brandy snifters and shot glasses.

Each woman wore a studded black leather collar and matching gauntlets on her wrists. They walked slowly, with measured steps. Lori saw that this geisha-like gait was produced by dainty chains attached to shackles around their ankles. The chains tinkled as they walked, creating a feminine music that underlay the coarser sounds of male laughter and rattling dice. Every detail in the room had been designed to titillate male senses, but Jean-Michel looked bored.

'There's nothing going on here,' he said to Lori and Danielle. 'Nothing but blue-collar distractions. Let's have dinner. Then we'll start the real entertainment.'

He led the women into an adjacent lounge, a cavern illuminated by a roaring fire. A solo saxophonist played sexy jazz, and at low tables guests sat dining and drinking. As Lori's eyes adjusted to the light, she caught the pearly glow of female skin at various booths. One nude woman was sliding down a man's lap; another undulated in a private dance. From the liquid sighs and groans that came from those tables, Lori guessed that the men were savouring more than the cuisine.

Jean-Michel and Danielle slid into a long booth. Lori started to follow.

'No,' Jean-Michel said. 'Take your clothes off. I want you kneeling on the floor, next to me.'

Undressing in front of strangers wasn't nearly as humiliating as it would have been two weeks ago, especially when the room was dim and most of the other women were already naked. Lori found herself getting turned on by the appreciative looks that came her way as she wriggled out of her leather dress, corset and stockings. She took off everything except the black velvet collar, laid the borrowed clothes carefully on the booth beside Danielle, then assumed one of the positions that Jean-Michel had taught her: legs folded under her body, feet under her buttocks, and her hands clasped behind her head with her elbows raised.

'Very good, little one,' he murmured, dandling one of her breasts. 'Your training is going even better than I hoped.'

One of the nude waitresses, a luscious redhead, stopped at their table and asked them for their order. She didn't even blink at the sight of Lori kneeling on the floor; she simply wrote down the food and drinks that Jean-Michel requested. Jean-Michel tipped the waitress with a gold coin from the velvet bag, then told her to turn around. He stroked the fine, smooth cheeks of her ass, then slid one finger between them. She stood still throughout the inspection, letting Jean-Michel fondle and finger her as he pleased.

'Not bad,' he commented to Danielle. 'Very tight.'

Danielle nodded. 'She's quite young.'

'I wouldn't mind using her later.'

'I wouldn't mind helping you,' Danielle said with a coy smile.

Jean-Michel dismissed the waitress. The redhead minced away as if the intimate inspection and discussion of her body were nothing more than a haircut. It would be easy to get used to this life, Lori realised, if you were able to cross those final boundaries. Jean-Michel's world was like the land behind a mirror, a territory where all values were reinvented, all judgments overturned. His world had its own language, its own laws and, in this private club, even its own currency.

Kneeling on the floor, Lori dined out of Jean-Michel's hand. He allowed her to put her arms down when he saw that they were beginning to shake. She placed her hands demurely on her knees and nibbled bits of rare filet mignon from his palm. Being fed was an unbelievably arousing experience; it was a form of intimacy that Lori hadn't experienced since early childhood, this time with the added electricity of sexual desire. Now and then Jean-Michel dipped his middle finger in his glass of single malt scotch and allowed her to suck. While she was sucking his finger, Lori noticed that Jean-Michel was fondling Danielle's cunt under the table.

'Lick her juices off my hand,' he told Lori, pulling his glistening fingers out of Danielle's pussy. Lori was happy to obey. After the tastes of rare beef and scotch, the flavour of Danielle's cunt was briny and exotic, like some unusual shellfish.

'I think you're both ready for tonight's entertainment,' he chuckled. 'Lori, you're going to go farther tonight than you ever have before. Are you ready?'

'*Oui, Monsieur,*' Lori said. Judging by the dense, wet heat in her cunt, she was more than ready for what the night had in store.

Lori never saw the room where she spent the rest of the evening.

After dinner the redhead waitress delivered several items on a wide silver tray: a black satin blindfold, a leash and a crop. Lori's cunt muscles tightened at the sight of the crop. Before Jean-Michel came into her life, she had never known that there were so many delicious varieties of pain. She could already feel the precise, burning lick of the thin leather strip against her ass.

Jean-Michel placed the blindfold over Lori's head, adjusting it snugly so that not even a sliver of light penetrated the cloth. He then attached the leash to the back of her collar. When he stood up, she tried to rise from the floor, but he pushed her back down.

'On all fours,' he said. 'Keep your back arched. There,

that's lovely. Pretend that you're a trained animal, a creature of great value and grace. Now follow me, my beautiful pet.'

'How can I be graceful when I can't see where we're going?' Lori asked.

'Don't worry about where you're going, just concentrate on each step. That's the nature of this game, no?'

Jean-Michel walked slowly, leading Lori along. Once she got used to the darkness behind the blindfold, it was easier to match her pace to Jean-Michel's. The humiliation of crawling on all fours faded as she began to feel more sure of herself. The soft, thick carpet was easy on her knees and palms. She held her head high and raised her backside, pretending that she was an Arabian mare or a prize-winning show dog. When she headed in the wrong direction, Jean-Michel would tap her ass with the crop, and she shuddered, imagining the torments that awaited her.

The raucous sounds of laughter and rattling dice died down when Jean-Michel brought Lori into the crowd. She could hear the men whispering to each other and sighing with longing as she passed. When she felt a door-frame brush against her waist, she knew that they had left the casino room. The texture of the carpet changed underneath her hands, becoming even more lush, and her fingers sank into the rug's velvety nap. Now she heard only a few masculine voices, the occasional hiss of a cigarette lighter and the muted clang of crystal on crystal. She pictured three or four men lounging around the room, pouring cognac out of carved decanters.

Jean-Michel stopped. Lori stood on all fours beside him, trying to look as confident as she could. A heavy door swung shut. Lori figured that this room must be soundproofed, because the racket from the casino was so effectively silenced that she might as well have been transported to another world.

'Thank you for your patience, gentlemen,' he said. 'I promise you that tonight's entertainment will be worth the wait.'

For the first time, Lori realised that *she* was the night's entertainment. She could smell the men's anticipation, spicy and strong, and knew that they were already naked. She could feel the electricity of their arousal, as if their cocks were lightning rods, pointing straight at her. The men – were there three of them, or four? – were still conversing, but their voices had taken on a hard, eager tone.

Lori was feeling more than a little nervous.

Jean-Michel knelt beside her, stroking her trembling flanks as he whispered into her ear.

'You will enjoy this, my love,' he said. 'I promise you. Concentrate on your sense of smell, your sense of touch. And trust me.'

He tugged Lori's leash and led her closer to the men. She heard bodies shifting, and the buttery creak of fine leather. In her mind's eye she saw a low couch, where Jean-Michel's guests were sitting back with their legs spread, pricks quivering. These strangers weren't going to attack her; they were simply waiting for her to service them.

Lori felt herself being guided into the warm canyon of a strong pair of male thighs. Powerful leg muscles enclosed her body, holding her in place. She nuzzled the man's groin, her lips and tongue feeling for his cock as if she were a pony licking a shiny red apple. When she found the swollen head, she was rewarded with a groan. But Jean-Michel didn't let her stay there for long. He tugged on the leash again, and she moved on to the next guest.

This man's stout inner thighs were covered with a wiry pelt of hair that tickled Lori's skin. In-between those legs was an amazing cushion of curls, smooth and fine, that Lori would have liked to explore with her fingers. His erection was much bigger than the first man's; the rod swung heavy and pendulous against her face as she tried to wrap her lips around it. The stranger waited for her mouth to find its goal.

Lori could have spent hours with the third guest. His smell, a combination of expensive cologne and his own natural civet, was as heady as incense. She would have liked to lose herself in the nook between his firm, smooth thighs. He was the only one who touched her, running his fingers through her hair. He murmured French endearments as she tongued his hard-on, which was just the right size for her willing mouth. Even without seeing him, she knew that she could happily make love with this man, and that he'd be as eager to please her as she was to arouse him. A runnel of sap was oozing out of her cunt-lips, and her own moans were beginning to form in her throat, when Jean-Michel yanked the leash again.

Was he jealous? The thought crossed Lori's mind, then faded as soon as Jean-Michel spoke.

'Now you've all met my little one. You're free to use her as you like. Lori, assume the third position.'

The third position was supposed to allow access to Lori's mouth, cunt and anus. She widened her stance, increasing the distance between her knees and palms, raised her head and opened her mouth wide. She felt a tremor of apprehension as she lifted her rump, thinking of the man with the monster prick.

Trust me, Jean-Michel had said. Did she have a choice?

She heard the men rise from the couch and begin to circle her. She felt their furry legs brushing her skin as the circle tightened; she knew that they were trying to determine which one of them would take her first. The tension of their barely concealed aggression was palpable. There was a brief struggle, with grunting and pushing, as two men tried to mount her at once. One of the men quickly won the skirmish. To Lori's relief, it wasn't the man with the enormous penis. This man's cock, as he slid into her passage, was just wide enough to fill her. His gentle grip on her hips told her that he was the man who had caressed her hair. Delighted, she pushed her ass back to meet his thrusts, but before she could get used to his rhythm, another prick was filling her open mouth.

It wasn't easy accommodating two men. Their bodies, their movements and their smells were so different that Lori felt that she was trying to be two women at once. The man fucking her clearly adored her body; his hands roved over her buttocks, waist and back, stroking her as if he were marvelling over a prize he'd won. The man in her mouth preferred to treat her like a cheap whore. He kept trying to cram more of his member down her throat, and he clutched handfuls of her hair, urging her to suck harder. But once she got used to the confusion, Lori began to like it. Then she began to love it. Why couldn't fucking always be this way? The rough and the gentle, the coarse and the sensual: if only they could be mingled every time!

To her amazement, Lori found that she loved being manhandled by the stranger with the cock in her mouth, loved the way he drove his massive prick in and out with little regard for her capacity to swallow him. She loved the way he called her 'slut' and slapped her cheek when her teeth scraped his rod. It soon grew so big that Lori couldn't do much more than lap and nibble at the head. The organ bobbed and ground against her tongue, its owner trying in vain to push it into Lori's aching mouth. Finally he pulled back and, after a few noisy tugs accompanied by guttural groans, sprayed her face with come. She let the mask of jism glide down her cheeks, loving the feeling of it, silken and degrading.

But she also loved the worshipful moans of the man riding her, and the considerate tempo of his thrusts. He was trying to time his pleasure to meet hers, so that they could come together. Lori didn't know if she could hold back that long; she was already wildly excited, her clit throbbing in an angry percussion. She longed to rub herself, but her position made that impossible.

Then the third man, who had been content so far to watch and wait his turn, joined in. One of his large hands mauled her breasts while the other furrowed in the folds of her cunt, fumbling for her clit like a bear's paw seeking a pearl. His thick fingers finally found their target, and Lori felt her orgasm rounding the bend, huge and ominous; she was almost scared of the intensity building inside her, but there was no turning back now.

The man fucking her was hitting his own peak, and the pounding of his hips against her ass was enough to send her over the edge. She cried out and reared back, her body grinding against his. The man with the broad hands held her as the spasms rushed through her. As she was recovering, he stood up and came across her breasts, while the man who had mounted her held her upright.

'Keep her up like that.' It was Jean-Michel's voice. 'My little whore enjoyed herself too much tonight. She needs to be punished.'

Lori's arms were held firmly behind her head. The man restraining her shoved a knee between her thighs, forcing her legs apart. Before she knew what was happening, Lori felt the sting of the crop against her right breast. She shrieked, more from the shock than from the pain. The first stroke was followed by another, excruciatingly delicate, across her left breast. She sobbed when the tail of the crop bit her nipple. One of the men chuckled. The crop struck her breasts several more times, before it laid burning trails across her belly and mound. Not even her pussy, softened by orgasm, was spared; as a grand finale, the crop flew up between her legs, biting into the tender flesh. Screaming, Lori threw her head back. In the burning aftermath of pain, she felt the most exquisite pleasure she'd ever experienced.

Drunk on these new sensations, Lori almost lost consciousness of the whir and snap of Jean-Michel's camera. Almost, but not quite.

19

Lori didn't know what time she left the club, but she saw the silvery light of a Parisian dawn as she slid into the back seat of Jean-Michel's car. Limp from the night's pleasures, she nestled back in the comfort of Danielle's arms and dozed while Jean-Michel drove through the city. She woke hours later to the aroma of coffee and found herself lying in satin sheets of the palest sea green.

'Hello, little one.'

Danielle stood above her, holding a bamboo tray. On the tray sat a white bowl filled with coffee.

'Where am I?' Lori asked. Groggy with sleep, she sat up against the deep pillows.

'My place. Jean-Michel wanted you to stay with me. He has something very special planned for you at my gallery tonight.'

'How could it be more special than last night?'

'You'll see.'

'Were you with me in the private room at the club?'

Danielle smiled. She sat down on the edge of the bed and stroked Lori's cheek. The glow in her eyes, a mixture of lust and pride, confirmed that she had definitely been there.

'Jean-Michel was overjoyed by your performance with his friends. He isn't going to let you go,' the French-woman said.

'He's going to have to. My vacation is almost over.'

'Maybe the vacation is over,' Danielle said, 'but your new life is just beginning.'

'What new life?' Lori laughed. 'This has been an amazing adventure, but it's not a life. Not *my* life, anyway. I've still got friends and family back home, not to mention a business.'

'Don't be surprised if Jean-Michel tries to convince you to stay.'

'He can try all he wants. When the game is over, I'm going back.'

'We'll see about that,' Danielle said. 'Now drink your coffee, then I'll help you get ready. I can't wait to see you in the dress that Jean-Michel bought for you to wear this evening. He had it made especially for you.'

'Evening?' Lori looked around in dismay. Through the sheer gauze curtains that covered Danielle's windows, she saw the early twilight of autumn. 'I slept all day, didn't I?'

Danielle patted Lori's hand. 'You were exhausted, little one. You needed your rest for tonight. Jean-Michel is going to introduce you to some of his friends. You'll be meeting people from the most exclusive social circles in Paris, not to mention artists, journalists, photographers. All of them belong to Jean-Michel's world, and all of them are gathering to admire you.'

'But Danielle, I'm no celebrity. I've never done anything to deserve that kind of attention.'

'Yes, you have,' Danielle said with a mysterious smile. 'Now let me show you the dress Jean-Michel chose for you.'

Danielle left the room and returned with a swathe of black satin draped across her arm. She held the dress up for Lori to see.

'*Et voilà.*'

Lori rubbed her eyes. The breathtaking evening gown could have come straight from one of her historical fantasies. For once, Jean-Michel had acknowledged her taste in vintage clothes. The dress resembled an original Chanel. Jean-Michel's guests might have no idea who

Lori Marwick was, but they would recognise the genius behind her evening gown.

'What do you think of the design? Does the cut look familiar?' Danielle asked.

Lori was too overwhelmed to examine the garment critically. 'It's stunning. That's all I can say. I can't believe that Jean-Michel had that made for me. It must have cost a fortune.'

'For Jean-Michel, it's worth it. He wants you to make a very specific impression tonight.'

Lori got out of bed and touched the dress hesitantly, as if it were a figment from a dream. 'My God, Danielle. This dress was copied from one of Lorelei's photos!'

Danielle beamed. 'Amazing reproduction, isn't it? When you walk into the room, everyone will recognise this dress. They'll think you're Lorelei Price herself.'

But I'm not, Lori thought. The old doubts returned. Would she be glamorous enough to pull off wearing this dress? Beautiful enough? Accomplished enough?

Then she realised that it didn't matter. Tonight, she would be playing Jean-Michel's game. She would masquerade as her great-aunt, and perhaps she would finally learn how it had felt to be a glamorous, beautiful adventuress living in 1930s Paris.

Danielle lived only a short distance from the Saskia, so the two women walked to the gallery that evening. Through the windows of the restaurants and cafés Lori saw the warm, friendly commotion of people beginning the night's adventures. This glimpse of bohemian Paris, she imagined, was not so very different from what her great-aunt had experienced. Here was Lori Marwick, a woman in an elegant dress straight out of a photo from the 30s, parading through the streets of Montparnasse. Men passing on the sidewalk turned to stare, and in the currents of their desire she felt her great-aunt's blood stirring in her veins. New secrets, vibrant and exciting, simmered under Lori's skin. This was what she had come to Paris for.

When Danielle led her down the secluded path to the gallery, Lori caught the shimmer of festivity in the air. Japanese lanterns edged the walkway, and through the gallery's open door light and noise spilled into the small courtyard. The cascading notes of jazz piano accompanied the music of conversation. Jean-Michel's lean, elegant silhouette filled the open doorway. Danielle stood back and let Lori go ahead, so that he could feast on her beauty.

'*Incroyable.*' His voice caught in his throat as he reached for Lori. She thought he was going to give her the customary French embrace, but he clutched her so tightly that she couldn't move.

'Don't wrinkle your dress!' she laughed.

'This is *your* dress,' he said, with a vehemence that startled her. He held Lori at arm's length and looked her up and down. 'No woman will ever wear this dress but you. No other woman could pull it off.'

'Jean-Michel,' Lori said, pulling herself free, 'we need to talk. I'll be going back to the States in a few days, and –'

'Hush.' He closed Lori's lips with his fingertip. 'After the party, we can talk. Right now your guests are waiting.'

He led Lori into the gallery. Danielle followed at a distance, letting Lori have the spotlight. When she stepped into the crowded room, Lori froze in a spasm of self-consciousness. The room was filled with people who exuded confidence, success and wealth. Celebrities, Danielle had said. Journalists, artists, politicians, all of them connected to Jean-Michel through the sadomasochistic pleasures they enjoyed in their private lives. Lori saw the signs of their affiliation everywhere: a studded leather collar around a woman's neck, a pair of handcuffs dangling from a man's coat pocket, women in astonishingly tight corsets and heels so high that they must have been designed in a fetishist's wet dream. Waiters in black tuxedos ducked in and out of the clusters of guests, distributing hors d'oeuvres and cocktails.

Jean-Michel cleared his throat. The music stopped. Conversation ceased. All heads turned towards Lori. The room was so quiet that she could hear the blood pounding in her veins.

'*Mes amis*,' Jean-Michel said, 'allow me to present my very own Lorelei.'

The clapping began sporadically, and soon the applause spread through the crowd. Lori blushed in confusion. When she was able to gather her wits and see the exhibits on the walls, she finally realised what this evening was about.

The room was lined with photographs. Immediately she recognised the photos that Jean-Michel had shown her on the day they first met, the shocking fetish shots taken by Lorelei Price. But as her gaze circled the room, Lori saw that her great-aunt's photos weren't the only works on display.

Hanging on the walls alongside her great-aunt's photographs were pictures of Lori herself. They were the shots that Jean-Michel had been taking of her in his studio, in the clubs and all over Paris. There were shots of Lori and Danielle making love, and shots of Lori exposing herself in the park. There were even scenes from the private orgy the night before. Lori saw herself on all fours, her blindfolded face raised in rapture to suck a man's cock. She saw her mouth twisted in pain as the blurred line of a crop fell across her bare breasts. Next to those humiliating images were photos of Lori looking like a fashion model in her white trouser suit; Lori climbing out of Jean-Michel's Mercedes, her long legs extended to the sidewalk; Lori gazing out over the Seine, her profile cutting a flawless white line against the cloudy Parisian sky.

It was clear that the photos were meant to portray two sides of Lori: the independent, self-possessed woman, and the submissive who craved domination. Looking at the array of images, Lori could see what Doran Cross had searched for in his portraits of Lorelei Price. He had tried to capture her transition from light to darkness, the illumination of her natural beauty versus the obscurity of her craving for humiliation. Ultimately, Lori realised, his purpose wasn't to establish a contrast, but to bring the two sides together into a single woman, beautiful and integrated, encompassing the pure and the profane.

Then Lori saw the photo that she had hoped she'd never see again, and her spirits crashed to the ground.

Set above all of the other photos was the portrait of Lorelei Price kissing the hand with the eagle ring. How could Lori have missed it? She had been so caught up in exploring her erotic fantasies that she had all but forgotten the horrifying reality of her great-aunt's past.

No one could mistake the intention behind the display of that photograph. It was the centrepiece of the show, the image that supplied the context for all the others. On either side of the photo, as if to emphasise the comparison, hung pictures of Lori practising her submissive positions, naked and humble, a slave to her desires. All of these people here tonight – total strangers – had seen Lori compared to her great-aunt. They believed that the two Loreleis were one and the same, two versions of one woman, separated by time.

'What do you think, little one?' Jean-Michel asked her.

She gaped at him, paralysed with shock. Jean-Michel's smug pride turned to irritation. 'What's the matter? Aren't you pleased?'

'I can't believe this.' Lori choked out the words. 'That picture – you know I can't stand it. It makes me sick.'

Lori whirled around, making a break for the door, but Jean-Michel's guests blocked her way. She shoved her way through the crowd in the opposite direction, glass shattering on the floor as she knocked drinks out of people's hands. With tears clouding her eyes, she groped her way through the throng to Danielle's private office. Inside, she closed the door and locked it behind her. She braced her hands against Danielle's desk and leaned forwards, gulping air, trying to keep herself from passing out.

This trip had been a terrible mistake. She should have listened to Melanie – the past was dangerous. Lori had waded into its depths like a trusting child, only to be dragged down by a brutal current. She had to push her way back to the surface before she drowned.

The doorknob rattled.

'Lori, open the door.' It was Jean-Michel's voice, low and urgent. 'Let me in.'

'Leave me alone!' Lori shouted.

A few minutes passed, then she heard a key scraping in the lock, and the door opened. Jean-Michel shut it behind him.

'Lori. Forgive me for displaying that photo. I thought that after all the work we've done, you would see that image in a different light. I wanted tonight to be a reconciliation with the past.'

Lori shook her head. 'There's nothing to forgive. You showed me the truth. I have the same desires as my great-aunt, and those desires are dangerous. I have to get out of here.'

'Dangerous?' He took both her wrists in his hands. 'But Lori, those desires brought you to life.'

'I *have* a perfectly good life back home. I want to go back. This game is over.'

Lori took off her velvet collar and dumped it on the desk. Jean-Michel stiffened.

'You don't know what you're saying,' he said quietly. The game isn't over until I end it. Tomorrow you will be moving out of your hotel. I will come to help you pack your things. You will stay with Danielle until I find a place for you to live.'

Panic gripped Lori's chest. 'Didn't you hear what I said? I'm going back to the States, Jean-Michel.'

Jean-Michel smiled. 'You can't go, little one. I haven't even begun to show you my fantasies.' He reached for Lori and kissed her on the mouth. His lips were hot.

Lori twisted in his arms. 'Let go of me.'

'No.' Jean-Michel's grasp tightened. 'You wanted this. You gave yourself to me.'

'I only wanted to understand Lorelei's past. I never gave myself to you or anyone else.'

'You let me photograph you. You wore the gifts I bought you. You did everything I told you to do.'

'Damn it, that doesn't mean you own me. Let me go!' Lori wrenched her arm free and punched Jean-Michel in the jaw.

Dead silence. Jean-Michel touched his face gingerly. Under his anger and pain, his face registered a certain admiration. Lori had never known that so much strength lay coiled in her slender arm. For a moment she thought he was going to hit her back, then his rage fled, replaced by sadness and defeat.

'You still haven't given up control,' he said. 'That's to be expected. We had less than three weeks together.'

'And they were wonderful, Jean-Michel. But this isn't who I am. I came here to learn about Lorelei Price, not to become her.'

'Give me one more chance, little one,' Jean-Michel murmured into Lori's hair. 'Let me show you what you came here to learn.'

Jean-Michel put his arms around Lori and covered her throat and lips with sweet, wild kisses, the kind she hadn't experienced since she was eighteen years old. She never would have guessed that a control addict like Jean-Michel could deliver such caresses: tender, expressive and, well, vanilla. Lori had to admit that they were very persuasive.

'I've already learned more than I can take,' Lori said.

'Take one more step with me,' Jean-Michel pleaded. 'Trust me just a little more.' He stroked her cheek, brushing a tear from her soft skin. 'Don't be deceived by that photo of Lorelei Price. Your great-aunt was a victim of Doran Cross. He made a practice of giving his women to other men. Sometimes he sold them for luxury items, or for food and shelter. Sometimes he traded them for political favours. Sometimes he gave them away just to seal their humiliation.'

'Jean-Michel, do you know what Doran Cross did to Lorelei? Have you known all along?'

Jean-Michel let Lori go. He lovingly arranged her evening gown, patting its folds into place. 'By midnight tomorrow, you'll know everything about Lorelei Price. Play the game one more night, Lori. Please? Then you'll go home knowing the truth.'

Even though the office was overheated, Lori was shivering. She couldn't tell if her tremors came from anticipation or fear. She knew that she should go straight back to her hotel and stay there until it was time to go home; but her craving for the truth still gnawed at her heart.

'All right,' she sighed. 'One more night.'

The concierge at Lori's hotel did not know where she spent her days, and the pudgy little man turned up his nose at Gavin's attempt to bribe him for information.

'I do not keep a dossier of our guests' activities.'

'Could you tell me the last time you saw her?' Gavin

pressed. Though he was jet-lagged, starving and desperate for caffeine, he wasn't about to satisfy any of his needs until he'd got at least a morsel of information about Lori.

'I am a busy man, Monsieur. How could I remember every time she comes and goes?'

'Lori Marwick isn't a woman you'd forget. Tall, strikingly beautiful. Curly blonde hair, down to her waist. Here. I have a photo.'

Gavin held out a photograph of Lori that Melanie had given him. The concierge shook his head. He had to be gay, Gavin thought, not to notice a woman like Lori. Then the man's eyes lit up.

'Ah. I do know your Miss Marwick.'

'Yes?' Gavin tried not to jump across the desk.

'I remember because she cut the hair. She looks nothing like she did when she came. Her clothes, everything has changed.'

'Changed? How so?'

'More sophisticated. More style.' He smirked.

'When you saw her, was anyone with her? A man?'

The concierge pursed his lips.

'Look, I know it's indiscreet, but I need to find out where this woman is. She could be in danger.'

'She does not appear to be in danger, Monsieur,' said the concierge. 'That much I can tell you. The times I have seen her, Miss Marwick seemed very content.'

The concierge gave Gavin a curt nod and slipped away from the desk.

Gavin rubbed his bristly jaw. His whole body craved a hot, pulsing shower. Plotting his strategy with Melanie before he left for Paris, they had agreed that he shouldn't book a room in Lori's hotel. Now that he was here, the precaution seemed futile. In fact, the whole trip seemed like a knee-jerk response to a foolish crush.

'Excuse me. Sir?'

An elderly woman with an American accent touched Gavin's sleeve.

'Yes?'

'I didn't mean to eavesdrop, dear, but I think I've seen the woman you asked about. The pretty blonde.' She lowered her voice. 'Is she your sweetheart?'

'She's ... she's my fiancée,' he heard himself saying. Where the hell did that come from?

'Ah. You poor thing.' Her eyes scanned Gavin's rumpled clothes. 'Just got off the plane, didn't you?'

'Can you tell me anything about this woman? Have you seen her this week?'

'We pass each other in the lobby every morning. She leaves with a Frenchman. He isn't as handsome as you. I doubt she's in love. It's probably just a foreign fling.'

'How would you say she looks? Anxious? Afraid?'

'Distracted. Doesn't seem to be taking in the atmosphere. I figured she's either been to Paris a hundred times, or she's under this man's spell.'

Gavin tensed. 'Why? Does it seem like he's coercing her?'

'No, but he leads her around like a little girl. Funny attitude to see, in a woman so tall and elegant. But I figure these models act differently from other women.'

'Models?'

'Well, she is a model, isn't she? The man is always taking her picture – in the street, in the courtyard.'

'When's the last time you saw her?'

'Why, it was yesterday evening, at a café nearby.'

'Which café was it?'

'Oh dear, I can't remember the name. It's right across from that strange little art gallery, the one that's tucked away behind all the plants.'

'The Galerie Saskia,' Gavin said.

'That's it.' The woman shuddered. 'I stumbled onto that place on my last visit. Some of the things on display

... well, all I can say is you wouldn't see that kind of thing in Iowa.'

'Thank you.' Gavin kissed the woman's cheek. 'You've helped me more than you know.'

The woman's faded face turned pink. 'I'd hurry up and find her, if I were you. Paris isn't always a good influence on a woman.'

'It's not Paris I'm worried about,' Gavin said. He picked up his bag and rushed out of the hotel.

Making his way through the labyrinthine garden of the Galerie Saskia, Gavin felt a pang of regret. He had wanted to be the one to introduce Lori to this enchanted place. In his fantasies he had imagined leading her on a tour of the private rooms, showing her the more unsettling treasures, exploring the limits of her sexual curiosity.

But Lori had got here without him. Gavin only hoped she hadn't seen the photos of Lorelei Price. He knew that Lori was mature enough to face the truth about her great-aunt's past; but he didn't think she should have to face that truth alone.

Last time he came to Paris, Gavin's search for Lorelei Price had reached a dead-end in this gallery. Remembering the afternoon he had viewed those photos of Lorelei, he felt a resurgence of that same sickening awareness. All of his admiration of the woman, his love for her work, had crumbled under a tidal wave of shock when he saw the photograph of Lorelei kissing the hand that wore the eagle ring.

Those photos weren't the end of Lorelei's story. But until someone uncovered the heart of the mystery, the images were the last evidence of what she had become.

The gallery was empty. Gavin stood in the centre of the main exhibition room, examining the installation. Bland, tastefully erotic photos in shades of silver and sepia lined the walls. Gavin knew that these images were a cover for the more controversial works that hung in the rest of the gallery. Those rooms weren't open to the general public, unless the general public offered a lot of money to enter.

He waited no more than five minutes before he heard the crisp staccato of Danielle's heels. Like an efficient spider, Danielle never left her prey dangling for long; especially when she recognised that prey on the security camera in her private office.

'Gavin! What a surprise. I'm delighted to see you again.'

Gavin smiled. The surprise, he knew, was genuine. He wasn't so sure about the delight. 'Likewise. You look gorgeous, Danielle.'

Danielle's lithe body had been poured into a one-piece bodysuit, in a shimmering snakeskin fabric that shifted between purple and green. Though the garment covered her from neck to ankles, it revealed the curves and clefts of her body so dramatically that she might as well have been nude. Her nipples were erect.

'I had no idea you were in France. What brings you back? Still searching for clues?'

'Yes, but it's an urgent search this time. I'm looking for a friend of mine. I think she might have come to the gallery. Her name is Lori Marwick.'

Gavin held out his photo of Lori. The Frenchwoman's face showed only the slightest disturbance, like the effect of a sigh ruffling cream.

'I don't know her.'

'Take a closer look,' Gavin urged. 'Go on.'

Danielle took the photo, gave it a perfunctory glance, and handed it back. 'She doesn't look familiar. Is this the end of the questions, Gavin? I'm very busy.'

'Look, Danielle. I've got a bad case of jet lag, and I'm in no condition to interrogate you. I just need to find this woman. You recently had a phone conversation with an American editor named Rayne Hughes. You told her you'd seen Lori Marwick with Jean-Michel Lacoste. Remember?'

Danielle shrugged.

'Goddamn it, this is important! I'm not a stalker, if that's what you think. And I'm not interested in exposing Lacoste. I only want to make sure that Lori's safe. Once I'm sure that she's acting of her own free will, I'll leave.'

'Why do you care so much about this woman?'

'I'm – hell, I'm in love with her.'

Danielle dropped the femme-fatale pose and wrapped her arms around her ribs like a child who had caught a chill.

'*Oui.* I've seen her.'

'How long ago?'

'Last night. We were with Jean-Michel.'

Gavin didn't have to work very hard to picture what they'd been doing. Danielle's stylish armour hid a ravenous sexual appetite. In spite of his fatigue and worry, he found his groin tightening at the thought of Danielle and Lori together. He shook himself out of it.

'Where is she now?'

'With Jean-Michel, I suppose.'

'Where does he live?'

Danielle's green eyes turned accusatory. 'I can't tell you that. He is a client of mine. I respect my clients' privacy.'

'Can you tell me anything? Anything. Please, Danielle. Don't forget, I've been a client of yours too.'

Danielle puffed her cheeks and blew out the air in a whoosh of exasperation. She stalked away into the back of the gallery. For a moment Gavin thought he'd been dismissed, but she soon returned. She gave Gavin a business card. Engraved on the card, in glittering black script, were the words 'Hard Blue Midnight', framed by a scythe-like crescent moon. Gavin recognised the name. He had heard of the nightclub in his wanderings through the fetish underground of Paris, but he'd never visited the place. Not even his Parisian friends would tell an American where it was.

'Tonight she will be at this club. Jean-Michel has arranged a special auction. It's very exclusive. Only a few are invited. The men will bid for Lori. One of them will take her home and do what he wants with her for twenty-four hours.'

'Are you serious?'

'Completely serious.'

'Why is he doing this?'

Danielle lowered her head into her hands, as if she couldn't bear the weight of her knowledge.

'Jean-Michel is recreating a scene from Lorelei Price's life. On her last night in Paris, Doran Cross offered her for sale at an auction for his friends in the SS. They were powerful men, men he wanted to impress. He gave her up to them because he wanted favours, status.'

'An auction? God, I had no idea.'

'Cross wanted to destroy Lorelei Price. She was a gifted woman, a strong woman. She threatened his sense of himself. He took her in as a pupil, then he tried to ruin her. Now Jean-Michel is trying to do the same thing to Lori.'

Gavin took Danielle by both arms. 'You wouldn't set me up, would you? All this is true?'

'Believe me, I wish it weren't.'

'How will I get into the club?'

'Give them that card, and tell them I sent you. But be careful. The men in the audience will be armed. Do you have a weapon?'

'No. I'll have to rely on my brain. And my wallet. I assume the bids will go high.'

Danielle nodded, her eyes glistening. If Gavin hadn't

known better, he would have sworn their emerald luminescence came from tears.

'You care about Lori, don't you?'

'More than you know,' said Danielle softly.

20

Lori stood nude in front of Jean-Michel. If she had been allowed to lift her eyes, she would have seen her reflection in one of the dressing-room's multiple mirrors. She would have seen a woman with a crown of blonde hair, artful stage makeup and a black velvet collar. A delicate gold chain hung across her breasts, attached to two loosely placed clips; its weight caused a stiffening awareness in her nipples. Her slim, taut legs were elongated by a pair of stiletto heels.

She wished she could see herself, but Jean-Michel had ordered her to keep her eyes lowered.

'It's a shame,' Jean-Michel said, 'that I'll have to sell you tonight. I hope the man who buys you appreciates what he's getting. Turn around.'

Lori turned, keeping her eyes focused on the floor.

'Perfect. If only you were really mine.'

Lori glanced up. Over the rim of his wine-glass, Jean-Michel was staring at her with alarming hunger. Quickly she lowered her gaze again.

'You see, I know you aren't devoted to me. You lower your eyes, but not in real submission. You're playing your part in my game. You've played it well. Now I want to bring you into my reality.'

Jean-Michel walked over to Lori. He dipped his finger in the glass of Merlot and held it out towards Lori's mouth.

'Suck.'

She opened her lips. He inserted his finger, and she tasted the wine.

'You only make me want to be more cruel when you obey. You make me want to whip your breasts, your thighs, your ass, and send you out into the streets so that everyone can see my marks.' Jean-Michel ran his fingertips along the chain between Lori's nipples. 'You let me train your body, and play with your mind. But you won't truly give yourself to me. You want someone else. You think you've hidden it, but you haven't. Who is he?'

'There's no one else.'

'Not true.' Jean-Michel placed his hand between Lori's thighs. 'You're hot down there. Wet. I made you think about him, didn't I?'

Lori shook her head.

'You think I'm still playing the game. I'm not.'

Jean-Michel turned sharply and hurled his glass. An arc of red wine sailed across the room before the glass smashed against the wall. Lori shrieked.

When Jean-Michel turned back to her, he was calm again. Lori held her breath. A pulse beat in Jean-Michel's jaw.

'Tonight you'll go home with a man you've never met. He'll do to you all the things I've dreamed about. He'll act out all the fantasies I've had about you. He'll go so far with you that you won't know yourself anymore. And that will be my revenge.'

'For what?'

Jean-Michel grabbed the back of Lori's neck and crushed his lips against hers. His tongue demanded entry, working its way into her mouth with such force that she lost her breath. He pushed the length of his body against hers, taunting her with the rock-hard bulge in his groin. Then he pushed her away.

'You used me, Lori. You wanted me to play Doran Cross for you. But you never learned to want me the way his Lorelei wanted him. She would have done anything for Cross. Anything. She gave him her body, her heart, her will.'

'But Jean-Michel, I'm *not* Lorelei,' she said helplessly. 'I'm a completely different woman. Last night you said you understood. You were lying, weren't you?'

Jean-Michel ignored her accusation. 'Put on your cloak. It's time to go on stage.'

He pulled Lori into the cramped backstage passageway, where they waited for Danielle's cue. Lori heard Jean-Michel breathing in the darkness – slow, measured breaths, with the occasional pause for a sip of whisky. He had not stopped drinking since he arrived at the club. Lori had never seen him consume more than a single glass of wine or champagne before; he was too attached to his self-control. He sat behind Lori in the shadows, but she could feel his stare burning through her velvet cloak, straight into her back. Those cool grey-blue eyes had turned into molten steel. In one hand he held a long leash, which was attached to a ring at the back of Lori's collar. He never released his hold on that leash, even to pour another drink.

Lori wished he would say something. Her stomach churned, and her thoughts raced. Would someone actually buy her tonight? Who would he be? What would he do to her?

Most importantly, how could she get the hell out of here?

Jean-Michel had given her pain, but never more than she could take. He had always known, through an intense observation of Lori's responses, when to ease off or stop. He had let her pleasure define the limits of their games. But tonight he was a different man. He hadn't even brought his camera with him. She had a feeling he was approaching some limit of his own, but she was afraid to think about what lay on the other side.

On the stage Danielle launched into her introduction.

Lori heard the husky notes of the Frenchwoman's voice, the mutter of the crowd and the clinking of ice in glasses: all sounds from another world. In Jean-Michel's world, Lori was a captive.

He stepped up behind her. She stiffened. He chuckled.

'You're afraid, aren't you? Don't worry. I'm not offering your life tonight, only the temporary use of your body. You'll be back with me within twenty-four hours.'

Jean-Michel's lips travelled up the base of Lori's neck. He embraced her from behind, his hands parting the folds of her cloak so he could reach inside and fondle her breasts. His fingers, usually as cool and smooth as stone, felt hot and coarse tonight. With his teeth he unclasped the leash, let go of Lori's breasts and rolled up the thin leather strap. He tucked the spooled leash into the pocket of Lori's cloak.

'I'm giving this to you. I know you'll come back,' he whispered into her ear. 'My sweet little one. Your life would never be the same if you ran away. Your friends, your colleagues, what would they think if they saw the photographs I've taken of you? If they knew what kind of woman you really are?'

He gave Lori a push, and she stumbled through the curtain and onto the stage. Danielle stood in the spotlight, addressing the men in the audience. Lori couldn't make out any individual faces, only a ring of lumpy silhouettes, like cavemen huddled around a prehistoric fire. Then the spotlight moved away from Danielle and settled on Lori, blinding her.

It wasn't 1930s Paris but, in the dark club vibrating with the rhythms of jazz, Gavin could almost believe that Lorelei Price would materialise out of the smoke. The room was largely empty; only the semicircle of tables at the foot of the stage was occupied. Gavin took a seat further back, close enough that his separation wouldn't seem obvious but far enough away to give himself some cover behind the clouds of cigar smoke. On the stage a scantily clad blonde was winding her way around a pole to the sensual beat of the music.

'Would you like a drink, Monsieur?'

A brunette waitress stood beside Gavin's table. As she bent over to take his order her tawny breasts, barely confined by a nylon halter top, brushed against his arm. She wobbled a little, pretending to lose her balance, and planted her hand on Gavin's thigh.

'I'm here for someone else,' he said. 'But I'll take a Scotch.'

The brunette pouted.

'When does the auction start?'

'Soon, Monsieur. The slave is waiting backstage.' She kneaded Gavin's thigh. 'But why wait for her? I can provide you with anything you need.'

'Just bring me my drink.'

The waitress nodded and walked away. She seemed sincerely put out, probably because the choice of clients in the club was so limited. The other men in the audience looked far too sinister to be appealing. Lacoste had done his work carefully. The air of underworld power that hovered around the stage was thicker than the cigar smoke. Gavin could easily imagine a row of black SS uniforms in place of the fine Italian suits. When the auction began, competition would be fierce.

On stage, the dancer broke her clinch with the pole, gave her apple-firm tits a final shake and blew the audience a kiss. The stage darkened, and the music faded. The sounds of clinking ice and harsh laughter died down as the beam of a spotlight parted the darkness. Onto the stage stepped Danielle, jarringly beautiful in a skin-tight ivory satin gown. Slit from floor to waist, the long skirt wafted open with each step, revealing alternating flashes of her snow-white buttocks and shaven mound. In her right hand she held a crop.

The spotlight followed Danielle to a lectern at the edge of the stage. She raised her chin, searching the audience, until her green eyes rested on Gavin. Then she began to speak in French.

'Good evening, gentlemen. Welcome to our exclusive auction. Because you are all acquainted with Jean-Michel Lacoste, I'm sure you're aware of the discretion he brings to his private events. And of the confidentiality he demands in return.'

'Enough talk. Show us the slave.'

'Bring out the whore!'

Gavin tasted bile. He wondered if he was going to be able to get through the auction without murdering one of these apes. Where was Lacoste? The coward was probably lurking backstage, jerking off to the sight of his cherished fantasy.

Danielle gave the men a brittle smile. 'Your wait is over, gentlemen. Allow me to present tonight's offering.'

She turned her head. The spotlight left her, travelling slowly until it reached the centre of the stage.

The light rested on Lori.

She wore a floor-length hooded cape in black velvet. From the folds of the hood, her eyes peered out at the crowd. Gavin drew back into the shadows.

'Bidding will begin at 5,000 euros,' Danielle announced. 'The highest bidder will take home his own personal slave for twenty-four hours. There are no limits to what you may do to her. She will perform whatever acts you desire. Fulfil your wildest fantasies. She is literally yours, to do with whatever you want.'

'So what the hell are we bidding on? She's covered from head to toe!'

Danielle crossed the stage. She pushed the hood away

from Lori's face, then untied the ribbon at her throat and whisked the cloak away.

A rumble of awe rose from the audience.

Gavin's heart stopped.

Lori's hair had been bobbed into a cap of curls. Her mouth was filled by a red ball-gag. Except for a black leather collar, Lori was naked. Against the darkness of the stage, her skin glowed. Her hands were bound behind her back, pushing her breasts forwards, her erect nipples linked by a fragile golden chain. Her belly sloped soft and smooth to the plume of pale curls that covered her mound. The spotlight turned her bare thighs and calves into molten silver. Gavin's heart began to beat like a jackhammer, and a corresponding pulse throbbed in his groin. An overpowering silence in the room told him that the rest of the men were feeling exactly the same thing. She was spectacular. Any man in the room would pay a fortune to take her home.

But none of those bastards was in love with her.

Lori's lips trembled around the slippery red ball. In her eyes Gavin saw the shimmer of fear. She was about to cross the inner line between pleasure and danger. Every muscle in Gavin's body ached to rush the stage like the hero out of an old melodrama, grab Lori and carry her out of this club.

Not yet, he warned himself. Not yet.

As her eyes adjusted to the bright spotlight, Lori could see nothing but floating clouds of smoke. She had been here before, in her Paris dreams, but her dreams hadn't prepared her for this tense, almost hostile silence. Her dreams hadn't prepared her for the reality of having her cloak whisked away, of feeling the heat of the spotlight on her bare flesh, of knowing that she was being watched by strangers.

'Turn around,' Danielle instructed Lori in English. 'Let the gentlemen see what they're bidding on.'

Lori turned. Her knees were shaking, but she managed not to fall in her high heels. The light and her nerves brought a light coating of sweat to her skin. She could feel the men coveting her, their desire as palpable as the heat of the spotlight. She could hear the jostling of their heavy bodies and the squeak of their chairs as they moved forwards to get a closer look. Danielle ordered her to walk back and forth across the stage. She felt the men staring at her pussy each time her thighs opened.

'The slave has been trained to accept moderate discipline,' Danielle said. 'I'll demonstrate.'

She ordered Lori to bend over a chair. With her hands tied behind her back, Lori leaned forwards at the waist, letting her breasts spill over the back of the chair. Danielle caressed Lori's bare bottom with her palm, then stood back and struck her lightly with a crop. Lori gasped as the blows gradually increased in intensity, until her flesh tingled. Then Danielle helped her stand upright. She reversed the chair and told Lori to sit down.

'Spread your legs.'

Lori parted her thighs, and Danielle shackled her ankles to the legs of the chair. With the tip of the crop, Danielle opened Lori's cunt-lips.

'Look at her pussy: pink, fresh and clean. Who wouldn't want to have such an exquisite slave? A fairy-tale princess who craves discipline and longs for the taste of pain. She will be at your disposal, gentlemen, for twenty-four hours, starting at midnight. For twenty-four hours, you will be at liberty to act out all of your desires with this delectable piece of flesh.'

'Ten thousand!' shouted a hoarse male voice.

Danielle smiled. 'Ah. Double the opening bid. Who will give me fifteen?'

'Fifteen!'

'Yes, sir. I see you. Do I hear twenty-five? You won't be disappointed, gentlemen. Have you ever seen such beauty in a submissive?' Danielle flicked Lori's nipple with the tip of the crop.

Lori listened to the bids rise to impossible heights. Thirty thousand euros. Forty thousand. Fifty thousand. The men mopped their brows with silk handkerchiefs and gulped expensive whisky to slake the thirst of desire. Each time someone raised the bid, fists pounded on the tables and groans of frustration burst from the audience.

Perspiration formed a slick, satiny sheen on Lori's breasts and belly. With her hands cuffed behind her back and her legs forced open by the shackles, she felt exposed to the core. Lorelei must have felt a similar emotion when she performed for her lover's cronies in the club – Jean-Michel had explained what had happened to her as they prepared for the auction. But how much more humiliating it must have been to offer herself as the prize in Cross's bid for favour with the SS!

This is only a game, Lori reminded herself. But her thoughts gave her little comfort as the bidders edged closer to the stage. Danielle's face, normally cool alabaster, was stained with pink as she urged the bidding higher.

'A hundred thousand euros!'

The bidder had loosened the tie around his plump, ruddy neck. His heavy features, possibly handsome twenty years ago, had been coarsened by spirits and rich food, and his eyes bulged in his effort to take in Lori's naked body. Here was a man who had exhausted all conventional appetites long ago; he was desperate to fulfil new ones.

Lori closed her eyes. *Not him*, she prayed. *Please, not him.*

'A hundred and fifty thousand.'

'Two hundred.'

He clenched his highball glass in his hamlike fist.

'A million euros.' The bid came from the back of the room.

The glass exploded. Blood filled the previous bidder's palm, but he seemed not to notice. All heads turned.

'A million euros,' the new bidder repeated in an American accent. A tall, lean male figure rose in the smoke and shadows.

It was Gavin MacLellan.

The ball-gag muffled Lori's cry. She bucked and twisted in the chair as she tried to squirm out of the spotlight. In its hard glare, she couldn't tell if his long shadow was real. Maybe her desperation was making her hallucinate.

'American bastard! That's not a fair bid! Get out of here!'

The drunk with the bleeding hand stood up and kicked over his chair. Two other men stood with him, hackles raised.

'I'm not leaving till I take her home,' Gavin said. 'That woman is mine.'

'Bullshit!'

With one heave the drunk shoved his table over, then all hell broke loose as he and his cronies rushed Gavin. Danielle's voice rose, trying in vain to make itself heard over the uproar. Three burly bouncers emerged from the gloom. Lori tried desperately to see what was going on. Her eyes couldn't make out anything but a fury of roiling bodies. The sickening sounds of fists meeting flesh, followed by shouts of pain and rage, filled the room.

A hood was yanked over Lori's head. Someone was freeing her from the chair. She was being wrapped in her cloak then rushed off the stage, through the backstage passageway and into the alley behind the club. She was shoved into the back seat of a car. The front door opened, then slammed shut. Relief rushed through her as she caught the heavy scent of Danielle's perfume and Gauloise cigarettes. Lori was in Danielle's Citroën. Everything was going to be all right.

Lori struggled to sit up, whimpering as she tried to breathe through the ball-gag. The hood was pulled off her head, and the gag was tugged out of her mouth.

'Danielle!' Lori cried. 'Where's Gavin? Is he all right?' She looked around the car, expecting to see Danielle's face.

Instead her eyes met the glitter of Jean-Michel's glasses.

'I don't know about your friend from the States,' he said, 'but Danielle is dead to me now. She betrayed me tonight. She told that American about the auction. Unfortunately, he tripped over his hard-on and missed his chance to get you.'

Jean-Michel started the engine. The car hurtled out of the alley and into the streets of Montparnasse. The city passed in a blur of light and motion. Lori prayed that a policeman would stop Jean-Michel. Even a collision might be better than whatever Jean-Michel had in store for her. She expected him to drive her to his neighbourhood, but the ride was taking much longer than it should. Lori's panic turned to stone-cold fear as she realised where Jean-Michel was going.

It would be next to impossible for anyone to follow me here, he had said when he first took Lori through that maze of suburban streets to Ilse Wilde's townhouse. As the black car ducked and twisted, taking wild detours through the city, Lori knew that he was right.

21

Lori had never seen pure insanity before, but she knew that she was witnessing it now. As he moved around the room arranging the photo shoot, Jean-Michel was as remote as a frozen planet orbiting its own dark sun.

'I never wanted to sell you,' he said. 'None of those animals would have known how to treat you.'

He held a light meter against Lori's face. She cringed.

'You don't trust me anymore.'

'I never really trusted you,' Lori said. 'Where is Ilse?'

Lori knew that Ilse Wilde wouldn't do anything to help her, but she would have felt safer with another woman in the room. Ilse was probably upstairs, sleeping soundly between satin sheets, her diamond collar nestling against her throat.

Lori wished that she could rip the collar off her own neck. The diamond's weight repulsed her.

'Ilse has been released,' Jean-Michel said.

'What?'

'I sold her to another man. I was tired of her. Aside from her beauty, she had very little to offer. Besides, I never keep two women in the same apartment. This place is yours now. You will live here.'

'You're mad, Jean-Michel,' Lori said, her voice soft with horror. 'You are completely mad.'

They were in a makeshift basement studio below the apartment that had previously housed Ilse Wilde. The room was dirty and stark, nothing like the state-of-the-art set-up in Jean-Michel's apartment. Lori sat in a straight-backed chair, her wrists tied with rope behind her back and her ankles tied to the chair legs. She was still nude, wearing only the dog collar, the stiletto heels and the golden chain between her nipples. But the sight of Gavin in the club, and the sound of his voice, had brought back the old Lori Marwick full force. If there'd ever been any chance of her becoming Jean-Michel's slave, Gavin had smashed the possibility.

She could see herself clearly now. Through the lens of his camera, Jean-Michel saw nothing more than a mannequin, a life-size doll. The qualities that made her a unique, flesh-and-blood woman were only accents to his entertainment. The emotion simmering in his mind was not love, as Lori had first believed, but a psychotic drive to possess any woman who captured his interest.

'So that was the man you're obsessed with,' Jean-Michel mused. 'The tall, dark American male with the tall, blonde American female. How predictable. The two of you could pose for a toothpaste advertisement.' The shutter clicked. He laughed. 'But these shots won't sell toothpaste. Spread your legs. Heels on the floor. There. Perfect. Now, let your head fall to one side. Like a broken doll.'

But Lori hadn't been broken, quite the opposite. Watching Jean-Michel behind his camera, she no longer saw a sexy, mysterious dominant, but a narcissist with an obsessive need to control everything and everyone around him.

'I checked you out of your hotel this afternoon,' he said, never stopping his work behind the camera. 'I took the liberty of leaving your things behind.' He paused to look straight into Lori's eyes. 'Except for your plane ticket. I took that with me. I burned it in the ashtray of my car.'

Lori kept her eyes lowered. By tiny increments, she edged her body forwards. She rolled her shoulders, as if to loosen a knot in her muscles, and found that she had room to move her arms. Jean-Michel had remarked that she didn't trust him; apparently he did trust her. Or he had too much confidence in his own power.

'Would you like a glass of champagne, Lori? How about some music? Or maybe a recording of Edith Piaf, something to remind you of the woman who brought you to Paris. No, too passionate. I feel like something more . . . rational.'

The prospect of running nude through the streets of a Paris suburb didn't thrill her, but the idea of the seething rage under Jean-Michel's composed surface pleased her even less. Though his movements were casual, as he walked around the studio toying with the stereo and pouring champagne, Lori could see his back and arm muscles straining against the fabric of his clothing. The tendons in his neck were as taut as strained rope.

Jean-Michel was going to punish her tonight. Once he started, he might not be able to stop.

The restrained measures of Couperin flowed from the speakers. The music seemed to calm him a little; Lori could see his muscles relax. Carrying a flute of champagne, he walked towards Lori.

'I shouldn't let you drink tonight. The alcohol will soften your pain, and you want to feel it, don't you? But one glass won't hurt, as a celebration of our new life together.'

He held out the glass. Lori pulled her leg back and drove the heel of her shoe into his kneecap. Jean-Michel howled, and the glass flew through the air. His face twisted into a red mask of rage. Lori stood up, kicking the chair back and lifting her bound arms. She fell forwards into Jean-Michel with her shoulder, sending him to the floor. Then she ran.

The flight through the townhouse was a nightmare. The rooms were a labyrinth of elegance, hallways leading from one lavish room into another. When she finally found herself in the marble foyer, she began to laugh in delirious, sobbing gasps. Her slippery fingers fumbled on the ornate doorknob. If only it would open . . .

Jean-Michel brought her down from behind. Lori's hands flew out to meet the marble floor, and a searing pain shot through her wrist. He smothered her screams and pinned her down with his entire body, his fury giving him such strength that she couldn't attack him with her elbows or knees. His face was a rictus of triumph and desire. Through his trousers, his erection dug into her inner thigh like a sword.

'You wanted those men at the club to lust after you,' he hissed. 'You opened your pussy for strangers, and you loved it. I watched you tremble, you wanted it so much.'

Lori shook her head. She hoped to loosen Jean-Michel's grip enough to bite his hand, but he only pressed harder.

'Yes, yes, you wanted it. You were being auctioned like an animal – your cunt, your tits, your pretty ass – and you loved every moment.'

Jean-Michel's hand bore down on her mouth and nose. She tried to buck up and down as she fought for breath, but his weight was holding her still. Her moans excited him even more. As he shifted his hips to penetrate her, she pulled her head free and screamed. He drew back as her shriek pierced his ears, and she shoved him off her. She began to kick, her feet pummelling him with a storm of sharp blows. One of her heels landed in the soft nook of his crotch, stabbing his balls a second time. Now he was the one screaming.

Voices rose outside the door, which then swung open.

'Lori! Thank God.'

A pair of strong arms were lifting her off the floor and wrapping her in coarse, heavy fabric. Lori recognised Danielle's voice and knew, in some corner of her mind, that she was safe, but she didn't stop thrashing until she realised that Jean-Michel was lying face-down on the ıarble. Beside him crouched Gavin, pinning his arms ehind his back. Gavin's cheek was swollen, his lower lip ·uffy and seamed with blood, but to Lori he was as eautiful as a divine visitation.

The scent of Gavin's skin filled her nostrils. She lutched at the fabric around her shoulders; she was vearing his coat. She closed her eyes and inhaled.

'She may be in shock,' Gavin said. 'Keep her covered.'

Danielle held Lori close, murmuring to her soothingly n French. Enveloped in the thick, scratchy wool of ;avin's coat and the cool white satin of Danielle's dress, ori let herself get lost in a mingling of male and female ensations. More people crowded into the foyer. Two nen in uniform dragged Jean-Michel to his feet, and)anielle's soft chest was replaced by Gavin's firmness as ıe took her in his arms. Lori buried her face in his shirt o that she wouldn't have to meet Jean-Michel's final tare.

'I treated Lori like a whore,' Jean-Michel taunted, 'and he loved it. It's in her blood. Try to satisfy her now!'

Gavin let go of Lori, but only long enough to silence ean-Michel with a jaw-cracking upper cut.

22

Gavin and Lori spent the next two days in bed. The pain of Gavin's bruised face and Lori's sprained wrist soon dissolved in the waves of pleasure that came from their lovemaking. Now that Lori was with Gavin again, she couldn't remember how she'd lived outside the dark compelling aura of his sensuality. No sooner had she climaxed with him than she needed him again: his taste, his smell, his hard, masculine substance. When her cunt was too raw for penetration, she grabbed handfuls of his thick hair and steered his tongue through the grooves and channels of her sex. Then she returned the favour, taking him into her mouth and coaxing him to orgasm after orgasm.

'I can't believe I let myself go so far,' she said. 'Melanie tried to warn me that I was getting obsessed with Lorelei, but I ignored her.'

They lay in Gavin's hotel room. Lori ran her fingertips along the seam of silken black hair that ran from Gavin's navel to his pubis. His cock stirred, but after two consecutive orgasms spirit couldn't sustain flesh. Gavin circled Lori's nipple with his thumb, then lowered his head to kiss the pink nub until it puckered.

'Do you want to hear about what happened?' Lori asked.

'Are you ready to talk about it?'

Since the night of the auction, they hadn't talked about Jean-Michel. Lori hadn't even spoken his name, and Gavin hadn't pressed. He had made a refuge for her in his hotel room, a place where she could fulfil her appetites without fear of punishment or control. He had pampered her with fine food, fresh flowers and hours of sensual stroking and lush kissing, all to bring her back to herself.

'He never hurt me, until the last night,' Lori said. 'He never forced me to do anything I didn't want to do. Everything I did with him turned me on. Even the auction aroused me, until I saw that there could be real danger involved. I never fell in love with Jean-Michel, but I must have trusted him. He was so authoritative, so in control. He knew how to give me pleasure, and when to take it away, and when I'd been pushed too far. At least I thought he knew.'

'Lacoste isn't an authentic dominant; he's a power junkie with a taste for kink. His control is just a front for a dangerously weak personality. Now that you've discovered you have a taste for submission, I'll show you the real thing.'

Lori winced. 'Let's keep things vanilla for now, OK? I've got a few kinky images in my mind that I'd rather forget. I let Jean-Michel take a lot of pictures of me. Some of them aren't quite, uh, tasteful.'

'Are you worried about them? I'd be happy to get the negatives for you. Break the guy's jaw again, while I'm at it.'

'No. The photos give me something in common with Lorelei. I still don't know what happened to her, or why she made the choices that she did, but I see the limits of the evidence. The photos of Lorelei are flashes of time. They aren't the whole woman, but they're powerful reflections of her sexuality. If she survived the war, I think she must have faced the reality of those pictures. Do you think she was strong enough to take responsibility for herself?'

'I don't know. I only know that *you* are. You'll need to be strong when you get back to Morne Bay. Melanie made a few changes in the inventory. Some of the more uptight residents aren't too happy about offering tourists a selection of vibrators and disciplinary toys.'

'Oh God,' Lori groaned. 'I told her the town wasn't ready.'

'Don't be too hard on her. Melanie deserves a chance to expose her sexuality too. Besides, as a woman who looks damn hot in a slave collar, you're not exactly in a position to pass judgment.'

'That reminds me. If you tell Melanie about those photographs of me, I'll kill you.'

'I'm sure you'll tell her yourself.'

The telephone on the bedside table rang. Gavin picked up the receiver. As he listened, the smile on his face froze. He said a few abrupt words in French, then hung up.

'Who was that?'

'Danielle.'

'Well? What did she want?'

Propped up on his elbow, Gavin stared down at Lori, saying nothing.

'What is it? You're scaring me. Is it about Jean-Michel?'

'No. It's about Lorelei Price. You're not going to believe this, but Nanette Pommier wants to see you.'

'*Nanette* Pommier?'

'Right. Geneviève Pommier's mother.'

'You mean she's still alive? She must be –' Lori paused as she tried to calculate the woman's age.

'She's at least ninety,' Gavin said. 'But she's not about to admit it. Danielle convinced Geneviève to tell her mother about you, and to show her your picture. Now Nanette wants to talk to you. She was very insistent. She wants to see you right away.' Gavin grinned. 'Dressed, of course.'

'My God.' Lori sat up. Feeling dizzy, she cradled her

ead in her hands. 'What if she knows what happened
o Lorelei in the end?'

'Then in about an hour,' Gavin said, 'you might know
oo.'

'I don't think I'm ready for this.'

'Of course you are.' He lifted Lori's chin and looked
nto her eyes. 'But you should also be ready for the
ossibility that this could be another dead-end.'

Lori took a deep breath. 'A dead-end, maybe. But not
he end.'

t felt strange to be standing in front of the Pommiers'
varnished door again. The woman who had knocked on
hat door three weeks ago had gone. The woman who
tood in her place knew herself much better, and was
leased with what she knew. Her knock was firm and
er voice confident as she introduced herself again.
Geneviève Pommier was as sour-faced as ever, but this
ime she let Lori in without hesitation.

'My mother is anxious to see you,' the Frenchwoman
aid. Her beady eyes glared at Lori. 'She is very frail.
Don't make her too excited.'

She led Lori through a tidy parlour and down a narrow
allway to a bedroom at the back of the apartment.
There, on a bed draped with an exotic embroidered
canopy, sat a tiny old woman dressed in a red brocade
bed-jacket, holding court amidst a sea of multicoloured
pillows and multicoloured cats. The red satin jacket
clashed with the startling orange tufts of her dyed hair,
but she held herself like a queen.

Her composure crumbled, however, when she saw
Lori. With quivering hands, she covered her painted
mouth.

'Mon Dieu. C'est toi, Li-li?'

'My mother is asking if you are Lorelei,' Geneviève

explained. 'Li-li was her pet name for her. They were very close. Sometimes my mother falls back into the past.'

'*Va-t-en!*' Nanette waved her hand at her daughter.

'She wants me to leave. Her English is poor, and she can't talk for long. If she struggles, call me at once.'

Geneviève left the room. Nanette held out her arms, but Lori hesitated.

'*Tu parles français, ma chère?*'

'*Un petit peu.*'

'We'll talk in English. Come.'

Lori made her way to the bed and leaned down into Nanette's open arms. She expected a fragile embrace, but the elderly woman hugged her as if she intended to merge her heart with Lori's. When she finally let Lori go, her eyes were moist and her mouth quivered.

'Switzerland,' she said. 'I last saw her at a small town. I don't remember the name ... there was a lake. A café. She sat outside at the café.'

'When was this?'

Nanette closed her papery eyelids. 'Twenty years. Or thirty? I had a lover then. Not my last. So it must be thirty years. Long after the war, but she was still hiding, my Li-li. Hiding her hair under a scarf. Her eyes behind dark glasses.'

'Hiding?' Lori asked cautiously.

'Yes. She was afraid. Always afraid. She left France, you see, with many hating her. French and Germans, wanting her dead. But I loved her. I helped her leave. Me and my friends.'

Lori squeezed the elderly woman's hand. The faded blue eyes scanned Lori's face, greedily taking in her features.

'Why did she have to leave France?' Lori asked.

Nanette's voice, rusty and deep, lowered even further

as she spoke three words, clutching Lori's hand for emphasis with each syllable: 'I never told.'

'I know. I know you didn't.'

'Her lover sold her. He sold her to a monster.'

'I know. The auction.'

'She was to go to him. The last night. But I told her no! You must leave. There is no choice. She loved me, too. She left because she loved me.'

'She went to Switzerland, you mean? Instead of meeting this man?'

The old woman's head nodded furiously. 'I went to him. Me.'

'You went in her place?'

'Yes. Yes. And I . . . I . . .' Nanette's voice cracked. A wild light burned in her eyes. Please hold on, Lori begged inwardly. Please hold on long enough to tell.

'What happened?'

'He knew I was not Li-li, but he took me, anyway. While he was on top of me, Li-li was leaving France. I let him use me. Vile. The things he did to me . . .'

Nanette's head sagged. Her brittle frame seemed to sink into itself, deflated now that her secret had left her lips. Her breath came in long, ragged gusts. Lori stood abruptly, ready to run for Geneviève, but Nanette took hold of her wrist and yanked her arm.

'I told him that she was dead. I had to tell him that. Do you understand?'

'Yes,' Lori said.

Nanette let out a long sigh and lay her head back against the pillows. One of the cats toyed with her sparse red curls. Underneath the folds of wrinkled, yellowed skin, Lori could see the bone structure of a beautiful woman, who still surrounded herself with satin and fur.

'I saw her in Switzerland,' Nanette repeated, 'after the war. Many years. At the café. She was drinking wine.'

Nanette lifted her head and smacked her lips. 'I want a glass of wine.'

'Did you speak to her?' Lori urged.

'My Li-li would not speak to me. She looked at me, then at the lake. After all that time, she was still afraid, you see.'

'Yes. I see.'

'I need water,' Nanette said. '*Je crève de soif.*' She tugged Lori's hand in consternation. '*Ma petite, je meurs.*'

'Geneviève!' Lori cried.

Geneviève Pommier opened the door so abruptly that Lori knew she must have been listening outside.

'I think she just said that she's dying.'

'She says that all the time,' Geneviève said with resignation. She poured water from a pitcher and steadied the glass against her mother's chin. The old woman swallowed the liquid in frantic gulps. 'She is speaking all her truths these days. *Ça suffit, Maman.* Enough truth for now.'

'Enough,' Lori echoed. In the overheated room, with its air of illness and confessions, she felt faint. 'More than enough.'

After they left Nanette to take her afternoon nap, Geneviève begrudgingly told Lori the name of the town in Switzerland where Nanette had last seen Lorelei Price. She even divulged the name of the café, explaining that her mother used to remember the incident very clearly, and knew exactly where the encounter had taken place.

'Your mother was a courageous woman,' Lori told Geneviève.

'She loved Lorelei,' Geneviève said. 'When she came to Paris from the country, Lorelei Price saved her life. My mother returned the favour.'

By the time she left the Pommiers' apartment, Lori was breathing more easily. She walked through the streets, trying to drink in every detail of Paris. In two days she would be back in Morne Bay. She would be followed by the haunting rasp of Nanette Pommier's confession, and the memory of her eyes as she scoured Lori's face for reminders of the lost Lorelei.

On the way back to Gavin's hotel Lori stopped at a boutique to buy a gift for her own best friend. If the town council hadn't stoned Melanie by now, sales at Chimera were probably skyrocketing. Melanie's business sense hadn't failed her yet. A good thing, too, because Melanie would be looking after the shop for most of the coming summer. Lori had already made up her mind to take one more step in her journey; she would go to Switzerland to look for any final traces of Lorelei Price.

Lori settled on an outrageously expensive negligée for Melanie, in a jungle green that would make her peachy skin glow. No vintage lingerie for that girl. Melanie could appreciate the past, but sexually she lived only in the present.

From now on, so would Lori.

Gavin was waiting for her in the hotel bar. He raised his eyebrows when she ordered champagne.

'We're celebrating? Must be good news.'

'Good and bad. The bad news is that Lorelei Price wasn't a feminist saint. The good news is that someone loved her enough to save her from betraying herself.'

'Nanette Pommier?'

Lori nodded as she sipped her champagne.

'Doran Cross tried to sell Lorelei at a private auction for his SS cronies. Apparently Nanette kept her from consummating the deal, and saved her life in the process. If her story's true, then Nanette was the brave one. And I believe her. She loved Lorelei; I could tell.'

'Are you going to tell me what happened to Lorelei after the war, or am I going to wait for your book?'

'*My* book?'

'I assume you're going to write one.'

'I thought we were working on the book together.'

'There are some things I want us to do together – repeatedly, in every possible position, until we drop dead from exhaustion. Writing a book is not one of them.'

Lori laughed. 'So we'll each write our own biography?'

'No. I'm turning the project over to you. Photos, letters, everything. It's your baby. Obelisk doesn't want to publish the book. Lorelei's life doesn't exactly fit into their Heroic Female Photographers series.'

'No,' Lori sighed. 'She wasn't a hero. But she was brave, in her own right. She was brave enough to face what she loved in art, and even braver to bring that into her own life. She just wasn't strong enough to resist Doran Cross. Submitting to a man was her fatal weakness.'

Gavin pulled Lori close. With one hand, he grasped both of her wrists. His breath was warm in her ear as his lips tickled the lobe. 'Submitting to a man isn't a fatal weakness,' he said. 'Not if it's the right man. Of course I'll have to train you all over again, to meet my personal needs.'

'And what would those be?'

Lori freed one hand and slipped it under the bar. Her fingers tunnelled between Gavin's thighs, first plunging into the soft heat of his balls then sliding upwards to trace the ridge of his erection. They lingered at the firm head, squeezing just below the crown then massaging the shaft until Gavin groaned. He fumbled for his wallet and threw a handful of bills onto the bar.

'I'll show you upstairs,' he said through clenched teeth. 'Right now.'

Lori smiled. 'I think you're about as right as they come.'

LOOK OUT FOR THE ALL-NEW BLACK LACE BOOKS – AVAILABLE NOW!

All books priced £6.99 in the UK. Please note publication dates apply to the UK only. For other territories, please contact your retailer.

THE NAME OF AN ANGEL
Laura Thornton
ISBN 0 352 33205 0

Clarissa Cornwall is a respectable university lecturer who has little time for romance until she encounters the insolently sexy Nicholas St Clair in her class on erotic literature. Suddenly her position – and the age gap between them – no longer matters as she finds herself becoming obsessed with this provocative young man. She tries to fight her desire but soon finds herself involved in a secret affair with this dangerously charismatic student. **Forbidden lusts and the appeal of young men.**

Coming in December 2003

ALWAYS THE BRIDEGROOM
Tesni Morgan
ISBN 0 352 33855 5

Jody Hamilton is a landscape gardener who has returned from the States to attend her best friend's wedding. All is well until Jody finds out what a sex-crazed rotter her best friend is about to marry. With too many people involved in the preparations for the big day, bickering, back-stabbing and infidelities soon ensue. But in the middle of the mayhem, Jody thinks she may have found the man of her dreams. **Erotica and chick-lit merge in this sizzling tale of wedding mayhem.**

DOCTOR'S ORDERS
Deanna Ashford
ISBN 0 352 33453 3

Helen Dawson is a dedicated doctor who has taken a short-term assignment at an exclusive private hospital that caters for the every need of its rich and famous clientele. The matron, Sandra Pope, ensures this includes their most curious sexual fantasies. When Helen risks an affair with a famous actor, she is drawn deeper into the hedonistic lifestyle of the clinic. **Naughty nurses get busy behind the screens!**

Coming in January 2004

WICKED WORDS 9
Various
ISBN 0352 33860 1

Wicked Words collections are the hottest anthologies of women's erotic writing to be found anywhere in the world. With settings and scenarios to suit all tastes, this is fun erotica at the cutting edge from the UK and USA. The diversity of themes and styles reflects the multi-faceted nature of the female sexual imagination. Combining humour, warmth and attitude with imaginative writing, these stories sizzle with horny action. **Another scorching collection of wild fantasies.**

THE AMULET
Lisette Allen
ISBN 0 352 33019 8

Roman Britain, near the end of the second century. Catarina, an orphan adopted by the pagan Celts, has grown into a beautiful young woman with the gift of second sight. When her tribe captures a Roman garrison, she falls in love with their hunky leader, Alexius. Yet he betrays her, stealing her precious amulet. Vowing revenge, Catarina follows Alexius to Rome, but the salacious pagan rituals and endless orgies prove to be a formidable distraction. **Wonderfully decadent fiction from a pioneer of female erotica.**

Black Lace Booklist

Information is correct at time of printing. To avoid disappointment check availability before ordering. Go to www.blacklace-books.co.uk. All books are priced £6.99 unless another price is given.

BLACK LACE BOOKS WITH A CONTEMPORARY SETTING

❑ IN THE FLESH Emma Holly ISBN 0 352 33498 3 £5.99
❑ SHAMELESS Stella Black ISBN 0 352 33485 1 £5.99
❑ INTENSE BLUE Lyn Wood ISBN 0 352 33496 7 £5.99
❑ THE NAKED TRUTH Natasha Rostova ISBN 0 352 33497 5 £5.99
❑ A SPORTING CHANCE Susie Raymond ISBN 0 352 33501 7 £5.99
❑ TAKING LIBERTIES Susie Raymond ISBN 0 352 33357 X £5.99
❑ A SCANDALOUS AFFAIR Holly Graham ISBN 0 352 33523 8 £5.99
❑ THE NAKED FLAME Crystalle Valentino ISBN 0 352 33528 9 £5.99
❑ ON THE EDGE Laura Hamilton ISBN 0 352 33534 3 £5.99
❑ LURED BY LUST Tania Picarda ISBN 0 352 33533 5 £5.99
❑ THE HOTTEST PLACE Tabitha Flyte ISBN 0 352 33536 X £5.99
❑ THE NINETY DAYS OF GENEVIEVE Lucinda Carrington ISBN 0 352 33070 8 £5.99
❑ DREAMING SPIRES Juliet Hastings ISBN 0 352 33584 X
❑ THE TRANSFORMATION Natasha Rostova ISBN 0 352 33311 1
❑ SIN.NET Helena Ravenscroft ISBN 0 352 33598 X
❑ TWO WEEKS IN TANGIER Annabel Lee ISBN 0 352 33599 8
❑ HIGHLAND FLING Jane Justine ISBN 0 352 33616 1
❑ PLAYING HARD Tina Troy ISBN 0 352 33617 X
❑ SYMPHONY X Jasmine Stone ISBN 0 352 33629 3
❑ SUMMER FEVER Anna Ricci ISBN 0 352 33625 0
❑ CONTINUUM Portia Da Costa ISBN 0 352 33120 8
❑ OPENING ACTS Suki Cunningham ISBN 0 352 33630 7
❑ FULL STEAM AHEAD Tabitha Flyte ISBN 0 352 33637 4
❑ A SECRET PLACE Ella Broussard ISBN 0 352 33307 3
❑ GAME FOR ANYTHING Lyn Wood ISBN 0 352 33639 0
❑ CHEAP TRICK Astrid Fox ISBN 0 352 33640 4
❑ ALL THE TRIMMINGS Tesni Morgan ISBN 0 352 33641 3

- ❑ THE GIFT OF SHAME Sara Hope-Walker ISBN 0 352 32935 1
- ❑ COMING UP ROSES Crystalle Valentino ISBN 0 352 33658 7
- ❑ GOING TOO FAR Laura Hamilton ISBN 0 352 33657 9
- ❑ THE STALLION Georgina Brown ISBN 0 352 33005 8
- ❑ DOWN UNDER Juliet Hastings ISBN 0 352 33663 3
- ❑ THE BITCH AND THE BASTARD Wendy Harris ISBN 0 352 33664 1
- ❑ ODALISQUE Fleur Reynolds ISBN 0 352 32887 8
- ❑ SWEET THING Alison Tyler ISBN 0 352 33682 X
- ❑ TIGER LILY Kimberley Dean ISBN 0 352 33685 4
- ❑ COOKING UP A STORM Emma Holly ISBN 0 352 33686 2
- ❑ RELEASE ME Suki Cunningham ISBN 0 352 33671 4
- ❑ KING'S PAWN Ruth Fox ISBN 0 352 33684 6
- ❑ FULL EXPOSURE Robyn Russell ISBN 0 352 33688 9
- ❑ SLAVE TO SUCCESS Kimberley Raines ISBN 0 352 33687 0
- ❑ STRIPPED TO THE BONE Jasmine Stone ISBN 0 352 33463 0
- ❑ HARD CORPS Claire Thompson ISBN 0 352 33491 6
- ❑ MANHATTAN PASSION Antoinette Powell ISBN 0 352 33691 9
- ❑ CABIN FEVER Emma Donaldson ISBN 0 352 33692 7
- ❑ WOLF AT THE DOOR Savannah Smythe ISBN 0 352 33693 5
- ❑ SHADOWPLAY Portia Da Costa ISBN 0 352 33313 8
- ❑ I KNOW YOU, JOANNA Ruth Fox ISBN 0 352 33727 3
- ❑ SNOW BLONDE Astrid Fox ISBN 0 352 33732 X
- ❑ QUEEN OF THE ROAD Lois Pheonix ISBN 0 352 33131 1
- ❑ THE HOUSE IN NEW ORLEANS Fleur Reynolds ISBN 0 352 32951 3
- ❑ HEAT OF THE MOMENT Tesni Morgan ISBN 0 352 33742 7
- ❑ STORMY HAVEN Savannah Smythe ISBN 0 352 33757 5
- ❑ STICKY FINGERS Alison Tyler ISBN 0 352 33756 7
- ❑ THE WICKED STEPDAUGHTER Wendy Harris ISBN 0 352 33777 X
- ❑ DRAWN TOGETHER Robyn Russell ISBN 0 352 33269 7
- ❑ LEARNING THE HARD WAY Jasmine Archer ISBN 0 352 33782 6
- ❑ VALENTINA'S RULES Monica Belle ISBN 0 352 33788 5
- ❑ VELVET GLOVE Emma Holly ISBN 0 352 33448 7
- ❑ UNKNOWN TERRITORY Annie O'Neill ISBN 0 352 33794 X
- ❑ VIRTUOSO Katrina Vincenzi-Thyre ISBN 0 352 32907 6
- ❑ FIGHTING OVER YOU Laura Hamilton ISBN 0 352 33795 8
- ❑ COUNTRY PLEASURES Primula Bond ISBN 0 352 33810 5

❑ ARIA APPASSIONATA Juliet Hastings ISBN 0 352 33056 2
❑ THE RELUCTANT PRINCESS Patty Glenn ISBN 0 352 33809 1
❑ WILD IN THE COUNTRY Monica Belle ISBN 0 352 33824 5
❑ THE TUTOR Portia Da Costa ISBN 0 352 32946 7
❑ SEXUAL STRATEGY Felice de Vere ISBN 0 352 33843 1
❑ THE NAME OF AN ANGEL Laura Thornton ISBN 0 352 33205 0

BLACK LACE BOOKS WITH AN HISTORICAL SETTING

❑ PRIMAL SKIN Leona Benkt Rhys ISBN 0 352 33500 9 £5.99
❑ DEVIL'S FIRE Melissa MacNeal ISBN 0 352 33527 0 £5.99
❑ DARKER THAN LOVE Kristina Lloyd ISBN 0 352 33279 4
❑ THE CAPTIVATION Natasha Rostova ISBN 0 352 33234 4
❑ MINX Megan Blythe ISBN 0 352 33638 2
❑ JULIET RISING Cleo Cordell ISBN 0 352 32938 6
❑ DEMON'S DARE Melissa MacNeal ISBN 0 352 33683 8
❑ DIVINE TORMENT Janine Ashbless ISBN 0 352 33719 2
❑ SATAN'S ANGEL Melissa MacNeal ISBN 0 352 33726 5
❑ THE INTIMATE EYE Georgia Angelis ISBN 0 352 33004 X
❑ OPAL DARKNESS Cleo Cordell ISBN 0 352 33033 3
❑ SILKEN CHAINS Jodi Nicol ISBN 0 352 33143 7
❑ EVIL'S NIECE Melissa MacNeal ISBN 0 352 33781 8
❑ ACE OF HEARTS Lisette Allen ISBN 0 352 33059 7
❑ A GENTLEMAN'S WAGER Madelynne Ellis ISBN 0 352 33800 8
❑ THE LION LOVER Mercedes Kelly ISBN 0 352 33162 3
❑ ARTISTIC LICENCE Vivienne La Fay ISBN 0 352 33210 7

BLACK LACE ANTHOLOGIES

❑ WICKED WORDS 6 Various ISBN 0 352 33590 0
❑ WICKED WORDS 8 Various ISBN 0 352 33787 7
❑ THE BEST OF BLACK LACE 2 Various ISBN 0 352 33718 4

BLACK LACE NON-FICTION

❑ THE BLACK LACE BOOK OF WOMEN'S SEXUAL FANTASIES Ed. Kerri Sharp ISBN 0 352 33793 1 £6.99

To find out the latest information about Black Lace titles, check out the website: www.blacklace-books.co.uk or send for a booklist with complete synopses by writing to:

Black Lace Booklist, Virgin Books Ltd
Thames Wharf Studios
Rainville Road
London W6 9HA

Please include an SAE of decent size. Please note only British stamps are valid.

Our privacy policy
We will not disclose information you supply us to any other parties. We will not disclose any information which identifies you personally to any person without your express consent.

From time to time we may send out information about Black Lace books and special offers. Please tick here if you do not wish to receive Black Lace information. ☐

Please send me the books I have ticked above.

Name ....

Address ....

....

....

....

Post Code ....

Send to: Cash Sales, Black Lace Books, Thames Wharf Studios, Rainville Road, London W6 9HA.

US customers: for prices and details of how to order books for delivery by mail, call 1-800-343-4499.

Please enclose a cheque or postal order, made payable to Virgin Books Ltd, to the value of the books you have ordered plus postage and packing costs as follows:

UK and BFPO – £1.00 for the first book, 50p for each subsequent book.

Overseas (including Republic of Ireland) – £2.00 for the first book, £1.00 for each subsequent book.

If you would prefer to pay by VISA, ACCESS/MASTERCARD, DINERS CLUB, AMEX or SWITCH, please write your card number and expiry date here:

....

Signature ....

Please allow up to 28 days for delivery.